D1008636

2021

NO LONGER PROPERTY OF
SEATTLE PUBLIC LIBRARY

WINTER GRAVE

Also by Helene Tursten

THE IRENE HUSS INVESTIGATIONS

Detective Inspector Huss
Night Rounds
The Torso
The Glass Devil
The Golden Calf
The Fire Dance
The Beige Man
The Treacherous Net
Who Watcheth
Protected by the Shadows

THE EMBLA NYSTRÖM INVESTIGATIONS

Hunting Game

An Elderly Lady Is Up to No Good: Stories

WINTER GRAVE

HELENE TURSTEN

Translated from the Swedish by Marlaine Delargy

First published in Swedish under the title *Sandgrav*
Copyright © 2016 by Helene Tursten. Published in agreement with Copenhagen Literary Agency, Copenhagen.
English translation copyright © 2019 by Marlaine Delargy.

All rights reserved.

First English translation published in 2019 by
Soho Press
227 W 17th Street
New York, NY 10011

Library of Congress Cataloging-in-Publication Data
Tursten, Helene, author.
Delargy, Marlaine, translator.

Winter grave / Helene Tursten ;
translated from the Swedish by Marlaine Delargy.
Other titles: Sandgrav. English.

I. Title

PT9876.3.U55 S2613 2019 | DDC 839.73/8—dc23

ISBN 978-1-64129-076-0
eISBN 978-1-64129-077-7

Printed in the United States of America

10 9 8 7 6 5 4 3 2 1

To Anneli Høier, with sincere thanks
for your friendship and professional support

WINTER GRAVE

PART I

DECEMBER

HER HEART WAS pounding and her stomach contracted with fear. Amelie was on the edge of her seat during the last ten minutes of the lesson. As soon as the bell rang, she leaped to her feet and raced out into the corridor, with Tuva right behind her.

"I'll come with you to the bus stop!" Tuva shouted.

The girls pulled on their jackets as they ran toward the door, pausing briefly on the stairs to zip them up and put on their hats. It was already dark outside, and the bitter wind blowing in off the sea was icy cold. On top of everything else, it was pouring. Only two weeks to go until Christmas Eve, and not a flake of snow in sight. *Horrible!* Amelie thought. She would have liked to turn around and rejoin her classmates, but she had to dash home to pick up her Lucia robe and her candle.

The music teacher had said that everyone had to get changed so that it would feel *real* when they practiced for the last time before the Christmas concert and the Lucia procession. *Dress rehearsal*, that's what she'd called it.

Things had been chaotic that morning. As usual her brother, Julien, hadn't wanted to go to preschool; he was always tired and grumpy when he woke up. Their mom had spent ages coaxing him into his clothes, and they had all been seriously stressed—and very late—by the time they left the house. In the rush Amelie had forgotten her Lucia bag, which was still sitting on the floor in the hallway.

She had her own bus pass because she didn't want to go to after-school club anymore. There was only one stop between the school and Önnaröd, where she lived, but it was dangerous to walk along the narrow road in the dark. Even though she had reflectors on both her boots and her coat sleeves, Mom insisted that she catch the bus. Tuva lived near school, so she didn't need a pass. The girls were best friends. Amelie would be ten in two months and three days, and she thought after-school club was for little kids. Tuva agreed, even though her birthday wasn't until May 5.

The girls could hear the bus pulling up at the stop. Or was it leaving?

"Wait!" they yelled.

They ran down the hill as fast as they could, only to see the red taillights disappearing into the distance. The next bus wasn't due for twenty minutes. *No!* She *had* to be back for the rehearsal in half an hour!

The girls stood at the deserted bus shelter for a couple of minutes, trying to catch their breath. Maybe Amelie should just run home—it would only take ten minutes. *But then I'll stink,* she thought. The familiar sound of a chugging engine cut through her thoughts. Kristoffer! He and Tuva were related, although Amelie wasn't quite sure how. He'd given them a ride on his EPA-tractor several times.

Tuva positioned herself by the side of the road,

frantically waving her arms as the slow, short truck approached. Amelie's heart started pounding as Kristoffer stopped. He wound down the window and gave them an inquiring look. Loud rockabilly music poured from the speakers, echoing around the bus shelter.

"Hi—can you give Amelie a ride? She missed the bus . . . Pleeease, Kristoffer!"

He nodded and Amelie ran around to the other side of the vehicle. She gave Tuva a cheerful wave before opening the door and jumping in. She sank down on the soft seat with a sigh of relief. White leather—cool. Kristoffer's EPA-tractor, no, A-tractor, was really nice. He was very particular about the names of cars, and apparently EPA-tractor was an old-fashioned term. There was a lovely smell from the fir-tree-shaped air freshener that dangled from the rearview mirror. Or maybe the smell was the gel Kristoffer used to keep his long hair in place? His "Elvis quiff," that's what Tuva called it. She thought it looked good, but Amelie wasn't impressed. She liked One Direction, and none of the boys in the band had that kind of hairstyle. Kristoffer's hoodie was covered in dirt and oil stains, as were his jeans. Amelie knew that he and his dad fixed up old cars.

She gave Tuva another wave as they set off.

"We've got a rehearsal and we have to wear our Lucia costumes, but we don't need any sparkle, not until tomorrow. It's the Christmas concert. All the parents come to watch. Me and Tuva are part of the procession. We sing all the time, and the little ones get to be sheep and shepherds, and we're like angels and . . ."

Amelie chattered away. She knew Kristoffer, after all, though she had never been alone with him since Tuva had always been there when he had given them a ride in the past. But he seemed the same as always, and maybe she kept on talking because she knew he wouldn't answer. He didn't say much. Hardly anything, in fact. He was nice, though. He was taking her home. She leaned back in her seat, secure in the knowledge that she'd be back at school in time.

JULIEN WAS EVERY bit as difficult in the afternoon when Maria arrived to pick him up from preschool. He flatly refused to go home. He and Malte were in the middle of building something with Legos, and there was no way it could wait until the following day. Maria felt the sweat trickling down her back as she tried to cajole and persuade him. Eventually she grabbed him and forced him into his outdoor clothes. He was cross and overtired. People talked about the terrible twos, but he was five years old now and had been behaving that way ever since he was born, Maria thought irritably. She exchanged a weary glance with the teacher, who had joined them in the entrance hall. Together they managed to get Julien into his jacket and boots, but they gave up on his thick waterproof over-trousers. Needless to say, he tripped and fell in a great big puddle on the way to the car. His jeans were soaked through, and he started whining again.

"We're just going to collect Amelie, then we'll go straight home. You can have hot chocolate with whipped cream, and I'll take some cinnamon buns out of the freezer. I think we've earned a treat after a day like this, don't you?"

She kissed his forehead and lifted him into the car.

She had a struggle with the child seat, of course—it was definitely one of those days! Only when she sank down in the driver's seat did she let out a long breath. Thank goodness they were only a few minutes away from Amelie's school. She could use a hot chocolate and a cinnamon bun herself.

MARIA LOOKED FROM Tuva to Therese Jansson, the girls' music teacher, in confusion. There were only the three of them in the hall where the concert was due to take place the next day. A strong smell of resin was coming from the tall Christmas tree in the corner, its branches weighed down with all the decorations the children had added.

"She didn't come back?"

"No. I called her like a thousand times, but there's no answer," Tuva said.

"I tried calling her, too, both on her cell and your home number, but I had my hands full with the rehearsal . . ." Therese Jansson made an apologetic gesture and swallowed hard. Maria noticed that her hand was shaking as she pushed her large horn-rimmed glasses up her nose. *She's worried, too.*

"Amelie wouldn't just not turn up," Maria said.

"Absolutely not, and she was really looking forward to singing her solo," the teacher agreed.

"She always answers her cell," Tuva said firmly.

She's right, Amelie always picks up, Maria thought, her anxiety growing.

"I'll drive you home, Tuva," she said quickly.

"Can you let me know when you find her? It doesn't matter how late it is," Therese Jansson said nervously.

"Sure."

Maria was already on her way to the car.

THEY'D SEARCHED THE house and garden. Julien had been happy to race around hunting for his sister. Hide-and-seek was his favorite game, so he knew all the best places. But he couldn't find Amelie anywhere.

On the counter there was a glass with a drop of milk in the bottom, and a banana skin was in the sink. Before Amelie left, she had gone to the bathroom to pee, and she'd forgotten to flush, presumably because she was in a hurry. There was no sign of the plastic bag containing her Lucia costume and the little battery-powered candle, so Maria knew that her daughter had been home, eaten something, gone to the toilet, grabbed the bag, and dashed off into the rain and darkness. But she hadn't made it back to school . . .

Mechanically Maria made hot chocolate and defrosted the promised cinnamon bun in the microwave for Julien. As he settled down contentedly with his snack, she called everyone she could think of. No one had seen or heard from Amelie. She tried her daughter's cell phone at regular intervals; the signal rang out, but there was no reply. Tuva was right—Amelie always answered her cell. Only recently she'd been given a new model, and she was so proud of it.

Fear constricted Maria's throat. Eventually she managed to pull herself together enough to contact her mother-in-law. Her hands shook as she keyed in the number. When she heard Iris Holm's calm voice, Maria's self-control gave way and she started to cry. She was relieved that Iris was home; she'd always been a reliable support. Between sobs Maria explained that Amelie was missing. She asked Iris if she could come over and look after Julien while she went out to search the area.

"HAVE YOU SPOKEN to Johannes?" was Iris's first question when she arrived.

"No, but I've called everyone else I can think of. I don't want to worry him. He can't do anything, given where he is."

"You're right, of course . . . If you don't find her within an hour, we'll contact the police."

Both personally and professionally Iris had the ability to maintain her composure and think clearly in difficult situations. She was due to retire in six months, but still worked full-time as a librarian. She gently put her arms around Maria and held her without saying another word. When her daughter-in-law's weeping began to subside, she patted her gently on the cheek.

"Okay. Off you go to find Amelie," she said.

Shortly afterward Maria hurried into the darkness and the pouring rain. She was carrying a powerful flashlight and set off along the left-hand side of the road, keeping the beam focused on the shoulder and the ditch. The rain was hammering down and the wind was even stronger now, making it hard to see anything. She found nothing out of the ordinary as she covered the short distance to the school. Every couple of minutes she tried Amelie's cell, but there was still no answer.

Suddenly she had an idea. She stopped and picked out a recent photo of her daughter on her phone: Amelie was smiling, eyes sparkling with happiness, her new barrette holding her hair in place. The picture made Maria start crying again. Her tears mingled with the rain that slashed against her face. With trembling fingers she posted the photo on Facebook, with a message asking people to contact her if they'd seen the girl after three o'clock that afternoon.

On the way back, she passed the recycling center a few hundred yards from the bus stop. Mechanically she tried Amelie's number yet again. *Please, please let her pick up this time! Please, God* . . . Her prayers were interrupted by the sound of "Jingle Bells" coming from inside one of the containers. Amelie had downloaded the ringtone a few weeks ago to remind herself and everyone else that Christmas was coming.

"Amelie? Amelie! Where are you?"

Maria's voice broke as she called out. She ran from one container to the next, her heart pounding. It took only a few seconds to locate the cheerful refrain. She pushed open the flap of the bins and shined her flashlight inside. The containers must have been emptied recently; she couldn't see any garbage, but the ringtone continued to reverberate. She realized that her child couldn't be in there, but she couldn't help shouting through the opening: "Amelie! Amelie!"

The only sound was the echo of her own voice and the mocking, tinny ringtone. Maria stepped back and tried to think. She ended the call just to stop the terrible din.

She keyed in 112, and when a calm female voice informed her that she had reached emergency services, it was as if her vocal chords seized up completely.

"Amelie . . . my daughter . . . she's missing!" she finally managed to stammer.

"How old is the child?"

"Nine . . ."

"And how long has she been gone?"

Maria tried in vain to work it out, but she couldn't concentrate.

"She went home from school to collect some stuff . . . there was a rehearsal for the Christmas concert . . . but she never made it back to school!"

"What time was this?"

"Three . . . about three o'clock."

"So almost four hours. Have you contacted friends and neighbors?"

"Yes, everyone I can think of! And I've searched the house, the garden, the area where we live. I've just walked along the road from our house to the school. With a flashlight. And—"

"How far would that be?"

"Just over half a mile. Right now I'm at the recycling station. I called her cell and heard her ringtone—it's coming from inside one of the containers!"

The last few words emerged as an involuntary shriek. There was a brief silence on the other end of the line, then the calm voice spoke again: "What's your name?"

"Maria Holm."

"Can you tell me exactly where you are right now?"

"At the recycling center between Önnaröd and Mällby."

"Nearest town?"

"Strömstad."

"How far from Strömstad are you?"

"Just to the north—a mile or so."

"Stay where you are—a patrol car will be with you shortly."

The police arrived ten minutes later. Maria showed the two officers the picture of Amelie and described what she'd been wearing: red padded jacket, white woolly hat, blue jeans, blue boots. The male officer introduced himself as Patrik Lind. He was in his early twenties and looked like he worked out, though he also seemed to be slightly overweight. He wasn't very tall and the jacket of his uniform was far too tight, giving him a somewhat stocky appearance.

He gazed at the photograph for a long time, then said, "She's quite dark-skinned. Have you received any threats?"

Maria stared uncomprehendingly at him, then realized what he meant.

"I was born in Guadeloupe—in the Caribbean. My husband is Swedish, he's from Strömstad. I've lived here for ten years, and I've had very few negative comments about the color of my skin. Amelie's never mentioned anything like that."

"I just thought it might be a hate crime," the young man said with a glance at his colleague, who was half a head taller than him, her coal-black hair tied up in a ponytail. It was hard to interpret the expression in her dark eyes when he said the words "hate crime." Patrik knew that Alice Åslund had been adopted from China. For the past year she'd been living with a slightly older woman on a stud farm outside Fjällbacka. With her unmistakably Asian appearance and her sexual orientation, Alice was familiar with every aspect of that particular concept.

Patrik sent the image of Amelie to his own phone and those of his colleagues, then gave the phone back to Maria. He stomped back to the car, arms dangling oddly by his sides, and slumped into the passenger seat. Before they drove off he managed to contact the manager of the company responsible for the recycling center. He explained the reason for the late call, and the manager promised to send someone out to unlock the container.

"We'll drive around, see if we can spot her," Patrik informed Maria through the open passenger window. He closed it quickly to stop the rain from getting in. Alice was already at the wheel. She started the car and pulled out onto the road.

Maria spent the next half hour standing alone in the darkness and the pouring rain. She was shaking with cold and fear but didn't dare move. In some strange way it felt important to keep vigil over the only trace she had of her daughter.

The man from the recycling company arrived just as the police car returned. Patrik and Alice gave Maria the depressing news that they had found no trace of Amelie, but another car was on the way to join the search.

The container was opened in seconds. A cell phone was lying on the bottom. Alice jumped in and carefully slid it into an evidence bag. Maria confirmed that the phone, with its pink case adorned with kittens, was Amelie's.

So now it's in an evidence bag, she thought. *Evidence of what?*

A MAJOR SEARCH was organized, with both extra police officers and the military. Several volunteers who had seen Maria's appeal on Facebook also turned up. Toward morning a helicopter with a thermal-imaging camera began to crisscross the area, with the promise that it would stay in the air until the girl was found.

MUCH TO MARIA'S relief, Iris stayed overnight. Her mother-in-law also called Johannes to tell him what had happened, in case he heard about it via social media. Needless to say, he was beside himself, but there was nothing he could do. A helicopter wasn't due to the oil platform where Johannes had been employed as a cook for the past four years until the following day, when it would drop off the new team of workers and shuttle those who had completed their three weeks back to the mainland. There was no other option. The platform was far out in the Norwegian Sea. The helicopter would take them to Kristiansund, and from there they would fly down to Oslo. Johannes usually caught the bus from Oslo, unless he was in luck and his friend Ted was traveling home to Strömstad from Gardermoen Airport, where he worked, and could offer him a ride. Fortunately, this was one of those occasions.

Maria woke from an uneasy doze when the house phone rang. At first she couldn't process where she was, or why she was sitting in the armchair, fully dressed. Then she ran into the hallway and almost dropped the receiver in her haste. Had they found Amelie? *Please God . . . Please, God . . .*

"Maria," she half-gasped, her heart in her mouth.

"Hi, it's Evelyn."

Tuva's mother. Maria knew her, even though they didn't really socialize.

"Hi." Maria could hear the disappointment in her voice.

"Any news?"

"No." Her response was curt, but Maria couldn't be bothered to make an effort.

Evelyn hesitated, then said, "Tuva's so upset—she's sitting here crying. She doesn't want to go to school or have anything to do with the Christmas concert. She didn't say anything yesterday, but this morning she told me . . . Apparently Amelie got a ride with Kristoffer."

It took a few seconds before Maria remembered Tuva's car-obsessed relative.

"Kristoffer Sjöberg?"

"That's right. His mom died a few years ago, but she and I were cousins, so Tuva and Kristoffer are second cousins. We—"

"Hang on—when did he give her a ride?" Maria interrupted. Her head was spinning with a mixture of fear and exhaustion; she couldn't handle a heap of useless information about family relationships.

"Yesterday, when Amelie was on her way home to fetch her Lucia costume. It was pouring, and she missed the bus. Tuva had gone with her to the bus stop, and apparently Kristoffer drove up. Tuva asked him if he could take Amelie home, and he agreed."

Maria's heart began to race. "Thanks for letting me know!" She slammed the phone down and grabbed her cell to call the direct line the police had given her. They'd told her to contact them at any time.

Patrik Lind and Alice Åslund were tasked with bringing Kristoffer Sjöberg in for questioning. Both officers had had only a few hours' sleep and neither was in a particularly good mood. Patrik's mouth opened so wide that Alice could hear his jawbones crack when he yawned, and he had to make a real effort to stop his eyelids from closing.

The wind had abated during the night, but the rain showed no sign of letting up. It was still dark, despite the fact that it was nine o'clock in the morning. The only light came from the Advent candles and stars in almost every window, and from the Christmas decorations outside most houses.

"He lives out toward Hällestrand—shortly before you get to the village. On the left-hand side—" Patrik said, but Alice interrupted him.

"I know. Everybody in Strömstad knows that place," she snapped.

No doubt she was right. Kristoffer's father, Olof Sjöberg, was something of a personality in and around Strömstad. The property where he and his son lived was a former slaughterhouse that he'd renovated and extended over the years, to the point that it was no longer recognizable; these days it looked like a manor house with two wings. Glassed-in verandas, one equipped with a hot tub and a sixty-foot swimming pool, made it bear more than a passing resemblance to a modern spa. There had been a major "At Home with . . ." feature in the local paper a couple of years earlier. Olof had proudly shown the reporter and photographer around, pointing out all the latest facilities he'd installed. People had reluctantly conceded that the renovation was tasteful, and in keeping with the style of the old house. The addition of the outbuildings, verandas, and pool meant the surface area had more than quadrupled. The only thing Olof Sjöberg hadn't changed was the name: Breidablick, which was displayed at the roadside on an old-fashioned cast-iron sign, with an arrow indicating the way. The house lay at the top of a steep hill, with a fantastic view in all directions. The road was lined with birch trees, and between the trees were lanterns on sturdy cast-iron posts.

In the middle of the courtyard a huge fir tree twinkled with Christmas lights, and shimmering LED icicles adorned the eaves. Advent candles or stars glowed in every window. Anything that could be lit up was shining.

When the police car drove into the yard, the double doors opened, and Olof Sjöberg emerged at the top of the impressive Bohuslän red granite steps, sparkling in the glow of the external lights on the wall. He turned and closed the door, then waited calmly beneath the portico, which was supported by granite pillars, as the two officers scuttled toward him through the freezing rain. There was no protection from the wind up there, apart from the house itself and a large barn a short distance away.

"Good day to you! Or maybe I should shay good morning?"

Olof Sjöberg had adopted a jovial tone, but Alice noticed a slight slurring—shay? The expansive gesture as he held out his hand to greet them confirmed her suspicion that Sjöberg was far from sober.

Both officers introduced themselves. Sjöberg was a big man, and the hand that squeezed theirs was rough and callused. His steel-gray hair was slicked back but couldn't quite hide the bald patch at the top of his head. On his feet was a pair of shabby clogs that contrasted sharply with the rest of his outfit: an elegant dark-blue jacket, dark-gray trousers, a dazzling white shirt, a tie, and a matching handkerchief that was tucked into his breast pocket. His clothes suggested that he was heading off to a business meeting rather than tackling everyday chores around the property. He was surrounded by a miasma of exclusive aftershave and gentleman's fragrance. *Possibly an attempt to hide the smell of booze,* Alice thought.

"So how can I help our wonderful police service?"

His tone remained genial, but he made no move to invite them in.

Alice got straight to the point. "Are you aware that a little girl went missing in this area yesterday afternoon?"

The pleasant expression was replaced by deep frown lines that made Sjöberg resemble a bulldog. "Yes, I saw it on the news this morning . . . such a tragedy. Have you found her?"

Patrik Lind cleared his throat and said authoritatively, "No, but we've discovered that your son, Kristoffer, gave her a ride, so we'd like him to answer a few questions down at the station."

Patrik unconsciously straightened his shoulders and looked Sjöberg directly in the eye.

Easy, Patrik, Alice thought with a sigh, which she tried to hide.

"Would you indeed?"

There was no mistaking the chill in those words. Any pretense at joviality was gone, and there was nothing in Sjöberg's voice now to indicate that he'd been drinking. He loomed over them like a dark, threatening shadow, lit from behind by the external lights. Even Patrik realized this wasn't going to be as easy as he'd thought.

"We're just gathering information. It's not a formal interview or . . ."

Alice did her best to smooth things over, but Sjöberg's body language made it clear that he wasn't interested.

"Not without my lawyer present," he snapped.

"There's really no need . . . Kristoffer isn't suspected of anything . . . As I said, we just want to ask him a few questions . . ."

"My son is not being dragged off to the police station in Strömstad to be interrogated by a fucking gang of incompetent cops unless my lawyer is present!" Sjöberg hissed, clenching both fists. Alice had the sense to keep quiet, but unfortunately the same couldn't be said of her colleague.

"They're detectives from Trollhättan. And the investigation is being led by the central regional unit in Gothenburg. Not Strömstad," Patrik explained, looking pleased at having had the opportunity to correct the pompous idiot. Too late he realized his mistake.

"You're the most incompetent fucker of the lot! You can tell those assholes from Trollhättan that my lawyer will contact them to arrange a meeting at the station. With me and my lawyer present!"

With those words Olof spun around on his heel and went inside, slamming the double doors behind him. Alice worried that the two beautiful Christmas wreaths might fall off, or that the glass in the leaded windows might crack.

"What the . . ."

Patrik stared incredulously at the closed doors.

"Come on, you incompetent fucker—let's get out of here," Alice said with a smile. Patrik didn't know whether to laugh or get mad.

"So we're supposed to sit here and wait until that asshole and his son feel like turning up? Why the hell didn't you stand your ground and bring the boy in?"

Roger Willén, the acting area chief superintendent for Trollhättan, glared at Patrik Lind and Alice Åslund. Before either of them had the chance to formulate a response, their boss, Detective Chief Inspector Sven-Ove Berglund, stepped in.

"Believe me, Roger, Olof Sjöberg isn't an easy man to deal with," he said, raising his bushy eyebrows meaningfully.

"What's the problem? Why does he deserve special treatment?" Willén demanded.

Berglund looked down at his hands, which were resting on the desk. They were wrinkled and marked with age spots. Alice wondered if he was praying to a higher power for strength and energy.

"Olof Sjöberg is what you might call a power player in Strömstad. I know him well; we grew up not far from each other, and we were classmates for many years. He's always . . . set the agenda, so to speak. We often see each other at various events—this is a small town. Sometimes we play golf together, and we've gone sailing several times over the years."

He glanced up at Willén, who was standing straight-backed in front of his desk. The chief superintendent's uniform sat perfectly across his broad shoulders, and the creases in his trousers were razor-sharp. His head was virtually clean-shaven, which no doubt contributed to the military impression he made on his subordinates. He appeared to be standing at attention.

Drop the refrigerator act, Alice thought sourly.

"And?" said Willén.

Berglund thought for a moment before he answered. It was obvious that he was choosing his words with care.

"He inherited a flourishing business from his father. I assume Olof takes after him. They've made a major contribution to the economic health of Strömstad. Entrepreneurs, both of them. They've created many job opportunities."

"What does Sjöberg actually do?" The chief superintendent's question carried an implied sneer. Inspector Berglund spread his hands wide and smiled.

"What doesn't he do? His father started up a large auto repair workshop, then partnered with the town's biggest car dealership. This was just after the war, but he was far-sighted and ambitious. He bought up as much land as he could and built apartment blocks and houses to rent out. Olof worked with his father until the old man died in the mid-eighties, then he took over. He's done a good job and expanded the business wherever possible. He sells cars, boats, and property. In recent years the Norwegians have been major clients."

Patrik coughed discreetly. To Alice's horror he had decided to say something.

"He was very unpleasant and obviously intoxicated, and it wasn't even nine-thirty in the morning," he announced.

Berglund immediately put him in his place, which wasn't what Patrik had been expecting.

"I'm not surprised. We were at the same Christmas party yesterday—the local branch of the Lions. There was plenty of mulled wine, among other things . . . If you'd breathalyzed me a few hours ago I'm sure you'd have gotten a positive result." He gave the chief superintendent an amused glance before adding, "It wouldn't have been a high reading, of course. After all, I had to come to work today. Although I did leave the car at home and walk in."

Roger Willén narrowed his eyes. "Did you know the girl was missing last night?"

Berglund shook his head. "No. I'm on the Lions' social committee, and we were at the venue by five. That's when the station closes, but I left an hour early, at four. The call came in at seven, so it went straight to the regional unit's central control. They chose to send you over from Trollhättan. Uddevalla has a problem with the stomach flu, plus they still haven't caught that serial rapist. One woman was almost strangled, so that investigation has top priority."

Willén was already aware of the situation, but he nodded in agreement. He had arrived in Strömstad that morning with two of his detectives, mainly to join the search for Amelie, but also to get to know the local team. He'd sent the detectives to speak to Amelie's teacher and classmates; when Paula Nilsson and Lars Engman returned to the station, they would be expecting to question Kristoffer Sjöberg on the events of the previous evening, but clearly that wasn't going to happen. They would have to wait until it pleased Olof Sjöberg and his lawyer to wander along with Kristoffer.

Willén was annoyed, but he tried to hide it.

"This station isn't manned on weekends, so Nilsson and Engman can base their operations here over the next couple of days. Is there a spare office they can use if they have to stay on into next week?"

He straightened his back even more. Alice could almost hear the seams of his uniform creaking.

"No problem," Berglund assured him.

If the inspector and Olof Sjöberg are the same age, that means Sjöberg is sixty-four, Alice thought. *But Berglund looks significantly older and more tired.* Willén was only about forty, but behaved like some crusty old general. Then again, he was the highest-ranking officer in the room, thanks to the new structure of the Swedish police service.

Following the reorganization a year or so ago, the country's twenty-one police districts had been brought together into seven regions. Strömstad was part of the Western Region and was under the jurisdiction of Fyrbodal, which also included Trollhättan, Vänersborg, and Uddevalla. The control center was based in Gothenburg and decided which area should be responsible for a particular investigation and which units should be brought in.

One effect of this restructuring was serious turbulence at every level. Units that had worked well for many years were broken up, with team members being dispersed to new departments. The union was highly critical of the reform, and those on the ground were very unhappy. A significant number of older officers had taken early retirement.

Roger Willén was an example of a younger man who had been moved up the promotion ladder, and the fact that he took his role extremely seriously was clear to everyone in the room. According to what Sven-Ove Berglund had heard, he was a good policeman. His former chief in Trollhättan, Ann-Katrin Svantesson, was now in charge at Fyrbodal. Berglund had heard nothing but positive comments about her, too. The new organization might function well in time, but personally he was sick of the whole thing. He had decided to retire at the end of June, but right now that seemed like a lifetime away.

The intercom on his desk buzzed, and Kicki on reception informed him that Olof Sjöberg's lawyer had called to say they'd be there between three and four.

Willén compressed his lips into a thin line. His ice-blue eyes appeared to be covered in a thin layer of frost, and the coldness in his voice was unmistakable when he spoke. "Is everyone at that man's beck and call?"

Sven-Ove Berglund smiled for the first time that morning. "I guess you could put it that way," he said.

Willén turned to Patrik and Alice. "You can go."

They didn't need telling twice. After they had closed the door behind them, Willén paced for a little while, then stopped in front of Berglund's desk.

"Why is Sjöberg doing this? Because he can, or because there's something suspicious about his son?"

Berglund remained silent for a moment, then he took a deep breath and looked up at his younger colleague. "Sit down," he said, gesturing toward the shabby chair.

Willén grasped the creases in his trousers between thumb and forefinger before cautiously lowering himself onto the rickety seat.

Berglund took his time before he began to speak. "I was at both of Olof's weddings," he finally said. "He divorced his first wife about twenty years ago, after he met Ann. She was younger than him, and she'd also been married before. Olof's daughter was almost grown up, but Ann didn't have any children. Eventually Kristoffer came along. He was premature and went straight into an incubator. The situation was critical, but he made it. He had to have heart surgery when he was a baby, I remember that. But he also suffers from a number of other . . . problems as a result of what he went through. He doesn't talk much and tends to keep to himself. He's phenomenal when it comes to anything mechanical, particularly veteran and old American cars. That's also Olof's main hobby, and the two of them spend a lot of time together tinkering around. As I said, for Olof it's a hobby, but it's Kristoffer's job, and his main interest in life. He's a genius!"

"So it's because the boy is mentally handicapped that Sjöberg is protecting him from us?" Willén said sharply.

"Kristoffer isn't mentally handicapped—quite the reverse. He's just a bit different," Berglund replied calmly as he contemplated the bandbox-neat chief superintendent perched on the visitor's chair. *Doesn't drop his guard for a second*, he thought. He decided not to mention that he was Kristoffer's godfather.

"There's a reason for Olof's protective attitude. Ann died ten years ago. She had a stroke while she was in the shower and collapsed. Dead, with no warning. Since then it's just been Olof and Kristoffer. They're very close," he said.

Willén gave his colleague a long look. "How old is the boy now?"

"Seventeen. Olof mentioned at the party last night that Kristoffer's about to go for his driver's license. Apparently there shouldn't be a problem. He reckons he'll be ready for his test in April, when he turns eighteen."

"But until then he drives around in a so-called A-tractor." Willén fell silent again, his expression pensive. Eventually he stood up. "I'll come back at three—I want to sit in on the interview. See you later."

He left the office, and Berglund heard his energetic footsteps hurrying down the stairs. The inspector remained where he was, contemplating an embroidered picture that had hung in the same spot on the wall ever since his predecessor's day. Over the years the stiff flowers had taken on a faded, grayish tone and did nothing to lighten the atmosphere in the room. However, the picture had always been there, and there it would stay. Nobody noticed it anymore anyway.

Berglund sat up a little straighter, took out his cell phone, and made a call. A mechanical voice asked him to leave a message after the tone. When the beep stopped, he said, "Olof—it's Sven-Ove. Call me on my personal cell as soon as you can."

AT TEN TO four Olof Sjöberg parked his specially imported Mercedes-Benz S-Class in the main square outside the police station. *That's almost a million kronor right there,* Willén thought, reluctantly admitting to himself that he was impressed. Which, of course, was the point. Charlotta Stark, Sjöberg's lawyer, had arrived in her bright red Jaguar XE five minutes earlier, so she must have known when her client was planning to turn up. Willén was irritated, but chose to say nothing. Even he knew who she was, and he didn't want to start off by alienating her. Charlotta Stark had quite an effect on those around her, and she was well aware of it.

When she walked into a room, she immediately became its center; everyone else faded into the wallpaper. She wasn't especially tall, but she carried her generous curves with a feminine assurance. Instead of hiding her figure in tent-like kaftans, she always wore close-fitting skirts or pantsuits together with low-cut tops or blouses, often in a silky fabric. It was part of her strategy to reveal just enough of the cleavage between her voluptuous breasts. Sometimes she almost crossed the line, but not quite. She often wore an expensive necklace to draw the eye to her décolletage. She wore high-heeled shoes or boots and had no problem walking in them. She was over fifty, but even the sternest male judge might find his hand trembling as he picked up the gavel. The odd female magistrate's hands might have trembled a little, too. Charlotta noticed these signs but ignored them, choosing instead to reward everyone with a big smile and the full beam of those sparkling blue eyes before fluffing up her dark-brown curls with practiced fingers. When she began to speak, that was the end of any coquettishness. She was razor-sharp and rarely lost a case.

"So, where are we?" she asked Inspector Berglund.

"You can use this office—it's the biggest. I've brought in some extra chairs," he said, getting to his feet. He gave Willén a little smile and went and stood in a corner, his entire body language making it clear that he was present only as an observer. The chief superintendent remained by the window, where he had positioned himself when he arrived forty-five minutes earlier. He leaned against the sill and tried to look relaxed. The truth was that Charlotta made him nervous, which irritated him even more. At the same time, he was fascinated by her; she was something of a legend in the legal world. And now she would be sitting here while he questioned Kristoffer Sjöberg.

Father and son entered the room along with one of the detectives from Trollhättan. Paula Nilsson had worked with Roger Willén for almost fifteen years. When they first met, both had been new on the job. After a few years he had been promoted to inspector, and now he was the area chief superintendent. Paula, on the other hand, still had the same rank, a divorced mother of three. *God works in mysterious ways*, Paula thought, but she no longer had the energy to feel bitter.

Olof Sjöberg went over to his lawyer and gave her a hug, accompanied by two enthusiastic air kisses. Willén saw her stiffen for a fraction of a second, before she freed herself from Sjöberg's embrace with a smile and turned to the teenager standing by the door.

"Hi, Kristoffer! I haven't seen you since the crayfish party," she said cheerfully.

She made no attempt to approach the boy. He didn't look at her; he just gave a brief nod.

Kristoffer was wearing a red checkered flannel shirt with a dark-blue T-shirt underneath, blue jeans, and sturdy boots. His clothes looked new and clean. He was skinny and gangly with long arms and legs. His hands were unusually large, and in one he clutched a blue baseball cap. His face was marked by a severe outbreak of acne, but he would probably be pretty good-looking when he was older. He was seventeen, almost eighteen, according to Berglund, but he seemed younger. His dark-blond hair was cut in what Willén would call a typical rockabilly style, with a long piece at the front combed up into a tall quiff and held in place by hair gel. His eyes were darting from side to side, but he kept his head down.

Olof went over to his son and gently put an arm around his shoulders.

"Come on, let's have a chat with these police officers. Then we'll go home and get back to work on the Pontiac."

The mention of the car produced a vague nod, but Kristoffer still didn't look up.

After general introductions Willén asked everyone to

take a seat. Tentatively he began to ask questions about what had happened almost exactly twenty-four hours earlier.

It was hard work from the start. Kristoffer gave one-word answers, nodded or shook his head, or didn't respond at all. He never made eye contact with anyone. He spent most of the time sitting motionless in his chair, staring down at the desk.

Willén managed to gain confirmation that Tuva, Kristoffer's second cousin, had waved him down at the bus stop near the school and asked him to give Amelie a ride home because she'd missed the bus. He'd dropped Amelie at the stop near her house, then driven straight home to Breidablick. When asked what he did when he got home, he simply said, "The Pontiac." Willén asked if he could give a little more detail, but Kristoffer shrugged and repeated, "The Pontiac."

Olof cleared his throat. "It's a Pontiac Firebird '68. The owner's coming to pick it up this evening, so we had a lot to do yesterday. We were together in the workshop until around six—that's right, isn't it, Kristoffer?"

The boy nodded, but didn't speak.

"Were you home when Kristoffer got back?" Willén asked.

Olof leaned back, totally at ease, which made the rickety chair creak ominously.

"No, I arrived just after. He doesn't have a driver's license yet, so I was out test-driving a car—a real restoration job. I hurried home to work on the Pontiac with Kristoffer for a while. I was at the Lions' Christmas party in the evening, but his friends Anton and Gabriel came over to help out before I left."

"What time would you say you got home in the afternoon?" Willén asked Olof.

"Around . . . quarter to four."

If that was true, then Kristoffer could hardly have had anything to do with the girl's disappearance. She'd eaten something and used the bathroom, which must have taken five or ten minutes. Kristoffer wouldn't have had time to wait for her at the bus stop and abduct her. Hypothetically he could have offered her a ride back to school, then taken her somewhere else and done something to her before disposing of her—but if he was home by quarter to four, that was impossible. He would have needed at least half an hour.

Or would he? It was around a mile and a half from Breidablick to the bus stop where Kristoffer had dropped off Amelie. Willén thought feverishly, but he just couldn't make it work. There just wasn't enough time. An A-tractor travels way too slowly, no more than twenty miles an hour. *If it hasn't been modified, of course—better check that out.*

"Okay, so we're done here!"

Everyone gave a start as Charlotta Stark stood up and smoothed her black skirt with a graceful movement. Her blood-red nails matched the large ruby sparkling in the décolletage of her cream silk blouse. She hadn't said a word during the interview, but suddenly she was the center of attention. With a regal wave she brought Olof and Kristoffer to their feet.

"If you wish to speak to Kristoffer again, please contact either me or Olof," she said before sailing out the door with father and son following in her wake.

None of the officers in the room managed to come up

with anything sensible to say before their interviewee was gone. Eventually Chief Superintendent Willén's brain started sputtering with rage.

"Get forensics on that fucking A-tractor—check if it's been modified," he barked.

Paula Nilsson nodded, then asked, "Did you notice that the father smelled of booze?"

"No . . . no, I didn't," Willén admitted. He and Paula knew each other well enough to allow him to do so without losing face.

"It hit me when we shook hands, and I think that dreadful Stark woman realized it, too, when he gave her a hug."

"That dreadful Stark woman." Yes, maybe. *But what fantastic tits!* Willén thought, blushing slightly.

IT WAS ALMOST seven—time to look for a place to eat before driving the seventy miles or so home. Willén stood up and yawned. It would be good to get out of these stuffy offices. Tomorrow he would follow the investigation from Trollhättan; his colleagues here in Strömstad could take over. So far the hunt for Amelie had produced nothing, but it would continue through the night. It was a race against the clock now as the search teams battled to find the child safe and well. Or dead.

Just as Willén stretched his whole body, the phone on the desk rang. Strange—there was no one else in the building. Everyone had gone home, including the receptionist. Who had put the call through? The incessant ringing sounded somehow challenging, and in the end he decided to pick up: a decision he immediately regretted.

"What the fuck do you think you're doing? Are you trying to break the kid? Playing fucking mind games!"

There was no need for the caller to introduce himself. Olof Sjöberg sounded far from sober; it was obvious that he'd poured yet more booze down his throat after the meeting at the police station.

"Okay, calm down. What do you mean by—"

"Calm down . . . you have no idea how fucking calm I am. If I wasn't calm, you'd fucking know about it!"

A tirade of curses and threats followed before Sjöberg realized the reason he was so upset. Kristoffer's A-tractor had been collected and transported down to Gothenburg for forensic examination. Kristoffer had also been asked to hand over the clothes he'd been wearing when he gave Amelie a ride—the jeans and hoodie he'd had on in the workshop when the police arrived.

"He had to strip in front of two fucking dumb cops! And one of them was a woman!" Sjöberg ranted.

"That certainly wasn't necessary . . ." Willén ventured, but Sjöberg wasn't listening.

"You're trying to frame him!" he roared.

Willén had to summon every ounce of self-control he had before he replied. "Once again, please calm down. You've got the wrong idea. By examining the vehicle and Kristoffer's clothing, we can confirm that he's innocent. We—"

"He *is* fucking innocent!"

"That's exactly what we want to establish, but Kristoffer was the last person to see Amelie, as far as we know. The gossips will soon have him down as guilty if we can't prove otherwise."

"You're going to plant evidence, I know it!"

Fatigue and hunger took over, and Willén knew he couldn't listen to this drunk any longer. At the same time, he could understand why Sjöberg was worried. As things stood Kristoffer was definitely implicated, and it was possible that he was responsible for Amelie's disappearance. Deep down Willén hoped forensics would find something. Kristoffer was strange. Who knew what someone like him might do?

"I've spoken to forensics in Gothenburg, and they've promised to prioritize this case. Tell Kristoffer he should have his vehicle back just after New Year's at the latest. Hopefully earlier, but of course it's getting close to Christmas and—"

"Exactly! So the poor kid's going to be without it for fucking weeks!"

Chief Superintendent Roger Willén had had enough. "Listen to me, and listen carefully. If we don't carry out this examination and we're not able to prove Kristoffer's innocence, then he's not going to need a vehicle for several years, never mind weeks. He'll be in jail—for a very long time!"

There was silence on the other end of the line, then the connection was broken abruptly.

Willén replaced the cordless phone on its base, then stared at it for quite a while. Something wasn't right. Suddenly he realized what it was: How come Olof Sjöberg had the number of Sven-Ove Berglund's direct line? The number wasn't listed anywhere, and the phone could only be reached via the main line, which was unmanned outside normal working hours. Next question: So how close were Olof Sjöberg and the inspector?

THE INTENSIVE SEARCH for Amelie was still fruitless. The decision was made to continue at full force over the weekend. A large number of volunteers had turned up and been allocated to various team leaders.

On Saturday morning Paula Nilsson and Lars Engman were the only two officers in the station at Strömstad.

"Did you see Kristoffer's A-tractor?" Lars asked.

"I did—my boy, Love, would have been drooling. He's already saying he wants one when he turns fifteen," Paula said with a sigh.

"I can understand that. Apparently the kid helped his father build it. Polished wood on either side of the flatbed, white leather seats, red metallic paint, and aluminum hubcaps . . . It's a long way from the beat-up old Puch Dakota I had when I was a teenager!"

"Sure, but it enabled you to get around, didn't it? I had to cycle. On the bright side, I was in really good shape then—emphasis on 'was.'"

With a wry grimace she pinched the small spare tire around her waist, while her colleague smiled and patted the rounded belly he had started to develop. He was determined to go on a diet, get himself to the gym. After New Year's. He'd made that same resolution for the past three years, and it was high time he followed it through. After New Year's.

"Okay, so we need to talk to Kristoffer again."

It wasn't something they were looking forward to, but Chief Superintendent Willén had been very clear on that point when he called shortly before.

"Find out if Kristoffer offered to wait for Amelie at the bus stop and give her a ride back to school. I've been wondering if he pulled in at the recycling center and turned his vehicle around. Maybe the girl got scared and took out her cell phone—he grabbed it and threw it in the nearest container before driving away. Bearing in mind that according to his father Kristoffer was home before quarter to four, Amelie should be somewhere along the road between the recycling center and his house. That's a distance of around a mile and a half. I know it's already been checked out, but I'm going to ask for a detailed search of that area today and tomorrow. And a search of every summer cottage and outbuilding anywhere nearby," he had said.

THE TWO OFFICERS from Trollhättan were driving to Breidablick to speak to Kristoffer and Olof Sjöberg. The rain had temporarily stopped, but the wind showed no sign of abating.

"One thing occurred to me," Paula said.

"What?" Lars asked.

"We and our colleagues have spoken to just about everyone who lives along that road, or has any connection with Amelie's school—both children and adults. They all know who Kristoffer is, and they all agree that he's a bit special, a bit different. But nobody's had a bad word to say about him. There's been no suggestion that he's unpleasant, has ever shown any violent tendencies, or has ever behaved inappropriately toward a child. Quite the reverse—he's regarded as a nice guy, totally harmless. A genius when it comes to dealing with engines and old cars. One of the mothers told me he helped fix her son's bicycle when someone accidentally ran over it. Kristoffer got a hold of new parts and spent several days working on it; when he brought it back, it was better than it had been before. As good as new, in fact. And he refused to take any payment. Kristoffer was only eleven years old at the time! Why would this slightly strange and technically gifted boy suddenly decide to abduct a nine-year-old girl?"

Lars Engman shrugged. "Hormones kicking in, maybe? Who knows what he's thinking. He's not exactly talkative—although his father more than makes up for that!"

"True, but I can understand why Olof Sjöberg is so protective. The boy has issues, and Olof is a single parent, after all."

They spent the rest of the journey in silence, mentally preparing for the forthcoming encounter.

Between the recycling center and Breidablick they saw parked cars all the way along the shoulders, and recognized two as belonging to the canine teams that had now joined the search party combing the area. There were almost four hundred people involved. If Amelie was here, they would find her.

As expected, Olof Sjöberg was far from pleased to see them. Reluctantly, he let them into the hallway. It was almost midday, but he was still wearing a full-length white bathrobe. His flip-flops made a slapping noise as he walked. He was surrounded by a faint aroma of chlorine; he must have gone swimming. Through the large window in the hallway the two officers could see the glass dome covering the heated pool. The underwater lighting was on, producing a magical glow.

"Don't you think it's time you stopped harassing Kristoffer?" Olof said with a hint of menace. The smell of booze on his breath was unmistakable.

Is this guy never sober? Paula thought crossly. The fact that he was under the influence didn't make their job any easier because he was obviously one of those people who became aggressive when they'd been drinking. Or was he behaving this way because he wanted to protect his son—did he know the boy was actually guilty? Did he know something he hadn't told them? Paula was far too experienced an investigator to start with the key questions, but she would get around to them in her own good time.

"Chief Superintendent Willén wants us to ask him a few supplementary questions," she said pleasantly. She deliberately left out "acting" from Willén's title. Olof glared suspiciously at her.

"What kind of shupp . . . shupp . . . What kind of questions?" he snapped.

"There are always one or two points to follow up on with a witness, and of course we're happy for you to be present," Lars said, doing his best to sound calm and matter-of-fact.

The big man stood in the middle of the granite floor tiles, swaying slightly in his fluffy robe. He frowned and peered at them through narrowed eyes before reaching a decision.

"Sit down. I'll go and get dressed." He gestured toward

two brown leather chairs on either side of a large stove. There was no fire burning behind the glass doors, but it wasn't necessary: the room was warm, and the temperature outside was above freezing. So far the winter had been surprisingly mild, bringing plenty of rain and wind, but little snow. The sea was warmer than usual for the time of year, which gave energy to the winds coming in from the west, according to the meteorologists on the local news. Climate change had been the subject of several lively debates in the media recently. *Too late shall the sinners awaken*, Paula thought.

She admired the stove, its upper section made of shimmering green soapstone, and wished she could afford to install something similar in her small terraced house. But it would have to wait; the children were growing up and getting more expensive by the day.

She and Lars took off their jackets and hung them inside the mirrored sliding doors of the closet. When they bent down to remove their shoes, Olof said:

"Don't bother. I have a cleaner."

With a squeaking sound he spun around and headed down the hall.

Lars and Paula sat down and gazed around the airy entryway. The high, white-painted ceiling created a wonderful sense of space; it was almost like being in a small church, Paula thought. The impression was reinforced by the wrought iron light fixture suspended from the main beam by a heavy chain. Beyond the glow of the pool she could see a large barn-like structure that must function as the garage and workshop. She went over to the window. Several vintage American cars were parked outside the building.

"The workshop," she said.

Lars merely grunted in response. His attention was focused on a large driftwood picture of a Bohuslän fishing village, with boats and boathouses. Small ceramic gulls hovered above the roofs or perched on the pilings on the quayside. It was a beautiful piece and fit in perfectly with its surroundings.

After a while they heard heavy footsteps approaching. Olof had opted for a white shirt, a pink knitted golf sweater, and pale-gray chinos. He had swapped his flip-flops for elegant dark-gray loafers. His hair was carefully arranged to cover the bald patch on the top of his head, and he was preceded by a powerful blast of gentleman's fragrance.

"I've called Kristoffer—he's on his way."

"Isn't he home?" Lars asked.

"Yes, but he's in the workshop. Here he comes." Olof nodded through the window. In silence the three of them watched as the gangling figure drew closer, hunched against the wind, one hand keeping a firm grip on his baseball cap, the other clutching his hoodie as it flapped around his skinny body. He didn't appear to be in a hurry. *I guess he isn't looking forward to this any more than we are*, Paula thought. His pale-gray hoodie had a large oil stain on one sleeve, and his jeans were covered in oily patches.

The door opened and Kristoffer came in, accompanied by a chilly gust of wind. Olof went over to him.

"Go and get changed. Put on the clothes you were wearing yesterday when we were in town. We'll be on the veranda," he said gently.

Kristoffer nodded without looking at any of them. He

stomped past in his muddy boots and disappeared. *The poor cleaner's certainly got her work cut out*, Paula thought sympathetically.

"This way."

Olof set off without looking back to see if the two officers were following him. They passed through a spacious living room furnished with several generous sofas and armchairs. On the walls hung huge paintings with maritime motifs. They continued through an inner hallway, where some of the doors stood open. One led to a big kitchen, and Paula caught a glimpse of dark granite counters, dazzling white cupboard doors, and a range of appliances in brushed steel. The kitchen looked bright even on this gloomy December day. Olof opened the door at the far end of the hallway, waving them through with exaggerated politeness.

With glass walls on three sides, the veranda was impressive. The temperature was as pleasant as it had been in the rest of the house. The front wall was made up of folding doors that led onto an extensive patio surrounded by plexiglass fencing.

Both Paula and Lars stood for a moment admiring the vista. The graphite-colored sea did not look particularly inviting, but the view of the rocks and skerries was spectacular, in spite of the mist and rain.

Olof came and stood beside them.

"People often ask why I don't move into Strömstad. The truth is, this is hard to beat. I never want to leave this place," he said.

Paula could understand why. But at the same time, sitting here enjoying the view had its pitfalls, she thought: too much booze, for example . . .

"Take a seat"—Olof pointed to the armchairs and sofa facing the sea—"I'll go track down Kristoffer."

The furnishings went well with the scenery. The upholstery was a fine cretonne with a floral pattern in blue and lime green. They each sank into a comfortable chair, and a short while later Olof returned and sat down on the sofa. Kristoffer ambled in after a minute or so, and hesitated uncertainly in the doorway.

"Come and sit beside me," Olof said, patting the cushion next to him. Without a word Kristoffer did as he was told. He was wearing exactly the same clothes he'd had on for his interview at the station the previous day. Paula noticed oil beneath his nails, and his hands seemed to be ingrained with black. Maybe he couldn't get them clean however hard he scrubbed. Or maybe he just didn't scrub them.

On the way over in the car, Paula and Lars had decided to start with Kristoffer's all-consuming interest: cars, and older American models in particular. Since Paula drove around in a ten-year-old VW Passat and had never had much interest in vehicles of any kind, she left it to her colleague.

"Hi, Kristoffer—sorry to disturb you when you're working. Lots of people have told us how brilliant you are when it comes to renovating old American cars, and that you're always busy."

Paula noticed Olof's face light up, but there was no reaction from Kristoffer.

"So what are you working on at the moment?"

Kristoffer glanced at his father, then mumbled: "Changing a windshield."

"And what's the car?" Lars continued, sounding genuinely interested.

"Buick Electra. Sixty-seven."

Kristoffer still hadn't made eye contact with either Lars or Paula.

Olof cleared his throat. "I don't suppose you came here to chat about cars?"

Paula took over. She smiled and tried to engage the boy's attention.

"No, we just wanted to clarify a couple of points. Is that okay with you, Kristoffer?"

An almost imperceptible nod.

"So you gave Amelie a ride from the bus stop outside her school to the stop in Önnaröd. That's what you told us yesterday, so I'm assuming that's correct?"

To say that Kristoffer had told them was stretching the truth. Olof had done most of the talking, and Kristoffer had mainly given one-word answers or failed to respond at all. Paula hoped the boy would feel more relaxed in his home environment and start to open up.

"I'm wondering whether you drove off right away when Amelie jumped out, or whether you waited for her?"

Kristoffer stared through the glass coffee table at the intricate patterns of the rug.

"Drove off," he said, looking up at her for a second.

His eyes were clear, but the moment was so fleeting that Paula barely had time to register it.

"You didn't wait so you could give her a ride back to school?" she went on, keeping her tone friendly.

"No."

The answer was instant, with no hesitation. *Sounds convincing*, Paula thought, but she decided to rephrase the question to see if he changed his mind.

"Did you see Amelie again after you'd dropped her off at the bus stop in Önnaröd?"

"No."

Again, no hesitation.

"Did you find her cell phone? After you drove away, I mean?"

For the first time he looked at her properly, completely taken aback.

"Cell phone?"

"Amelie's cell phone. It—"

"What the hell are you talking about? Kids lose their phones all the time! Kristoffer has his own cell—he doesn't need to take anyone else's!" Olof interrupted her, placing a protective arm around his son's shoulders.

With a huge effort Paula managed to control her irritation. "I'm not accusing Kristoffer of taking Amelie's phone, but it's all we have to go on. It was found, as I'm sure you've read or heard, in a bin at the recycling center. But there are no other traces of her," she said, keeping her voice calm. She took a deep breath before turning back to Kristoffer.

"Did you find Amelie's phone in your truck? Had she dropped it?"

"No."

His answer was equally firm, but this time he was staring out the window. No more eye contact.

Both Paula and Lars tried to get Kristoffer to contradict himself, but without success. He was adamant: Amelie had jumped out of the truck, closed the door, and run off toward the house where she lived. Kristoffer had pulled away from the bus stop and driven straight home. When he got back he had gone to the workshop and continued working on the Pontiac that was due to be collected the following day. That was where Olof had found him when he arrived home, along with his friends Anton and Gabriel.

"So that's the end of the matter. I'd like you to leave us in peace from now on," Olof said. He had remained surprisingly composed during the interview. Paula had seen his eyelids drooping occasionally and assumed that the constant boozing must make him tired.

She and Lars exchanged a quick glance; they both realized they weren't going to get much further. They stood up and prepared to take their leave.

Kristoffer remained seated. Suddenly he looked at his father and said, "I almost crashed into Eva."

Olof frowned, clearly confused. "Aunt Eva?"

The boy nodded.

Olof straightened his back, any trace of drowsiness swept away. He turned to the two officers and said, "Wait here. I need to make a call."

Kristoffer immediately got to his feet and followed his father out of the room.

"What's going on?" Lars raised his eyebrows inquiringly, but Paula was equally puzzled and merely shrugged.

A few minutes later Olof reappeared. "You need to speak to Eva! She can confirm that Kristoffer's telling the truth, that he came straight home after he'd dropped Amelie at the bus stop!"

He looked triumphant; there was no other word for it.

"Who's Eva?" Lars asked.

Olof seemed surprised, then gave a wry smile. "Of course, you're not from around here. Eva's my sister—she lives over there." He gestured toward the south-facing glass wall. "There. You can see the roof of her house," he said.

Through the mist and rain, the upper part of a black slate roof was just visible.

"I got ahold of her just as she was leaving Gardermoen—she was in the car. She's been in Copenhagen. She'll be home around three."

"How do we get to her house?" Lars asked.

"You need to go back about a hundred yards, then it's the first turn on the right. There's no sign, but there's a big silver fir at the end of the drive. She lives on a hill, just like me."

Through the window Paula saw Kristoffer slide in through the door of the workshop. He was back in his dirty clothes, one hand clamped on top of his baseball cap. The wind hadn't eased—in fact it seemed to have increased in strength. On impulse, she gave Olof her most charming smile. "Mind if we take a look in the workshop?" she asked. "Those fantastic cars . . ."

"Yes, I do mind. You're not hassling the boy in there," Olof snapped.

As they didn't have a search warrant, they had no choice but to leave and head back to Strömstad. They would have to find something else to do before it was time to come back and speak to this new witness, Eva, who had suddenly cropped up. Lars suggested they go and get some lunch, which Paula thought was an excellent idea.

THE WHITE BRICK house seemed to glow in the darkness at the top of the hill. There was a detached garage to one side; they parked in the driveway and walked over to the front door. Despite the fact that darkness was falling and nature was in her washed-out winter garb, Paula could see that the garden was well-cared for. It wasn't hard to imagine how glorious it would look in the summer. There were fruit trees, raspberry canes, and currant bushes, as well as several beds of roses and perennials that were now unrecognizable. Not that she would have been able to name them anyhow. A short distance away was a large vegetable patch. It was obvious that Eva loved her garden and had a green thumb. However, she didn't seem to be as keen on Christmas decorations as her brother; the only concession was an Advent candle bridge in two of the windows.

The door abruptly swung open when they reached the steps.

"Welcome—I'm Eva Sjöberg. I believe you're the officers who interviewed Kristoffer?" the woman in the doorway said. She smiled and stepped aside to let them in. Like her brother, Eva was tall and well-built. Lars and Paula knew she was three years younger than Olof, but she looked to be the same age. The lines on her face were deeply marked, as if she'd spent a lot of time in strong sunlight and hadn't bothered with sunscreen. She wore no makeup, and her hair was gray. Her body gave an impression of heaviness, although she wasn't necessarily overweight. *Strong* was the word that came to Paula; Eva's handshake was firm—perhaps a little too firm.

The pleasant aroma of coffee and freshly baked Christmas cookies greeted them as they followed her through the house. Paula noticed a harmonious blend of old and new in the décor, with touches from exotic lands. Two long spears with feathers on the shafts were displayed on one wall next to African masks and decorative shields. A collection of drums of various sizes stood in one corner. The African elements carried over to Eva's clothing and footwear; she wore leather sandals and a beautifully patterned full-length kaftan. She had thick shoulder-length hair that she wore loose, and her square-cut bangs suggested that she didn't frequent the salon too often.

"Please take a seat while I go and get the coffee," she said. Her smile was warm and genuine. There was a sincere friendliness about this woman, with not a hint of her brother's blunt aggression.

They found themselves in a large living room with enormous picture windows. Even though it was almost dark they could sense that the view was at least as fantastic as the one from Breidablick—although it was just about the only thing the two houses had in common.

Lars and Paula settled into comfortable dark-brown leather armchairs that, like the matching sofa, were smooth and well-used. The coffee table was actually a black wooden chest covered in intricate carvings. With their camels and other animals, the motifs also looked African. The top of the coffee table was protected by a thick sheet of glass, and a red dish containing lit pillar candles sat in the center, spreading an atmospheric glow. Beneath the chest was a zebra skin that also looked somewhat the worse for wear.

"You're in luck—the cookies are ready. When I heard you were coming I took the dough out of the freezer and did some baking—although the buns were already made. I just had to defrost those," Eva said cheerfully when she returned carrying a tray.

Paula wasn't surprised to see the sturdy handmade mugs in different colors. No dainty little porcelain cups here! In a woven bread basket lay saffron buns and a pile of Christmas gingerbread cookies, which smelled amazing. Eva set everything out on the table and urged her two guests to help themselves.

"I only heard about the missing girl today. Olof told me when he called me at the airport. It's terrible!" Eva said, her expression serious.

"How could you have missed the news? There's been a hell of a search operation around here for almost forty-eight hours now," Lars said.

Eva picked at a strand of hair that had fallen over her face and attached itself to the sugar on her saffron bun. She sucked the hair thoughtfully for a couple of seconds before answering. "I've been away—a reunion with my old college friends. We graduated just before Christmas 1975. We usually meet once a year to celebrate, and this time it was Berit's turn. She married a Danish orthopedic consultant almost forty years ago and still lives in Copenhagen even though he died a while ago. Her children live there and—"

"Do you still work?" Lars interrupted her.

"No—although I do volunteer for the Red Cross. I'm retired."

"What did you do?" Paula asked.

The question slipped out involuntarily, but Eva didn't seem to mind.

"I'm a trained intensive-care nurse, and I've worked in both Sweden and overseas for a number of different organizations. I've seen a great deal of human suffering, but I've also had a lot of fantastic experiences. Met people who . . ." She broke off and grew serious once more. "I loved my job, but ten years ago Kristoffer's mother died."

She fell silent and swallowed hard before continuing. "Olof and Kristoffer were devastated. Ann's death was completely unexpected; she was only forty-three. A stroke. I took care of Kristoffer. He's never had it easy, not since he was born."

She stood up and started topping off the coffee cups, offering the buns and cookies around again. She sat down and composed herself.

"He was born ten weeks premature. The doctors discovered a hole in his heart, but it was very small, thank God. He only needed one operation. But as he grew older it became clear that he's almost deaf in his left ear and has reduced vision in his left eye. He also has Asperger's syndrome, or high-functioning autism, as it's called these days. Olof and Ann consulted a series of experts in this type of neuropsychiatric disability."

She paused and took a bite of her bun.

"You say disability, but he doesn't appear to be particularly disabled . . . I mean he's brilliant with cars and so on," Paula said.

"Absolutely! Olof realized very early on that Kristoffer is phenomenally gifted in that area. I remember when he'd just turned three, and they were here for dinner. I'd recently come back from Somalia, and as we were sitting chatting, Kristoffer sneaked into my guest room, where I had a floor lamp with an adjustable arm so you can change the angle. When we went looking for him he'd taken the lamp apart and neatly laid out all the pieces on the floor. Ann was horrified, but Olof simply asked him if he could put it back together. Kristoffer nodded and got started. In no time the job was done, and the lamp worked! And it still does to this day."

"Three years old?" Paula said skeptically. At that age her own kids were building with Duplos. They didn't move on to Legos until they were older, so they wouldn't put the small pieces in their mouths and choke.

"Yes, and Olof encouraged him. He let Kristoffer tinker with all kinds of things, and he was really good!"

Eva smiled proudly, deepening the lines in her face.

"What about friends?" Paula asked.

The smile disappeared.

"There were a few problems when he started school because he is a little different, but he's always had friends. Maybe not many, but he's never been bullied. The other kids admire his technical skills, and for the past few years he's really focused on cars. Old American cars are Olof's main passion, and he's developed that interest along with Kristoffer. People come from all over western Sweden to get their cars fixed up. Kristoffer's good at paint jobs, too, though he's not interested in leather or interiors. He only wants to work with metal."

There was no mistaking the pride in her voice.

"You don't have any children of your own?" Paula asked tentatively.

A fleeting shadow passed over Eva's face. "No."

Lars reached for a third saffron bun. Before he took a bite he looked searchingly at Eva. "So how come you saw Kristoffer on Thursday afternoon? You just said you were in Copenhagen."

"I didn't fly out until the evening. It only takes ninety minutes to drive from here to Oslo; I caught a late flight down to Copenhagen."

"What time did you leave here?"

"Just before four. It was around ten past three when I saw Kristoffer drive away from the bus stop in Önnaröd. The little girl was running up the slope toward her house. Kristoffer's usually very careful in traffic, but he must have been in a hurry to get home because he pulled out right in front of me. I had to slam the brakes on, and I beeped my horn at him. I wagged my finger at him, too, but he knew I was only kidding. When I got home I changed my clothes, then grabbed my suitcase and headed off to Gardermoen. From Kastrup, I took a cab to my hotel and fell straight into bed. I spent all of Friday with my college friends in Copenhagen. We had a fantastic day, with a traditional Danish Christmas feast in the evening. Today I caught a morning flight back to Oslo and arrived home about an hour ago."

What an amazing woman—the first thing she does when she gets home from a busy trip is bake cookies, Paula thought. But now it was time to ask the question that had come up at regular intervals; it had to be done.

"Your brother . . ."

Eva looked at her and sighed.

"I can guess what this is about. Everyone notices . . . when he's like this."

"We couldn't help it. He seems to have a problem with alcohol."

Another shadow passed over Eva's coarse features, and she looked down at the work-worn hands resting on her lap. When she raised her head, tears glinted in her eyes. She met Paula's gaze. "Olof is an intermittent alcoholic," she said quietly. "He always liked to party, but since he lost Ann . . . This time of year is the worst. Ann died on Christmas Day, and he can't cope. The trigger is all those holiday parties and festive dinners, and from then on he carries on drinking for several weeks. It's gotten worse over the last couple of years. He also had an episode last summer, though it was pretty short."

"How does Kristoffer deal with it?"

There was deep sorrow in Eva's eyes when she answered.

"When he was younger he used to come and stay with me during the worst periods, but Olof has never mistreated his son. Never! He just couldn't manage to take care of the boy—cook meals, make sure he had clean clothes, and so on. But when he stopped drinking he'd come and pick him up."

"Does Kristoffer still come here when his father's drinking? We spoke to him at home earlier today."

Unconsciously, Eva straightened her back. "He's perfectly capable of handling the situation these days. He's old enough to understand that his father's sick. He turns up and stays the night occasionally, but that's happening less and less often. Then again, he likes to sleep over now and again even when Olof isn't drinking."

"He doesn't drink at all between episodes?"

"Not a drop."

LARS AND PAULA were driving back to the center of Strömstad. The rain had stopped, and it looked as if it was going to be a damp but snow-free Lucia Eve.

"What do you think? Is Eva telling the truth, or have she and her brother cooked this up between them?" Lars asked.

"I don't know. We need to follow up on this college reunion; she gave us contact info for her friend Berit and the hotel. I'll take a look at the passenger list for the flight, too, although something tells me it will all check out. She made a very . . . solid impression," Paula said.

"And she bakes fantastic saffron buns. I don't need any dinner!"

PART II

JANUARY

WITH A SIGH of relief Detective Embla Nyström sank down onto the seat of her old Volvo 245. The tension across her shoulders eased, and she was filled with a mixture of calmness and anticipation. It had been a hectic week at work, and she really ought to spend the weekend relaxing, but nothing was going to stop her from driving up to her family home in northern Dalsland because it was time for the January wild boar hunt. It was a relatively new tradition, introduced by her hunting club.

Hunting wild boar is easier in winter than during the summer months; it's more difficult for the boar to hide among the vegetation, and the mosquitoes and blackflies aren't around. The club had decided to shoot in two specific locations that had been prepped ahead of time, so no dogs were needed.

The two youngest members, Embla and Tobias, were childhood friends. According to tradition they should have taken care of providing food for the animals, but since Embla lived in Gothenburg, Tobias had set up two sites, just over half a mile apart. During the fall he had started putting out food. The whole club had helped gather natural fodder such as potatoes, carrots, seeds, and fruit. Anything processed, like bread or leftover Christmas cakes and cookies had been banned; they wanted only what was good for the boar.

The hunt was scheduled for the beginning of the year because it wasn't permitted to hunt adult boar between February 16 and April 15, so this would be their last opportunity until late spring/early summer. Until three years ago a winter hunt hadn't been necessary since there weren't many wild boar in their area, northwest Dalsland. But now they were everywhere—literally! Their numbers were increasing at an alarming speed, and therefore they had become an important quarry for the hunters.

There was no snow left in Gothenburg. The thin layer that had been covering the ground had been washed away by the rain between Christmas and New Year's. The first weeks of January had been cold, wet, and windy. Gloomy and depressing. It rained all the way up to Mellerud, but when Embla turned northwest toward Bäckefors, the rain changed to snow.

Thick flakes were falling on the well-cleared yard when she skidded to a halt in front of her uncle's house. He flung the door wide open before she'd even climbed out of the car. With the light behind him, he looked like a great big shadow.

"Hey there, hot-rod girl!" he yelled.

He'd been welcoming her with the same words for the past ten years, ever since she first drove all the way from Gothenburg on her own in the '90 Volvo 245 he'd given her. Back then Aunt Ann-Sofi had stood beside him, but she had died almost four years ago, so now he was alone.

Embla ran up the steps and Nisse gave her a great big bear hug. Eventually he loosened his grip and asked the obligatory question:

"How's the Veteran running?"

Her reply was always the same:

"Like clockwork!"

That was what he wanted to hear, but it wasn't entirely true. Neither the fuel gauge nor the speedometer were functioning properly. Despite repeated visits to various repair workshops, both instruments were still unreliable. Plus, a banging noise seemed to be coming from the engine. Or maybe it had something to do with the axle. Sometimes the car seemed to pull when she was going around a bend. In all honesty, the old Volvo that had served her so well was starting to reach retirement age since she couldn't afford to have it serviced. It had just passed 180,000 miles. Occasionally she considered getting a new car, but that would be pure blasphemy. She had no intention of mentioning it to Nisse; she wasn't sure how he'd take it.

As they walked in the house, Embla inhaled deeply. The house was filled with the wonderful smell of meat and frying onions. "My favorite—moose steaks!" she exclaimed.

"Of course. It's important to make an effort when there are special visitors. Go on up to your room while I finish making dinner."

She took the stairs two at a time. Decorated in shades of yellow, the guest room was ready for her as always. Nisse had managed to outfit a former closet with a small toilet and shower. There was just enough space under the sloping roof for Embla to stand up in the shower, but she had to stoop a little when using the sink. An exhaust fan and a tiny window kept the dampness at bay. It was perfect.

She took a quick shower and put on a cornflower-blue long-sleeved T-shirt and a pale-gray fleece body warmer with her tight blue jeans. She left her hair loose to dry.

Nisse came into the hallway as she ran down the stairs. He smiled and shook his head.

"You're so like Sonja."

"People often say that."

"Yes, but I mean when she was young. She used to wear her hair loose, too—all the girls did in the seventies. Everyone admired her long curly hair. And the color . . ."

"Chestnut. And yours was the same shade," Embla said quickly.

"Chestnut . . . I'd have said dark red. Mine's long gone, of course."

He ran a callused hand over his bald head. He had shaved off the small amount that remained around his ears and at the back of his neck; Embla had convinced him that it looked better that way.

"You know she was only eighteen when she went down to Gothenburg to apply to drama school—and she got in!" he said.

Embla had heard the story many times over the years: how her amazing mom had impressed the board and gotten in at her first attempt. She was expected to have a brilliant career. After a year or so she met Örjan, Embla's father, an arts journalist specializing in theater. They married in a civil ceremony and had a big hippie wedding celebration for family and friends. They had three boys within six years. Seven years after the youngest boy a little bonus came along—Embla. Her mother's acting career never really got going again after the children began to arrive, but Sonja wasn't one to complain. She had plenty of other projects. She would soon be eligible for her state pension, but nobody was expecting her to slow down. She still had her organic food store in Haga, which she ran with a friend, and she was an active politician, serving on the town council in Linnéstaden as a representative for the Green Party. She also looked after her retired, absentminded husband and loved spending time with her eldest son's two children.

Embla had often wondered whether Sonja would have gone back to acting if Embla hadn't been born—not that her mother ever hinted as much. Embla had never really felt like she fit in with her artistic, creative family. Her choice of profession had been met with bewilderment. A police officer? What sane person wanted to become an officer? As activists who attended demonstrations against the US's involvement in the Vietnam War, both her parents had come into close contact with police batons on more than one occasion. Not that anyone said anything. In the Nyström family, *tolerance* was a key word.

They sat down at Nisse's rustic pine table, where he had set out a tempting array of food. Perfectly fried moose steaks ("You shot it yourself!") with plenty of fried onions in a delicious sauce, boiled potatoes, and lingonberry conserve ("I picked the berries"). Embla stuck to water while Nisse partied with a low-alcohol beer.

"I'll need a steady hand tomorrow," he said with a wink as he poured the beer.

The meal was excellent, and they ate in silence for a while. Eventually Embla leaned back to let the food go down better. As usual when she came to visit Nisse, she'd eaten too much too fast; her uncle was a phenomenal cook. It had to be good, plain Swedish food, though—he wasn't interested in any fancy French cuisine.

"How's Ingela?" she asked.

Nisse's face lit up at the mention of his partner. "Great. She's got her grandkids over this weekend, so our hunting trip fits in very well." He emptied his glass, and as he put it down he gave her a sly look. "We've booked a trip."

"Cool—where and when?"

"Gran Canaria—the week after Easter. It's cheaper then."

Embla raised her eyebrows. As far as she was aware, her uncle had never set foot outside Sweden. As a young man he had been tied to the farm because of the animals, and just when he and Ann-Sofi had begun to think of retirement, she'd gotten sick and passed away very quickly. Nisse had never flown before—she knew that for certain.

"Fantastic! Who's going to look after the farm?"

"Tobias—he doesn't have any animals these days. I've only got four youngsters left after the autumn slaughter, but I'm not sure if I'll bother getting any more in the summer. We'll see." He fell silent for a moment, his expression suddenly serious. "Did you know that Tobias is going to buy Hansgården?"

This was news to Embla, and she simply shook her head. She still shuddered whenever she heard the name of that place. The events of last fall came crowding in; she had almost lost her life there. With an enormous effort she pushed the unpleasant thoughts aside and tried to concentrate on what Nisse was saying.

"It's on the market for next to nothing. Nobody wants to live there after . . . what happened," he said grimly.

Embla regained the power of speech, and even managed a small smile. "It'll be fine. Baby number three will be along soon, so they need a bigger house. And no doubt Tobias will buy the land as well so that he can concentrate on farming full-time."

"Let's hope so. He enjoys selling agricultural machinery, but commuting to Åmål every day isn't easy."

Despite his words, Nisse looked far from convinced. He felt the same way as Embla about Hansgården: it was haunted by bad luck. No one who'd lived there had been happy. Hopefully Tobias's growing family would change all that.

Switching to a different subject, Embla said, "I want to fit in a serious session with your punching bag and the speedball tomorrow morning. I've only managed to train twice this week."

"Are you starting to feel better?"

"Absolutely."

Nisse looked searchingly at his niece. He knew her too well and could probably hear that she wasn't being entirely honest.

"How about the concussion?" he asked quietly.

Embla preferred not to talk about the injuries she'd sustained while working a case during the previous year's moose hunt, but at the same time she realized that if there was anyone who would understand, it was Nisse.

"I . . . I took a really hard blow to the back of the head. The doctors said I must have an unusually thick skull. They've done all kinds of tests, run an EEG, and so on. It's looking much better, but I must never take the risk of receiving another blow like that. Never. I could suffer a brain hemorrhage and end up in a vegetative state."

She fell silent and swallowed, trying to get rid of the lump in her throat. She had gone through a severe trauma, and the consequences would affect her for the rest of her life.

"Does that mean you can't compete anymore?"

"Yes."

The answer was muffled. Six months ago, she'd become Nordic light welterweight champion. The whole of Scandinavia had bubbled over with jubilation. It had been the happiest day ever, the result of many years of rock-hard discipline and relentless training. And now she wouldn't be able to defend her title. It was a bitter pill to swallow, but at the same time she was grateful that she'd survived the attack.

"That's a shame, but I'm so pleased you've managed to recover."

As usual Nisse seemed to have read her mind. He stood up and began to clear the table.

"Time for coffee and a piece of Ingela's Tosca cake. Did I say she sends her love? If not, I'm telling you now."

THESE DAYS THERE were only six active members of the hunting club. Former leader Sixten Svensson's injured shoulder would never be the same again, and he was now living in the local assisted-living home. He was happy there, and his hunting friends visited him on a regular basis. They had reached an agreement allowing the club to lease his land and hunting rights, and after each hunt he would receive a share of the meat. Really, it would be handed over to the cook at the home, who was delighted at the opportunity to prepare a special meal for all the residents. Sixten enjoyed living with people his own age, chatting about times gone by. He realized now how lonely he'd been in that dilapidated house on the edge of the village.

When darkness fell late on Saturday afternoon, Embla and Nisse began to make their preparations for the hunt. It was a few degrees below freezing, with a light breeze. Ideal conditions—not bitterly cold, and with good visibility. However, they could well be sitting motionless for long periods, so they needed thick socks and long underwear, several tops and sweaters layered beneath their padded jackets, plus warm hats and fur-lined gloves. The worst thing about hunting in the winter was that you always ended up with frozen hands; when it came to shooting, only fingerless gloves would do.

The club had decided that three or four boar would be enough. This expedition was designed to fulfill their own needs in terms of meat; they weren't intending to sell any to restaurants. They had split into two teams, one for each feeding site. Embla and Nisse were with Karin Bergström, Embla's cousin. She was the daughter of Nisse's oldest sister, Embla the daughter of his youngest. The two of them had been close ever since childhood, despite an age difference of almost seven years. They always enjoyed hunting together. Karin's husband, Björn, was with Tobias and his father, Einar.

They parked the car a short distance away on the track, which had been cleared by the snowplow. They moved along silently until they reached a smaller forest track where the ground had been churned up by broad tires. This was where Tobias had driven his Nissan Navara SE when he came to feed the boar. Cautiously, with the wind in their faces, the three hunters edged closer to the site. It was only fifty yards off the track, but it was dark among the fir trees, and they had to be careful where they put their feet.

Before long they could hear the animals slurping and grunting. Good—they were making enough noise to drown out any sound from the approaching hunters. The site was behind a wall that was tall enough to allow them to stand. As silently as possible they positioned themselves a few feet apart and looked through the night vision sights. They were also able to rest their rifles on the wall, which made life easier.

Around twenty boar were enjoying the food, squabbling over the tastiest morsels. A large sow had a number of piglets with her. She and her offspring were protected, but there were several yearlings that looked perfect. However, it was hard to get a clear shot. The boar were moving around, close together, and it was against the law to fire if there was a risk that another boar could be hit by the bullet or the ricochet.

After fifteen minutes, Embla's fingers had begun to stiffen. The fingerless gloves didn't stop the cold from penetrating into her bones. It was high time to take out a suitable animal, but they were still crowding together. Suddenly the sow snapped at a yearling. He squealed and skittered away. Embla took aim and fired, and the yearling went down immediately. The others took fright and fled. Nisse seized his chance and shot a small sow that became separated from the others in the confusion.

Seconds later they heard distant shots from the other site.

"Yes! At least three, maybe more!" Karin exclaimed delightedly. Her husband and three kids loved their food back home, so a decent share of wild boar meat was more than welcome. However, first they would have to wait for the results of the trichinella or roundworm tests, which they were legally obliged to submit to a lab. Only when the samples yielded a negative result would they be permitted to eat the meat.

They finished up with four wild boar—three yearlings and Nisse's little sow. The perfect amount to fill up everyone's freezer.

EMBLA FELT BOTH rested and happy when she set off back to Gothenburg. The sense of well-being lasted all the way to just north of Nödinge, at which point the Veteran's engine seized up. All she could do was call for a tow truck.

It was definitely time to start thinking about a new car.

ACTING CHIEF SUPERINTENDENT Roger Willén was back in Strömstad. Just like before, he was in DCI Sven-Ove Berglund's office. Also present were detectives Paula Nilsson and Lars Engman, along with officers Patrik Lind and Alice Åslund. Everyone in the room looked serious. Willén took a sip from the mug adorned with the words THE EIGHTH WONDER OF THE WORLD. Alice had set out coffee and a plate of cinnamon buns; she couldn't possibly have known that the chief superintendent would choose that particular seat. *A chance occurrence that seemed to be deliberate*, Alice thought with a smile. She had ended up with MOTHER'S LITTLE HELPER. You had to wonder what kind of wit had once bought these mugs. Sven-Ove had WORLD'S BEST GRANDPA, but that one belonged to him; it had been a Father's Day present from his three-year-old grandson, Ivar.

Willén cleared his throat to indicate that he was ready to start.

"It's now been almost six weeks since Amelie Holm went missing. We've worked intensively, including over Christmas and New Year's, brought in extra resources, widened the search with additional manpower. We haven't found a single trace apart from her cell phone, which has only Amelie's fingerprints on it. In some places the prints are smudged, but that could be because Amelie herself held it with her gloves on. Or because whoever took her was wearing gloves when he or she threw it in the container."

He paused and took another sip of coffee. Paula Nilsson also spotted the logo and had to clamp her lips together to hide a smile.

"No suspicious calls or messages have been found in her phone records. Her computer has also been examined—nothing out of the ordinary there either." Willén paused to finish his cinnamon bun. "Forensics found nothing unexpected in Kristoffer Sjöberg's A-tractor, which hasn't been modified, by the way," he continued. "The girl was wearing a hat, which is presumably why no hairs were discovered. There's a small amount of fabric residue from her gloves on the car seat and mud from the shoulder by the bus shelter in the foot well on the passenger side. That's it. Whatever happened, it didn't happen inside that vehicle. The question is where he took her."

"So you still think it was Kristoffer?" Berglund said. His icy tone escaped no one in the room.

"Who else could it have been? He's the only person who was seen with Amelie."

After a few seconds of extremely tense silence, Berglund took a deep breath.

"The triangle between the recycling center, Knarrevik, and Hällestrand has been searched with a fine-tooth comb. Every single square foot that's accessible with an A-tractor has been checked out. Plus the search area has been extended to include every forest glade, every ravine, every empty house . . . We're talking about several square miles here. We've used a helicopter with a thermal-imaging camera, the Home Guard, trained police officers, dog patrols, the organization Missing People, and hundreds of volunteers over the past six weeks. There is absolutely no trace of Amelie. She's not there," he said firmly.

The lines around Willén's mouth tightened. "So where is she, then?"

Berglund gave him a sharp glance. "The bus driver and the passengers have confirmed that she didn't travel back to school on the bus, which means she must have missed it. I think someone picked her up in a car as she was walking along the road—it was pouring, remember. Maybe she waved her arms, just like Tuva did when she stopped Kristoffer," he suggested.

"Would a nine-year-old girl really get into a stranger's car? I can understand her accepting a ride with Kristoffer because she knew him, but hitchhiking . . . I'm not sure," Paula said.

"I don't believe it was a stranger. Either she knew the person, or she was taken against her will. But no one saw or heard a thing. I'm leaning toward the idea that Amelie knew the driver," Berglund said grimly.

"You mean someone who isn't in our database," Willén said, eyes fixed on his colleague.

"I know you're busy checking out every pedophile in western Sweden and Norway. I also know that nothing has come up that can be linked to Amelie."

Patrik Lind unexpectedly waved his hand, and Willén gave him a nod.

"Could it be a hate crime? I mean, she's pretty dark-skinned . . ."

Berglund suddenly looked just as old and tired as he felt. The child's disappearance and the suspicions against Kristoffer had taken their toll. Were they supposed to check every racist in Norway and in western and central Sweden as well as every pedophile? Not to mention Copenhagen—there's a ferry from Oslo. An investigation of that scale could easily involve around a third of Sweden's police service, plus colleagues in Oslo and Copenhagen. Impossible! The very idea made his head spin.

"We can't rule anything out under the circumstances," he said vaguely.

Willén was having none of it. "Before we start speculating," he said, "I suggest we stick to the lead we have—Kristoffer Sjöberg."

Berglund responded with alacrity. "We've had both Olof and Kristoffer under surveillance. They hardly left Breidablick over the Christmas and New Year's period. The boy spent most of his time in the workshop. Olof's sister, Eva, has been over pretty often, as have Kristoffer's two friends who also like tinkering with cars. But no one else has been there."

He had no intention of mentioning the fact that he'd visited three times over the holiday.

He could see that Willén wasn't convinced, although the others didn't look quite so skeptical. There was absolutely no proof that Kristoffer had had anything to do with Amelie's disappearance. The case was beginning to look increasingly hopeless. It had swallowed up an enormous quantity of resources, even though so many volunteers had come forward. As if that weren't enough, there had been a serious attempted homicide on New

Year's Eve: a Norwegian partying in Strömstad had been stabbed. It turned out that the guy had a criminal record a mile long and was well-known to the Oslo police, which meant that Berglund was now under considerable pressure from his colleagues in Norway.

"By the way, Robert Halvorsen is still in critical condition. He's been in a coma ever since he was brought in, and the doctors don't hold out much hope. If he dies we have a homicide investigation on our hands." Berglund sounded even more weary, if that were possible.

"In that case you'll be pleased to hear that the Norwegians have taken over the case," Willén informed him. "We don't need to give it another thought."

He looked very pleased with himself as he delivered the news, and the smug look lingered as he continued, "I spoke to an Inspector Gilstrup from the Oslo narcotics unit yesterday. They've been watching Halvorsen and his gang for a long time. Maybe that's why they decided to party over here on New Year's. The house they were staying in belongs to a Swede, Hans Joffsén. He's made a fortune in finance selling some kind of fund. He's around forty, no criminal record, but he and Halvorsen obviously know each other, as he rented the house to Halvorsen, and—"

He was interrupted by the shrill signal of the intercom. Berglund leaned forward and pressed the button.

"Yes?"

"Sorry to disturb you, but Inspector Gilstrup would like to speak to you," Kicki's voice informed him.

"Okay, put him through."

Berglund's phone rang and he picked up the receiver. His expression grew even grimmer during the course of the conversation. Eventually he thanked his colleague and ended the call.

"Halvorsen died about an hour ago."

What a way to end the work week, he thought.

The Working Dogs Association in Skee had started its Saturday evening session. That evening the dogs were being trained to track down game with just their senses of smell to guide them. The only light sources allowed were flashlights or headlamps, but the owners were operating under strict instruction not to help their teammates out. To make things even more difficult, the exercise took place on a forest track outside the town. Earlier in the day the trainer had placed tufts of fur from various wild animals in the terrain along the track. The pouring rain—though of course unplanned—added to the challenge.

At the trainer's signal, the dogs set off with their owners at regular intervals, a few minutes apart. There were eight dogs of assorted breeds and their masters and mistresses. The clear star of the night was one of the smaller dogs—a border terrier named Baltsar.

When the pairs reached the end of the track, they continued left on the 164 and followed the road for around a hundred yards in the direction of Skee, before turning right onto a well-lit dirt road that would take them back to the association's modest clubhouse. They were all familiar with the route, even though they had mostly used it in daylight until then.

There was a small parking lot where the track met the 164. The first pair to arrive were Baltsar and his master. The dog started pulling on the leash and yapping excitedly, making it clear that he wanted to investigate something interesting in the opposite direction of the clubhouse. His master was cold and wet and just wanted to get indoors, but Baltsar started whining and refused to cooperate. It was unusual behavior, even for the strong-willed terrier, so after a little while, his master gave in and loosened his grip on the extending leash. The dog immediately ran over to the side, still barking like crazy. His master followed and shined his flashlight down into the ditch.

The report of a dead man in a ditch outside Skee to the east of Strömstad came into the Regional Crime Center in Gothenburg at 5:14 p.m. The caller introduced herself as the trainer with the Working Dogs Association, and she was extremely upset.

"The whole ditch is full of blood!" she repeated over and over again.

The only squad car on duty in northern Bohuslän was manned by Patrik Lind and Alice Åslund. They both felt a surge of adrenaline when they heard that a body had been found. They took the name of the person who'd made the discovery, then headed to the scene to cordon off the area in case it turned out to be a suspicious death and wait for backup.

"The 164 to the west of Skee. No one lives out there—well, hardly anyone," Patrik commented.

Nothing was going to stop him. He raced toward the location, blue lights flashing, siren screaming. Neither of them had been first on the scene of a death before, let alone a person who had died in unexplained circumstances, as Patrik rather dramatically put it.

They sped past Skee, traveling way too fast, and were soon out in the country. They could see the flashlights from some distance away, waving back and forth to show them where to go.

"Shit. Eight flashlights," Alice muttered.

They were surrounded as soon as they got out of the car. Both owners and dogs were shocked, and the atmosphere was fraught. The dogs barked and whimpered, making it difficult for Alice and Patrik to get a clear picture of what had happened. Confusion reigned until a powerful woman in a yellow high-vis jacket managed to shut everyone up, enabling her to explain who they all were. Clearly she was the group leader and trainer. The two officers had already worked out that they must be dealing with some kind of dog club. The trainer, who introduced herself as Rigmor, asked the others to move aside so that the police could get to the ditch to look at the dead man. In an authoritative tone she informed them that she was a nurse and used to seeing dead bodies. Because he was definitely dead, there was no doubt about that. She had examined him already and established that the cause of death was a blunt force trauma to the head.

Patrik and Alice let their flashlights play over the body. A man was lying facedown in the sodden ditch. The water around his head was colored red with his blood. He was wearing dark running shorts and a reflective jacket. His hat might once have been white, with a small multicolored bobble. The back of the hat was drenched with blood, but it was just possible to make out a broad wound.

"He's wearing a headlamp," Rigmor pointed out.

Alice noticed the beam next to hers wobble, and spun around just in time to see Patrik collapse. With Rigmor's help, she managed to lay him on his back and raise his feet to get the blood flowing to his head. After a minute or so he began to mumble something unintelligible; it took a while before Alice could make out what he was saying.

"Hat . . . my hat," he slurred, then he passed out again.

A REPORT OF a missing boy reached the Regional Crime Center at 5:50. His name was Viggo Andersson, a six-year-old from Strömstad. He had disappeared from the family's garden just over an hour earlier; he'd been out playing alone. The boy's father, Ted Andersson, made the call. He was agitated to say the least.

"I would have gone on looking for a while longer if . . . but Amelie Holm went missing . . . I know her parents . . . And now Viggo . . . What the hell are the police doing? Everyone knows who took her—that kid who's sick in the head!" he yelled down the phone.

He had already searched the immediate area and called everyone he could think of, but to no avail, so his distress was understandable. The decision was made to contact Acting Chief Superintendent Roger Willén; he was responsible for the investigation into the disappearance of Amelie Holm before Christmas, so it made sense to pass on Viggo's details to him.

The only available radio car was north of Uddevalla and was immediately redirected to Skee in order to relieve the two officers from Strömstad who were there;

they were now needed to search for the boy. A team with local knowledge was better suited to the task.

Willén called the contacts who had organized the search party for Amelie. He explained that another child had gone missing in Strömstad—a little boy this time.

The Home Guard, a number of volunteers, and the police dog team would start looking for Viggo immediately. Missing People would be there early the next morning if he hadn't been found by then.

Willén then called Sven-Ove Berglund to tell him what had happened. Without any great enthusiasm the inspector agreed to drive over to Skee. During their conversation, Willén could hear voices and laughter in the background. Sven-Ove and his wife obviously had guests, but in circumstances like these, all resources must be mobilized as quickly as possible.

When he'd put the phone down, Willén sent for Paula Nilsson and Lars Engman. They wouldn't be enjoying a cozy Saturday night at home either.

THEY WERE ON the way to Strömstad when Willén's cell phone rang. He answered immediately, then sat in silence for a long time, listening. Paula was driving; she could hear a man's voice on the other end of the line, but not what he was saying. Willén ended the call, his expression grim.

"That was Sven-Ove. It seems as if the guy in the ditch is a cop. And it looks like homicide."

Both Paula and Lars were shocked, and couldn't think of anything to say. The silence in the car was almost palpable.

"A colleague—who is it?" Paula managed eventually.

"His name is Viktor Jansson—he's based in Strömstad. Thirty-four years old, lived in Skee. One of the officers in the patrol car recognized his hat. Either of you know Jansson?"

Paula and Lars shook their heads. They knew a lot of their colleagues in the four towns, but it was impossible to know everyone.

After a brief discussion it was decided that Paula would drop off Lars and the chief superintendent at the crime scene in Skee, then she would head over to see Viggo Andersson's parents to try to get a clearer idea of what had gone on.

The CSIs arrived at the tiny parking lot at the same time. The ditch at the side of the road was illuminated by the headlights of a blue-and-white patrol car, and three silhouettes could be seen next to the vehicle.

"The big guy must be Patrik Lind, and the other uniformed officer is Alice Åslund. Sven-Ove is plainclothes," Willén said. He felt it was important to remember the names of those he was working with. It showed you cared—that's what he learned on a course after he'd gotten the job of acting area chief superintendent.

Paula Nilsson had entered the Anderssons' address into the car's GPS. The wind picked up as she got closer to the sea, and the rain started to come down even harder. She had to tighten her grip on the wheel as fierce gusts repeatedly took a hold of the car, threatening to sweep it off the road. The darkness was so dense that it seemed to absorb the least glimmer of light. She longed for snow to brighten things up. There was nothing left of the snow that had fallen between Christmas and New Year's.

Her thoughts turned to the missing boy. As far as he was concerned, it was a good thing the temperature hadn't dropped too low. Hopefully he would soon be found. Surely two children couldn't disappear within six weeks in the peaceful little town of Strömstad. It felt as unreal as the idea that a cop had just been murdered. Plus there had been a serious stabbing on New Year's Eve, which had now been classified as a homicide. Although according to Willén, that was no longer their concern because the case had been taken over by Oslo.

She glanced at the clock on the dashboard. Viggo had only been gone for around four hours. If it hadn't been for Amelie, the police might not have reacted so quickly, but the hypothesis that there could be a pedophile operating in the area had come up several times during the course of the investigation. It was good that the search parties were already set up and had been mobilized immediately. If the child was out there in the darkness, they would find him. He must be so frightened . . .

Paula felt a mixture of sorrow and anxiety when she thought about Viggo. She blessed the fact that her own children were fourteen, twelve, and nine. Amelie and her daughter were the same age . . . What if something happened to Tilde . . . ? A shudder ran down her spine. The danger wasn't over. It would never be over. *You remain a worried mom until the day you die*, she thought with a sigh. The children were with their father this weekend. Anders was also a cop, and they'd managed to work out their shifts so that they were free on different weekends. It worked very well, even though his new partner didn't really get along with the kids. Sometimes Tilde didn't want to go to her dad's, which made life difficult for everyone.

Paula sighed in the darkness. Guided by the GPS, she passed a train station, then Uddevallavägen, heading for the churchyard. After a couple of hundred yards she turned onto a side street and parked outside the address she'd been given.

There were lights showing in every window of the small two-story house. It was a typical 1950s property, the kind Paula and her siblings had grown up in. The garden was large, with several flourishing fruit trees. In the birch nearest the gate was a wobbly looking tree house, no more than three feet off the ground. Two swings moved to and fro in the wind beside a yellow slide, which had fallen over. A red spade stuck up from the waterlogged sandbox. There were signs of the child who had played there, but no sign of the child, Paula thought gloomily.

She cautiously made her way up the slippery path to the steps, but before she had time to set foot on the first one, the door flew open. A woman of around thirty stared at her, wide-eyed.

"Have you found him!"

It wasn't a question, it was a cry of anguish.

"Hi, I'm Detective Paula Nilsson. I'm afraid Viggo hasn't been found yet, as far as I'm aware."

She walked up the steps, holding out her hand. The woman didn't move an inch, she just kept running her hands through her bleached hair. Her mascara had run, giving her a panda-like appearance, and her eyes were filled with sheer panic. Her foundation was also badly streaked. She was wearing short nylon overalls, which strained over her generous bust, and a name badge that said *Pernilla.*

Paula gently placed a hand on the distressed mother's arm. "We will find him," she said, "but we need your help, and all the information we can get. May I come in?"

She wasn't sure if Pernilla had heard the question, but at least she stepped aside to let Paula pass. The hallway was narrow, the floor cluttered with shoes, bags, umbrellas, and an assortment of toys. Next to the door lay a large old-fashioned flashlight. The coatrack was full, so Paula draped her jacket over her arm as she went into the kitchen. A fairly old countertop dishwasher was humming away laboriously on the draining board, which looked clean. There were two pancakes on a plate on the table.

"He had pancakes before . . . before he went out."

Pernilla stared at the cold pancakes, her eyes full of tears.

"My kids love them, too," Paula said.

"They're Viggo's favorite, with lots and lots of jelly and sugar. Way too sweet, but that's how he likes them . . ."

Pernilla broke off and went over to the sink. She grabbed a piece of paper towel and blew her nose.

"Shall we sit down?" Paula suggested, pulling out a chair.

Pernilla nodded and took a seat opposite her, constantly plucking at the paper towel in her hand.

"Have you come straight from work?" Paula asked, pointing to the badge.

"Yes. I don't finish until eight on Saturdays, but I left as soon as Ted called. I forgot to change." She tried to smile, but managed only a pale grimace.

"Is your husband here?"

"No, he's out searching. I wanted to go with him, but they called and said a cop . . . a police officer was coming over, so I had to stay home. And someone has to be here in case . . . in case Viggo finds his own way back . . ." Her lower lip began to tremble, and tears rolled slowly down her cheeks.

"Okay, Pernilla, so we've been given a description of Viggo. Six years old, blond curly hair, blue eyes. Wearing a camouflage-patterned jacket, green waterproof trousers, green hat. Black Wellington boots. Correct?"

"Yes . . . yes. He turned six on December nineteenth," she sobbed in despair.

Only just six, might be better to regard him as a five-year-old, Paula thought. That wasn't good, but she hid her concern.

"Viggo had been gone for about an hour when your husband called us, which means he must have disappeared at around quarter to five."

A nod.

"I'm wondering why Viggo was playing outside alone. It would have been dark by then. And of course it's been raining all day today—it hasn't really gotten properly light at all."

Pernilla blew her nose again, then she took a deep breath and met Paula's gaze. "Viggo loves being out in the dark with his flashlight—running around, shining the beam on different things. Ted was out there with him at first, but then Ted started to feel cold and wanted to come in. He tried to get Viggo to come in as well, but he didn't want to, so Ted told him he could have another fifteen minutes. When he went out to fetch him . . . Viggo was gone!"

The last sentence unleashed a fresh flood of tears.

"Was that when Ted started searching the local area?"

"Yes, and he called everyone we know. He checked with the neighbors . . . drove around in the car . . ." She wiped her eyes and nose, then exclaimed angrily, "Why didn't you lock up that idiot? He's a retard! First he took Amelie, and now Viggo!"

For a few seconds Paula was taken aback by the woman's aggression and choice of words. She straightened up and said authoritatively, "There is nothing to connect Kristoffer Sjöberg to Amelie's disappearance. And he certainly isn't a retard."

"But he attacks kids! How many does he have to take before you realize!" Pernilla yelled, lurching forward across the table.

Paula felt a few drops of saliva land on her cheek. Keeping her tone reasonable, she replied, "We don't know what's happened to Viggo. We don't believe there's a link to Amelie. It—"

Pernilla interrupted her with a loud snort. "Johannes thinks it was Kristoffer who abducted Amelie—that's what he said to Ted weeks ago!"

Paula realized she was talking about the girl's father. "You've heard Johannes Holm say this?"

"No. Ted told me." Pernilla seemed more hesitant now, but she still looked ready for a fight.

"So he and Johannes are friends?"

"They've known each other all their lives, so I know what Johannes and Maria have been going through. And now it's happening to us!"

Pernilla started sobbing again. Paula was at a loss. How could she conduct a sensible interview with this hysterical woman? Pernilla's anxiety was understandable, but she would have to pull herself together if she was going to be any use in the search. The smallest piece of the puzzle is important, and it's vital to work fast during the first few hours after a disappearance. Right now, however, Pernilla was in no state to cooperate.

Both women gave a start when the doorbell rang. Pernilla leaped to her feet and raced into the hallway. Paula heard agitated voices, then Pernilla came back into the kitchen with Amelie's parents. They nodded to Paula, their expressions grave. Johannes was tall and thin, with wispy fair hair and blue eyes—the polar opposite of his small, dark-skinned wife, Maria, with her halo of frizzy black hair. However, when he put his arm around her shoulders and she leaned into him, the warmth between them was unmistakable.

"Where's Julien?" Pernilla asked, her voice trembling.

"With my mom. We came as soon as we heard about Viggo. Our neighbor saw it on Facebook," Johannes said.

That was one of the advantages of social media: information could be spread quickly, Paula thought. It was time she left, but first she had a question for Johannes.

"Pernilla tells me you and Ted have been friends all your lives . . ."

He looked at her suspiciously. "What's that got to do with the fact that our kids are missing?"

"The police always look for patterns. Sometimes there isn't one, but we still like to check things out. It goes with the territory when you're a cop," Paula said with a little smile.

Johannes didn't smile back. He sized her up for a moment before he answered. "Ted and I have known each other since preschool and went to the same high school, though we took different classes. Now we both work in Norway, but not in the same place. Our families get together occasionally."

He gestured toward the two women, who nodded in agreement.

Paula stood up. "Okay, thank you. Please contact me if you think of anything that might be helpful."

She gave her card to Pernilla, who slipped it in the pocket of her nylon overalls. It was obvious that she'd forgotten about it within a second. Johannes Holm refused a card—the family had already been given several by different officers.

When the door closed behind Paula, she remained standing on the top step. She'd thought of something, but it had slipped out of her mind just as quickly as it had appeared. Could she retrieve it? She made an effort, but nothing popped up; she was probably too tired. Best to wait, see if it came back later. She shivered as the cold crept inside her collar. The wind was even stronger now, and the rain lashed her face as she set off toward the car, her shoulders hunched.

When she reached the tree house she stopped and shined the beam of her flashlight on it. A rickety little ladder led up to the floor. It was clumsily made, but no doubt it was good enough to allow a little boy to clamber up and down. The weeping birch had three trunks, and the cabin had been built to fit among them. Paula didn't go any closer because she knew CSI would want to check for footprints. The tree was around three yards from the gate. If Viggo had been playing there with his flashlight, it would have been natural for someone passing by to stop and chat with him. If the boy then came over to the gate, it would have been easy to grab him—a hand over his mouth, maybe a chloroform pad, then into a car. It would have taken seconds.

Paula started knocking on doors, but no one had seen or heard anything suspicious. Most of the neighbors were elderly and hadn't been tempted to venture out in the wind and rain. By the time she'd worked her way up and down the small street, she was soaked to the skin and frozen. She decided it was time to liaise with her colleagues at the station, find out how the search for

Viggo was going, and get an update on the murder of Viktor Jansson. For at least the hundredth time that evening she wondered how the hell all this could happen *at the same time* in peaceful little Strömstad. Surely so many terrible things wouldn't befall the idyllic town by the sea over the course of the entire next decade.

On Sunday all available officers in Trollhättan and Strömstad were brought in, along with extra resources from Uddevalla. Not only were they dealing with two missing children, but also the murder of a police officer. On top of that, colder weather was forecast. During the day the temperature would drop below freezing, the wind would remain strong with icy gusts, and the rain would turn to snow.

The Home Guard, dog teams, Missing People, and other volunteers were still searching for the children. The focus was on Viggo, but there was a faint hope that they would find a lead on Amelie. Or her body. No one really believed she was still alive.

The previous evening Roger Willén had spoken to Patrik Lind at the scene of Viktor Jansson's murder. Patrik was still feeling dizzy, but Willén wanted to know how Patrik had realized right away that the victim was a colleague.

"The hat. We play for the same indoor bandy team, Viktor and I. Back in the fall our main sponsor bought a new jersey with our logo and their advertising. The hat . . . with the bobble . . . It's our . . . the team . . . colors."

Patrik fell silent and took a swig of water from the bottle he'd been given by one of the paramedics.

"But how did you know it was Viktor?"

"I knew right away. It's only our team that has those particular colors on the bobble, and Viktor's the only member of the team who goes running all year round and lives in Skee," Patrik replied, his voice far from steady. He was deeply shocked and upset by the murder of his friend and colleague. They all were, and the atmosphere at the scene was oppressive. The dog owners had been sent away as soon as Alice had taken their names and contact info.

When the CSIs arrived they immediately started complaining that any possible evidence on the wet ground had been trampled into oblivion by both humans and their four-footed companions. They erected a tent to protect both the body and themselves from the rain, but they were still working in extremely challenging conditions. The ditch was deep and overflowing with water.

"This is the worst January I can remember," one of the technicians muttered as he passed Willén. "Either that or it's the longest fucking November ever."

Willén had to agree.

THE SEARCH FOR Viggo continued. A fresh contingent of Home Guard soldiers was brought in, and the exhausted dog teams were replaced after working for twelve hours in the appalling weather. A helicopter with a thermal-imaging camera had been deployed, but to no avail.

THE FIREFIGHTERS WERE faced with an inferno when they arrived on the scene. The entire structure was already alight, flames crackling against the dark sky. Sparks swirled in the strong wind, and there was a considerable risk that the fire could spread to the nearby house. The burning building looked like a large barn, but they could see several vehicles both inside and outside. An acetylene tank had already exploded, and they had no idea if there were more. All they could do was try to contain the blaze.

Within minutes an Audi A3 came racing up the hill. It screeched to a halt in the yard, and the driver, a middle-aged woman, got out. She ran over to the firefighters with surprising speed.

"Where are Olof and Kristoffer?" she shouted.

It was hard to make out what she'd said over the roar of the flames. The incident commander went over to her, mainly to stop her from getting too close. When he realized she was related to the owner of the property, he drew her to one side.

"Who lives in the house?" he asked.

"My brother, Olof, and his son, Kristoffer," the woman said between coughs. "Where are they?"

"Do you know if they're home?"

After a fresh bout of coughing, she said, "They should be. Both of them." Her voice was hoarse and her eyes filled with tears.

"So why haven't they come out? We assumed no one was home because no one came to meet us when we got here. We've got our hands full with the blaze, so we haven't had time to knock on the door yet," the commander said, turning toward the house.

The woman gave him a sharp glance, her lips compressed into a thin line. She spun around on her heel. "I have keys."

Without waiting for a response, the woman ran toward Breidablick's impressive double front door. She could see it was ajar; the light from a lamp in the hallway window was seeping out through the narrow gap. With the commander close behind, she ran up the steps and yanked the door open. She pressed the switch just inside and remained standing on the threshold for a few seconds. The commander looked over her shoulder at the macabre scene now illuminated by the ceiling light.

On the floor about three feet from the door lay a badly injured teenage boy. There was a significant amount of blood on the floor, and he appeared to be unconscious. At first the commander feared they were too late, and he was already dead. The woman quickly moved forward and knelt down beside the boy, checking his throat for a pulse. It was clear that she'd done it before.

"Call an ambulance!" she said.

At the touch of her fingers, the boy grunted.

"It's okay, Kristoffer. It's me," the woman said gently.

Untroubled by the blood, she began to check him

over, while at the same time stroking his uninjured right cheek with one hand. The left side of his face was a bloody mess. His body jerked when she touched his right arm and hand.

"His right wrist and ulna—the bone in the forearm—are fractured. His left cheekbone is shattered, and there may be some damage to the eye. Injuries to the sternum. He's lost a lot of blood."

The commander passed on this information to the Regional Crime Center. At first, the person who'd taken the call about the fire outside Strömstad at 10:55 thought it must be some kind of hoax, but when the incident commander contacted them to say that he needed an ambulance, his request was immediately implemented. So during one weekend, a police officer was murdered, a six-year-old went missing, and now there was a major fire with at least one person badly beaten. What the hell was going on in Strömstad? That was what everyone at the Regional Crime Center was wondering.

Without looking up from the injured boy, the woman said, "Can you try to find Olof? He's probably asleep on the sofa, or in his bed. Drunk."

The bitterness was clear. The commander trudged off in his heavy boots and began to search the big house, but he couldn't find the boy's father anywhere. He returned to the hallway and the woman who was still kneeling beside her nephew, desperately trying to communicate with him.

"Kristoffer! Kristoffer! Where's Dad? Do you know where he is?"

The boy's only visible eye began to twitch. He raised his uninjured left arm and pointed at the window with a trembling hand. Outside the fire was still raging. The glow of the flames danced over the walls in the hallway, making the gulls in the driftwood picture look as if they were moving their wings.

ON WEDNESDAY MORNING sleet fell over Gothenburg. It was the kind of morning when you just want to stay in a nice warm bed and carry on sleeping. To tell the truth, Inspector Irene Huss didn't like any mornings. If it were up to her, the working day would begin at noon at the earliest. Actually, after lunch—even better. She had no objection to working late into the evening or at night. That was the way her daily rhythm had always been.

In my next life I'm going to open a nightclub, she thought as she contemplated the coffee machine. That was her usual retort when her colleagues commented on the fact that she was half-asleep in the mornings. She needed two mugs of black coffee during morning prayer, which was what they had taken to calling the daily briefing sessions. As usual Irene was the last to arrive in the conference room.

The others were already seated, and Chief Inspector Tommy Persson was ready and waiting in front of the whiteboard. His laptop was open on the table, suggesting that he would be showing pictures or diagrams. *Please don't let me nod off*, Irene prayed as she sat down next to the newest member of the team. Although she wasn't really new. Embla Nyström had spent a few months working with the Violent Crimes Unit a year or so ago before moving to VGM, or Västra Götaland County Bureau of Investigation's Mobile Unit, to give it its full title. After the major reorganization within the police service, VGM had been disbanded and the three members of the team redeployed.

Irene was pleased that Embla had returned, this time in a permanent post. She was young and energetic and gave a real boost to the somewhat aging department. Even the resident hunk, Fredrik Stridh, was approaching forty and was a settled father of two these days.

With her lustrous dark red hair and toned body, Embla had more than a hint of glamour about her, but she was down to earth, impulsive and full of ideas, physically strong, and very smart. An excellent cop, to put it simply. Recently Irene had noticed a gravitas about her that hadn't been there before, but that was hardly surprising given what she'd gone through the previous fall. She'd almost died, for God's sake! Embla was only a few years older than Irene's twin girls; maybe that was why they got along so well. However, this was no mother-daughter relationship. They had a mutual respect for each other, and the chemistry between them just worked.

"Hi. Mmm—I don't drink coffee, but it smells wonderful. I kind of inhale the caffeine," Embla whispered.

"Inhale? I'd prefer an intravenous drip."

They laughed quietly; Irene's coffee consumption was a standing joke between them. They pulled themselves together and focused on the chief inspector. Embla felt guilty when she realized he was looking straight at her. Had her whispering and laughing disturbed him?

"Embla, you need to call Roger Willén, the acting area chief superintendent in Trollhättan," he informed her.

Embla was surprised. Admittedly Willén had spoken to her a few times after the events of last year, but once he was sure she'd fully recovered from her injuries, he hadn't contacted her again. What did he want? He seemed to have acquired a fancy new title since they'd last met. Something told her he'd be really pleased about that.

"Is it urgent?" she asked.

"Yes—he said you have his number."

True—she hadn't deleted it from her contact list. Irene raised an eyebrow when their eyes met, but Embla could only shake her head and shrug. She had no idea what it was about.

"I'VE BEEN GIVEN permission to reassemble VGM on a temporary basis. Fyrbodal is in an impossible position, and we need help. I'd like you to come up to Strömstad as soon as possible—you need to be here by three-thirty at the latest," the chief superintendent informed her.

It took a few seconds before Embla was able to speak. Obviously she was aware of what had gone on in Strömstad recently.

"Is this about the missing children? And the murder of Viktor Jansson?"

"Yes. Plus a couple of other things."

Other things? Surely that was more than enough?

"Have you spoken to Göran and Hampus?" she asked.

"Yes. They've also been released from their normal duties. Göran will be contacting you and Hampus." He paused, but before Embla had the chance to say anything, he added, "It will be good to meet up again, but the circumstances could have been better. See you later. Goodbye."

"Bye . . ."

But he'd already hung up.

SUPERINTENDENT GÖRAN KRANTZ had returned to his former role in the technical department. These days it was under the supervision of the National Forensics Center, but the seven regions worked independently to a large extent. As Göran was something of a computer genius he had a number of special tasks within the department. In order to keep up to date with developments, he was sometimes involved in practical assignments out in the field and also worked in the different laboratories.

When the call came from Willén asking him to take charge of VGM once more, his heart gave a little leap of joy, much to his surprise. Until that moment he hadn't realized how much he'd missed the freedom of those days. As soon as he'd finished speaking to Willén, he contacted Hampus Stahre, who was lead interrogator with the narcotics unit. After a whole raft of objections from Hampus's chief, he was given permission to return to VGM.

All three were surprised, but full of anticipation. The idea that the team would get back together, if only for a short time, was more than any of them could have imagined or hoped for.

First they had to go home and pack. They also had to check the car before they set off. This was pure routine, something they always did when they were called to help out in an investigation in the Västra Götaland region. Their specially equipped Volvo XC90 was still in the garage at Police HQ; the new management hadn't decided what to do with it yet. Other issues took higher priority. Or maybe they'd just forgotten about it, as Hampus said.

JUST BEFORE THREE o'clock Embla parked the black Volvo in the square outside the police station in Strömstad. When they rang the bell, Roger Willén himself came to open the door.

He must have been at the window waiting for us, Embla thought.

They all shook hands, and Willén greeted them warmly.

"Good to see you. There's a meeting at four. All the units involved in the various investigations will be there. They'll brief you, then you'll have the opportunity to ask questions. There are so many of us we had to borrow a room over at the town hall," he told them.

There was a spring in his step as he led the way upstairs and showed them into Sven-Ove Berglund's office. The inspector wasn't there; he'd called in sick that morning. Willén assumed Berglund had fallen victim to the flu epidemic that was raging in Strömstad just like in the rest of the country.

Kicki on reception organized coffee and cookies for the team from Gothenburg. All three of them had eaten lunch before setting off, but they weren't about to refuse a snack. Except for Embla, of course, who according to Hampus always had to make a fuss with her herbal tea. As usual she had brought her own tea bags, so all she asked for was some hot water. She never ate cakes or cookies. Embla trained hard and was very conscious of what she consumed. Unfortunately Göran didn't have the same restrictive attitude to sweet things.

Embla was wearing light boots with a low heel, tight jeans, and a steel-blue polo shirt, the same color as her eyes. During last year's investigation Willén had mostly seen her in hunting gear: thick trousers, heavy boots, gray sweater, and body warmer. Today's outfit was definitely sexier, but he thought it best to keep his opinion to himself.

Over coffee—and herbal tea—Willén gave a rough outline of what had gone on in the town over the past six weeks, before summarizing the situation: "So we're talking about two missing children, a fatal stabbing, arson with a presumed fatality as a result, a serious assault, and the murder of a police officer. All at once. It's too much!"

He glanced at the clock and got to his feet.

"Time to go."

THE MEETING WAS held in a conference room with plenty of space for the thirty or so officers who had gathered there. They were seated on comfortable chairs facing a podium. From the walls, the luminaries of the town through the ages gazed down at them from dark oil paintings in heavy gilded frames.

Acting Chief Superintendent Roger Willén welcomed everyone and introduced the three members of the VGM team, who were then given an in-depth account of each investigation by their respective colleagues.

Since the Oslo police had taken over the stabbing of Robert Halvorsen, they touched on the events of New Year's Eve only briefly. The general consensus was that the homicide had nothing to do with the other crimes but was due to some kind of feud between Norwegian gangs in the capital. There was an ongoing investigation into an extensive narcotics ring that involved both the murder victim and a number of the partygoers.

Seventeen-year-old Kristoffer Sjöberg was still in rough shape. The contusions all over his body indicated that he had received several vicious kicks, one of which had ruptured his spleen. During the night doctors had carried out emergency surgery to remove the damaged organ. The operation seemed to have gone well, but the boy's general condition was still poor. He had also suffered a concussion, and there was some swelling of the brain, but at least there was no evidence of a hemorrhage. He would remain in an induced coma for a while. Willén couldn't hide his irritation as he passed on this detail, and Embla could understand why: you can't interview a person in a coma.

The fire investigation team announced that they had established that the blaze at Breidablick had been started deliberately. They had found traces of an accelerant among the debris. An hour or so earlier, Olof Sjöberg's charred body had been recovered. He had been lying on a sofa in a room that had apparently been used as an office. His sister, Eva Sjöberg, had said he would probably be there. Without mincing her words, she had described the office as the "booze room." When he was in a bad way, he would shut himself in there and drink for several days. "There was a toilet and a refrigerator—that's all he needed," she'd said.

The fire department had been alerted on Sunday evening when the automatic alarm in the workshop went off. The only witnesses who had called the emergency number were an elderly couple visiting friends in Strömstad. They had been on their way home to Hällestrand when they saw the flames up at Breidablick, clearly visible against the dark sky. The man had been in touch again a few hours ago because he'd suddenly remembered something. Just before the turn off for Mällby they had met a pretty big car speeding toward Strömstad. He had no idea what kind of car it was—maybe a station wagon? When asked if it could be an SUV, he'd said he didn't really know what an SUV was.

As far as the timing went, the encounter could well fit in with the assault and the arson attack. Willén allocated two officers to follow up this lead; they would start by checking the CCTV cameras at the train station and ferry terminal. There wasn't much traffic in Strömstad on a Sunday evening in January, particularly between 10:40 and 11:00.

The mood darkened when they moved on to the murder of Viktor Jansson. He had been born and raised in Strömstad, completed his training at the police academy in Stockholm, then served in the capital for a few years. The opportunity to return home had come along two years ago. For the first few months, Viktor and his fiancée, Jessica, had rented an apartment in town, but after a while they had found the house in Skee. Viktor was a cheerful, sporty guy. He played indoor bandy, went running on a regular basis, and did strength-training workouts at the gym. He ran all year round and had been on one of his usual circuits on Saturday. Darkness was no obstacle; he simply wore a headlamp.

Jessica had gone down to Gothenburg to visit a cousin who'd just had a baby. She'd arrived back in Skee shortly after five o'clock Saturday afternoon and had been surprised that Viktor wasn't home. She wasn't really worried; she just assumed he was getting in some extra training. When the doorbell rang later and she opened it to find two police officers standing there, she knew right away that something had happened. She was still in deep shock.

The preliminary report from the autopsy gave blunt force trauma to the back of the head as the cause of death. Several brutal blows had been delivered using a heavy object, and the whole of the back of the skull was more or less crushed. The wound would be analyzed in more detail, but the initial view was that the weapon had been rounded, like some sort of cudgel. A considerable amount of force had been used. The weapon had not been found at the site, which was also the scene of Viktor Jansson's murder. The killer had attacked him from behind, then pushed him into the water-filled ditch. The medical examiner didn't believe he'd drowned; the injury to his head was so severe that he was probably already dead by the time his face ended up underwater.

There was nothing new on Amelie Holm.

Viggo's disappearance was equally mysterious. He had gone missing during a period of fifteen to twenty minutes while he was alone in the garden, playing with his flashlight. The neighbors hadn't seen or heard anything suspicious. There had been no unfamiliar cars in the area, and no one had noticed a stranger in the street. The darkness and the bad weather had of course contributed to the fact that no one had been paying much attention to what was going on outdoors.

During the subsequent discussion Willén decided that the three officers from VGM should focus on the search for the two children.

"Take a look at Viggo first because the trail is still fresh. We've put a hell of a lot of resources into Amelie's case, but we're still stuck on square one," he said.

Göran Krantz nodded. "Okay, we'll make a start right away."

"Good." The relief in Willén's voice was unmistakable.

"Where can we set up?" Hampus asked.

The relieved expression on Willén's face vanished in a second.

"The thing is . . . we have a slight problem. The Laholm Hotel has rooms for you, but only for tonight. From tomorrow until the weekend every bed in Strömstad is booked for a major Norwegian conference—some oil company. But of course we'll find you a decent place to stay."

He didn't sound quite as convinced as he was trying to appear. The team wasn't worried. They could usually sort out a roof over their heads.

"Embla, I'd like you to go and speak to Kristoffer's aunt, Eva Sjöberg," Göran said.

"Sounds like a good start."

"Hampus, maybe you could have a chat with Viggo's parents."

Hampus nodded without looking up; he was busy tapping away feverishly on his cell phone. He hadn't said much during the journey, but Embla had assumed he was tired. Was something else going on?

They were sitting at a window table in the hotel's spacious foyer, which was sparsely populated. Two large gas-powered stoves gave an illusion of warmth, with flickering flames behind the glass doors. From her seat right by the window, Embla could look down onto the open-air pool. People emerged from the changing rooms and the steaming sauna and stepped into the black water. In January! It must be freezing cold! The wind had dropped a little, but the water was far from still.

Her thoughts were interrupted as Göran got to his feet.

"We'll meet back here for dinner at nine," he said.

AT FIRST GLANCE it didn't look as if Eva Sjöberg was home. The exterior lights were on, but Embla couldn't see any sign of life from inside. She drove up slowly and parked at the bottom of the steps. As she switched off the engine, a light came on in the hallway; she could see the glow through the frosted glass in the front door. She got out of the car, walked up the steps, and rang the bell.

"Who is it?" a faint voice asked.

Eva must have been standing right behind the door, but after what had happened to her relatives, Embla could understand her caution. She took out her ID and held it up.

"My name is Embla Nyström and I'm a detective from Gothenburg. I'm here to help with the investigation."

The door opened a fraction of an inch and a pale, haggard face appeared in the gap.

"A Superintendent Krantz called to say you were coming," Eva said, opening the door. Embla stepped inside, hung up her jacket, and took off her shoes. Eva's thick gray hair was tousled and uncombed. She was wearing a green-and-white patterned loose-fitting full-length dress and bobbled gray cardigan. Shuffling along in thin sandals, she led the way through the house, switching on lamps as she went. The décor was an intriguing mix of the old and the exotic. The living room was furnished with a well-used leather sofa and armchairs. Eva clicked on the ceiling light, as well as several small lamps in the huge picture window, making it impossible to see anything outside. There was only darkness.

"Tea?" Eva asked wearily.

Tea, not coffee. Fantastic!

"Please."

Embla looked at Eva's pallid complexion and noted the dullness in her eyes. She probably hadn't slept for the last twenty-four hours, and maybe she hadn't eaten either.

"I'll come and give you a hand," Embla offered.

Together they went into the spacious kitchen. The cupboard doors were made of dark wood, as were the table and chairs. Above the table hung a conical lamp that looked like it was made from woven birch bark. Embla filled the kettle and spooned tea leaves out of a shiny packet labeled ORGANIC ASSAM GOLDEN while trying to make small talk with Eva, but it ended up being more of a monologue. The older woman mostly just mumbled unintelligible things, interspersed with the occasional "yes" or "no" in response to a question. She took out some bread and dropped four slices into a toaster with a retro design. She placed butter and cheese on a tray—a fine, mature cheese. *Delicious*, Embla thought. *And excellent tea.*

They added the teapot, mugs, plates, and toast to the tray and returned to the welcoming living room. The zebra-skin rug had seen better days, but both the rug and the beautifully carved chest that served as a coffee table seemed very modern. *I could imagine having these things in my living room*, Embla thought. Her gaze fell on an open fireplace in the corner, with plenty of wood in a copper pan beside it.

"Would you like me to light a fire?" she asked.

She caught a faint glimmer of interest in Eva's eyes. "Yes, I think that would make me feel . . . better."

There was such sorrow in her voice that Embla felt her throat tighten with sympathy. Eva's grief was understandable; the family had suffered a terrible blow. But she had to start functioning again. Her help was vital to the investigation.

Embla quickly got the fire going, then poured the aromatic tea into the generous hand-painted mugs before settling down in a comfortable armchair. She made a cheese sandwich with the toasted bread and ate it before tentatively asking a few questions.

"Any news on Kristoffer?" she began.

Tears sprang to Eva's eyes. She swallowed hard several times before she was able to answer. "He's . . . he's still in intensive care. I'm not allowed to see him. Apparently they're going to keep him in an induced coma for a few days because of the pain . . . and the swelling on his brain. How could anyone do something like this?" She let out a sob and fumbled in the pocket of her cardigan for a packet of tissues. She wiped her eyes, blew her nose, and tried to compose herself.

"Is he in Uddevalla or NÄL?" Embla asked.

"NÄL. It's not exactly local, but I'm used to driving. I've driven through savannas and deserts . . . places where there are no roads. A long time ago . . ."

Norra Älvsborgs Länssjukhus—that was the hospital where Embla had been treated after the injuries she'd sustained during the moose hunt in October. She shuddered involuntarily, but tried to hide it from Eva. With a huge mental effort, she pushed aside those dark memories.

The older woman remained silent for a while, but Embla was glad she'd started talking a little more. Just as Embla was formulating another question, Eva took a deep breath and continued.

"They operated on him last night. His spleen was ruptured beyond repair. And his face . . . They've stabilized the cheekbone and the lower jaw with titanium. The jaw was broken in two places. They've also put his arm in plaster."

Distress had brought color to her pale cheeks. Maybe the hot tea and toast were also helping to get her circulation going again. Tears were running down her cheeks, but she didn't seem to notice them.

"It's appalling, but of course we're doing our best to track down whoever's responsible," Embla assured her. "Do you have any idea who could have done such a thing?"

Eva snorted. "It could be just about anybody! There's been so much gossip since Amelie disappeared—Kristoffer's crazy; he better not approach girls of his own age; he's shown signs of being a pedophile in the past. It's all lies, every single word of it!"

Her cheeks were bright red now. Embla nodded to show that she was on Eva's side. "Have people said these things to you? Or to Kristoffer?"

"Do you think they'd say that kind of stuff to our face?

Not a chance! It's all on the Internet. On Facebook. People have posted so many lies about Kristoffer, and he's gotten some terrible text messages. His friends Anton and Gabriel told me. Kristoffer doesn't say a word—he just gets . . . quieter."

Eva blew her nose again. She seemed more present, somehow. She looked angry, which Embla felt was a good sign. She made a mental note to ask Göran to check out what had been posted online; there might be leads to the arsonist.

"Since your brother died in the fire, I've been wondering if he was the intended victim. Kristoffer might have seen someone setting fire to the barn and was beaten up to stop him from talking. Do you know if Olof had any enemies?"

Eva thought hard and weighed her words carefully. "Over the years, Olof has had a number of disagreements with various business associates. He is . . . was . . . the nicest man in the world, but when it came to business he was as hard as nails. The biggest disputes were over Sandgrav, I guess, but we inherited those from our father. Or, rather, our grandfather."

A hint of a smile flitted across her face, but then she grew serious again.

"Our paternal grandparents were farmers, and they lived at Breidablick. They died soon after each other at the beginning of the 1950s. Our father was their only child, and he was a very skilled businessman. He'd already set up his workshop and started selling cars. He had no interest whatsoever in farming, although he held on to Breidablick and some of the land. He sold the rest and invested the money in his business; he also bought and built a number of houses in Strömstad. The land he kept is the area surrounding my house and Breidablick. He also retained the meadows by the shore and the cliffs at Sandgrav. His father had acquired that particular tract for next to nothing to use as grazing land. My father later built a summer cottage right by the water. There didn't seem to be a problem with the house itself, but then he claimed he owned the rights to the water off Sandgrav. A lot of people tried to prove that the original purchase was invalid, but it was part of my grandfather's estate when he died. It was set in stone, so to speak!"

Eva looked very pleased with herself as she uttered the last sentence. Embla realized it was doing her good to talk about Olof and the family.

"So why is the place called Sandgrav?" she asked.

"It's always been called that. For hundreds of years, I assume. Back in the day, *grav* in Swedish meant the same as *deep*. The shore out there isn't very big, but it's surrounded by steep cliffs. So it lies deep down, if you will. There's a natural deep channel that originates in what is known today as Kosterhavet National Park. Plenty of people wanted to get their hands on Sandgrav to turn it into a fishing harbor, and later a marina for yachts and other leisure craft; it's ideal because it's so sheltered. But neither our father nor Olof would sell. Olof renovated and extended the summer cottage, and today it has both water and sewage mains. He also built a service marina for larger yachts and commercial vessels. There aren't many places along this coastline where the bigger boats can get close to the shore. The owners can get their repairs done and buy various nautical bits and pieces. There are also gas pumps, of course, and a small store that sells food and whatever else they might need at sea."

Eva paused to catch her breath and take a sip of her tea, which was lukewarm at best by then.

"Would you like me to top off your tea?" Embla asked.

"No thanks, I'm done."

Embla poured the last few drops left in the pot into her own mug. "So where exactly is Sandgrav?"

"It's about nine miles from here, south of the town. Not far from Dillehuvudflo. I've always thought that's an amusing name for an inlet. Sandgrav is in a sheltered spot behind Tjärnö, Rundö, and Rossö. These days several entrepreneurs are keen to exploit the area, build houses and jetties. But Olof has always said no, and just to make things worse, he called the summer cottage Strandvillan—the Shore House. It was because a building firm tried to accuse him of flouting the planning regulations when he extended the place. But since it was all done at the same time as the construction of the marina, Olof provided plenty of new jobs for the community, so nothing came of the complaint."

Eva looked really smug once more. Better to think about this than all the terrible things that had happened over the past few days.

"So there could still be a motive for these businessmen to want Olof out of the way. Then again, building firms in Sweden don't usually kill people . . . What about personal enemies?" Embla asked.

Eva pulled a face. "The only one I can think of is Carina, Olof's first wife. She's never forgiven him for leaving her for Ann. Carina's a very bitter woman."

"Surely a lot of time has passed since they split."

"Yes, almost twenty years, but she's still just as angry. She also managed to turn Evelina against us."

Tears shimmered in her eyes.

"Who's Evelina?"

"Olof and Carina's daughter. She was eighteen when they divorced. Carina got herself a smart apartment in Strömstad—all thanks to Olof, of course—and persuaded the girl to join her. She was in her last year of high school and I guess she preferred to live in town."

"So Kristoffer and Evelina are half-siblings?"

"Yes, although Olof's had very little contact with Evelina. She and I used to be close, but after the divorce she refused to have anything to do with me. She's never shown any interest in Kristoffer, which is a terrible shame."

Embla needed more information about this daughter who'd suddenly popped up.

"How old would she be now . . . let me think . . ."

Mental arithmetic had never been her strong point.

"Thirty-eight. She's married to an Australian, and she's been living in Sydney for the past fifteen years. Two kids. She's been back four or five times and Carina's been over there, but Olof was never invited to visit, which made him very sad. He only saw his grandkids when Evelina and her family came to Strömstad, and only for very short periods of time."

"Does she know he's dead?"

"Yes. Our lawyer has taken care of all the practical details."

Eva's tone became dismissive; Evelina was obviously a sensitive subject, but Embla wasn't done yet.

"I assume Evelina stands to inherit a considerable amount from her father?" she said tentatively.

Eva narrowed her eyes, evaluating Embla. "Olof was a strategist," she said after a few moments. "He planned everything because he knew there was a chance he'd die before Kristoffer reached adulthood. Most of the money is in his various businesses. Kristoffer will inherit all the businesses when he turns eighteen in April. In order to help him, Olof set up an administration company, which is run by his lawyer, Charlotta Stark. The board is made up of trusted individuals chosen by Olof. A sum of money will be divided between Kristoffer and Evelina, but it's not a ridiculous amount—four or five million each at the most. She's going to be disappointed if she thinks she's going to get her hands on the business side of things."

Embla had one more question. She hesitated to ask, but she had to know.

"Don't you inherit anything?"

Eva raised her eyebrows and gave a faint smile. "We've already taken care of that. I received my inheritance when Mom and Dad died. I used some of it to build this house. Over the years Olof has given me money and invested in stocks and shares and private pensions on my behalf because I've helped him with Kristoffer. I've also worked full-time throughout my career, so I have enough to get by. More than enough."

They sat and chatted for a while longer, but when Embla glanced at her watch, she realized it was time to head back to town to meet her colleagues for dinner. She stood up and carried the tray into the kitchen, ignoring Eva's protests.

"Thank you for the tea and toast," Embla said. When she had put on her boots and jacket, she was struck by a thought. "By the way, do you know of a place we might be able to rent for a few days? There are three of us, all police officers from Gothenburg. Every hotel room in the town is booked up until the weekend—some Norwegian oil conference, apparently."

"Where are you staying tonight?"

"The Laholm—we can have rooms for one night."

Eva seemed to be considering something. After a few seconds she said, "You can use the Shore House. It's clean and heated. There's bed linen, towels—everything you need."

Embla was surprised, but when she thought about it, maybe it wasn't such a bad idea. "That would be fantastic!"

Except . . . Her boss would want to know the answer to one very important question.

"How much will it be? Per night?"

"Nothing. You're here to catch whoever killed Olof and beat up Kristoffer. In any case, nobody uses the place during the winter."

"That's so kind of you!" Embla exclaimed, giving Eva a spontaneous hug.

Tears shimmered in the other woman's eyes again, but she was smiling as she said, "It's me who should be thanking you. You arrived like an angel and . . . thawed me out." She wiped her nose with a crumpled tissue, then straightened her shoulders. "I'll come over to the Laholm tomorrow at nine. I'll give you the keys and show you around the house, give you the alarm code and so on."

IT WAS STILL raining on Thursday morning, but the wind had died down. Embla, Göran, and Hampus made the most of a fantastic breakfast buffet, which was almost as good as the previous night's dinner. They all agreed that the hotel had a brilliant chef.

"This is amazing—there's everything you could possibly want!" Göran exclaimed as he munched happily on a chocolate Danish. It wasn't exactly what his dietician had recommended, but it was definitely Göran's idea of the perfect conclusion to breakfast.

"We need to do some food shopping if we're going to stay in that house," Hampus pointed out.

He still hadn't said much. Embla was getting worried; he wasn't being himself at all. Not that he was usually very talkative, but he was generally more sociable. She knocked back her vitamin shot of crushed ginger, raspberries, and orange juice.

Göran paused with his Danish halfway to his mouth. "You need to be careful. Those shots contain a whole lot of allergenic substances," he said, sounding concerned. He stuffed the last piece of the chocolate-covered pastry into his mouth. Breakfast was over as far as he was concerned. "Shall we go and sit in the foyer?" he suggested.

They went and sat at the table by the window again. Reception was busy with arrivals and departures, but the three of them had already checked out.

As on the previous day, no one else was making use of the spacious foyer. A person suffering from agoraphobia might well be at risk of an attack, but it was ideal if you wanted to talk without being overheard.

"I've done some digging into Olof Sjöberg," Göran began, opening up his laptop. "All I could find were two drunk-driving convictions. The first was nine years ago, on New Year's Day. He hadn't sobered up from New Year's Eve. He was fined. The second incident was last summer. His blood alcohol concentration was much higher that time, plus the penalties had been increased, so he lost his license for two months and was fined sixty thousand kronor. He was also told that if it happened again, he would have to have an Alcolock ignition immobilizer fitted to his vehicle. That's it, there's nothing else in our records."

He scrolled down the page and continued reading.

"However, there's plenty about all the trouble concerning Sandgrav. There have been complaints and counter-complaints ever since the Second World War, but no one's ever gotten anywhere in a fight with the Sjöberg clan. They've kept the land, and Olof has established a flourishing business."

He broke off and nodded to Embla. "I think your friend's here."

Embla glanced toward the glass doors, which opened automatically as Eva approached. She was wearing a dark blue coat, black trousers, and sturdy boots, with a pink and lime green shawl wound around her neck. On her head was a fluffy angora beret in the same shade of lime green. She was striding along, and her eyes were bright and clear as she scanned the foyer. Her face lit up when she spotted Embla, and she came straight over. The three officers got to their feet and Embla introduced her colleagues.

As they headed for their respective cars, Eva said, "I spoke to Kristoffer's doctor this morning. His condition is still serious, but he's much more stable. They're going to keep him sedated today and possibly tomorrow, but they're going to let me be there when they bring him around. They'll call and let me know when it's time."

There was a glint in her eye and fresh energy in her voice as she spoke about her nephew. The broken woman Embla had met the previous evening was nowhere to be seen.

Eva got into her silver-gray Audi A3 and led the way. Apparently it wasn't that easy to find Sandgrav. Göran, Embla, and Hampus followed in the Volvo. Less than a mile to the south of Strömstad, it was clear they were out in the country. The farther south they traveled, the more isolated the area became. They passed several minor roads leading toward the coast, with signs advertising campsites and beaches, but the Audi kept on going.

When they reached a desolate stretch of the 176, where the flat landscape stretched in all directions, the Audi slowed down and signaled right. They turned onto a narrow dirt track; there was just about room for two cars to pass. There were no houses in sight, apart from a farm in the distance on the other side of the 176.

After a few hundred yards the track split in two. Two

yellow arrows on a post pointed to Rävö in one direction, Sandgrav in the other. This track was no more than the width of a single vehicle, with fields and low-lying bushes on both sides. They hadn't seen a house or any sign of activity since leaving the main road, apart from an information board about a nature reserve.

They took a sharp bend, and there it was. They could see why it was known as the Shore House. It was painted white and built in the style of a typical archipelago manor house from the early 1900s. It was all there: the leaded windows, the glassed-in veranda, the white façade, the ornate blue eaves, the tiled roof. It was in an elevated position on a flat rock. Presumably Olof had had some excavation work done for the original summer cottage.

Even on a gray and windy January day, the view of the sea was fantastic. The skerries and islands were quite close, but the deep channel was well-marked. It reached land around a hundred yards away, where the service marina was located.

The Audi stopped on the drive and Eva jumped out. "You can see why most people arrive by sea," she said as the three officers joined her.

"Is that what your brother usually did?" Göran asked her.

"Yes. The boat's moored in the boathouse." She pointed to a roof that was just visible down below. "Of course it's out of the water for the winter," she continued. "It's over in the boatyard; we'll go there later."

While Eva was talking, Embla took the opportunity to fill her lungs with the salty air. The smell of seaweed was strong, but not at all unpleasant.

They headed for the bright-blue front door. On either

side of the steps were large concrete pots containing heather and spruce. A sticker on the door informed visitors that the house had an alarm.

"The alarm is just inside the door. The code is zero zero seven six. Olof was a fan of James Bond, hence the first three numbers. And . . . six."

She smiled, and Embla felt it might be the right time to ask a question that hadn't seemed appropriate the previous evening.

"Six . . . *sex* in Swedish. I was wondering . . . did Olof have a girlfriend?"

Eva had inserted the key in the lock, but paused for a moment. "He went on a few dates, but nothing worked out. A few years ago, he told me he'd given up on the idea of a steady relationship. He worked hard and wanted to spend his free time with Kristoffer."

She turned the key and opened the door. An uninterrupted beep told them the alarm was activated. She keyed in the code and the noise stopped immediately.

"Come on in," she said.

They took off their coats and hung them on a rack in the hallway. The place was a little chilly and there was a stuffy smell, but Eva showed them how to turn up the heat. There were beautiful rag rugs in white and various shades of blue on the polished floorboards. The kitchen had large windows overlooking the sea. It was ultramodern, but with old-world appeal. The cupboards were white, as were the big table and chairs—Embla counted ten. The wallpaper was blue and white, and there were more rag rugs on the floor. The chair cushions were also blue. A lovely, fresh nautical theme. Embla felt the need to comment.

"This is fabulous! Olof has . . . had . . . a real flair for this kind of thing."

Eva nodded. "To be honest, it was Ann who was responsible for the décor both here and at Breidablick. She was an interior designer; that was how they met. He asked her to fix up his office when he moved into the new office block down by the river. I say new, but that was twenty years ago . . ." She sighed. "The years go so fast."

It was obvious she was talking to herself, and didn't expect an answer.

She showed them around the place. The big living room had sliding glass doors that led out onto a huge sun terrace. Just as at Breidablick, the fence was made of plexiglass so that the sea view was uninterrupted. At the moment the idea of sitting out there was far from tempting, but it wasn't hard to imagine how wonderful it would be on a warm, sunny day.

On the ground floor there was also a bedroom and a bathroom with blue and white tiles. Next door was a sauna with a separate shower. There were three bedrooms and another bathroom upstairs, plus a furnished landing with a window and glass double doors, beyond which they could see a glassed-in balcony.

"If you take the downstairs room, Hampus and I will camp up here," Göran said to Embla. She was about to protest, in view of the stairs and his physical bulk, but then she thought it would do him good to go up and down. Involuntary exercise, so to speak. She kept quiet and merely nodded.

They carried in their overnight bags plus the three bags of equipment that were always kept in the Volvo, then they locked the door and accompanied Eva down to the marina. Apparently sailors from all over Bohuslän and southern Norway knew the name Sandgrav Marina, and exactly where it was.

It was an impressive facility, with gas pumps, a grocery store, and a chandlery. A notice informed them the stores would be open on April first, and anyone wishing to order from the chandler before then could do so online. There was a large building on the pontoons out in the water, and they could hear the screech of tools slicing through metal coming from inside it. A slipway ran down into the sea; this was obviously the boatyard Eva had mentioned.

They walked along the wide quayside, which Embla guessed must be almost two hundred yards long. A series of jetties provided berths for boats of different sizes.

"There are no permanent berths; only visitors to the marina are allowed to moor here. The jetty at the far end is for boats in need of repair. As you can hear, the boatyard is open for business. Three men work there all year round—more during the high season. But it doesn't look as if there's going to be any ice this year, so they'll probably be at full stretch by the beginning of March. Olof says . . ."

Eva fell silent and her eyes filled with tears. A combination of grief and the biting wind perhaps. All four were hunched against the gusts blowing in off the lead-gray sea.

"Shall we take a look at the boathouse?" Hampus suggested.

"Good idea." Eva led the way back to the Shore House, around the patio, and down some steps to a jetty.

The boathouse had the same look as the main

building. On the wall hung a fishing net and some green glass floats. Embla had the feeling this was more for decoration than everyday use. In the center of the broad jetty stood a wood-fired hot tub. Needless to say, the cover was on it right now, but again it was easy to imagine sitting in the warm water, gazing out over the sea and the skerries. There was a small deck at the side, and Embla could see a flight of steps leading downward. She went and looked over the fence. The steps provided access to a small inlet with a beautiful sandy shore. The cliffs all around were tall and steep; there was no way someone could clamber down the rock face without climbing equipment. Outsiders would have to come by boat, so in fact this was more or less a private beach for the residents of the Shore House.

She went back to the boathouse, running a hand over the attractive glass floats as she passed.

"I've got the key," Eva said. She unlocked the door and went inside.

A loud thud and a stream of curses made Eva stop dead. She turned and saw Göran Krantz sitting on the wet jetty, clutching one foot, as Embla and Hampus stared at him in horror.

It must really hurt—I've never heard him swear before, Embla thought as she rushed over. "What happened?"

"I tripped. I think I've sprained my ankle," he groaned, pointing to a large padlock securing a trapdoor in the jetty.

"Oh my goodness, I forgot to warn you . . . That's Olof's lobster trap." Eva knelt down beside him. Gently she checked the foot and ankle. "Nothing broken, just a sprain. I've got a support bandage in the house; we need to go back," she said firmly.

With the support of Hampus and Embla, Göran managed to make it back to the house. They parked him in a comfortable armchair with a matching footstool.

"I keep a first-aid kit out here," Eva explained. "Sometimes one of the sailors needs a little help. Of course if it's anything serious I send them to town."

She disappeared into the hallway and they heard her rummaging around in a closet. When she came back she carefully removed Göran's shoe and sock. He couldn't suppress a groan when she felt his foot. With practiced movements she rubbed in a colorless, odorless gel.

"What's that?" Göran wanted to know.

"It's an analgesic, plus it reduces inflammation and swelling. It's very effective. It contains diclofenac diethylamine."

The inspector raised an eyebrow. "Of course it does."

Eva smiled, but didn't expand on the ingredients of the magic gel. "What's your shoe size?" she asked.

"Forty-four."

"Excellent, I have that size." She chose a support bandage from the small pile she'd brought in with her and slipped it over his foot and ankle. "You need to rest today. You can put some weight on the foot, but don't attempt to walk far," she said in a professional tone.

"Do I have to sleep with the bandage on?"

"For tonight, yes, and make sure you keep it on during the day. And take it easy for the next few days."

"Okay."

Göran didn't sound too upset; Eva's instructions didn't involve much deviation from his normal lifestyle.

Hampus was standing by the glass doors looking out

over the choppy sea. After a while he turned and asked Eva, "Are there any lobster down there now?"

"No. Olof always has a lobster feast at the end of October, and it's empty from then on. You're allowed to keep them until May, but he thinks that's cruel. He fishes for a few weeks from the first day of the season in September, then he has a big party. It's great."

"You're there, too," Hampus said.

It was more of a statement than a question.

"Yes. I usually take Kristoffer home after a couple of hours. He doesn't like parties. Too many people. He'd rather be back at Breidablick."

"Does he spend much time in this house?"

"No. He might come over once or twice in the summer on a really hot day. Which means Olof isn't here too often either."

"I suppose it's not exactly kid-friendly, given how deep the water is," Göran commented.

Eva smiled, clearly amused. "Actually Kristoffer's always been a real water baby. He's won every swimming badge there is. He can't ride a bike at all, though—his balance is very poor. That's why Olof wanted him to have an A-tractor; a moped was never an option." She glanced at her watch. "I have to get back to town to meet with my lawyer."

She said her goodbyes and hurried out. After a minute or so they heard the Audi start up and drive away.

"I suggest we unpack first, then we can have a coffee and work out what we're going to do," Göran said.

"You'd better take the downstairs bedroom," Embla said, nodding toward his bandaged foot.

He didn't object.

WHEN ALL THREE had settled in to their rooms they divided up the tasks. Embla was to interview Carina Sjöberg, Olof's ex-wife. According to Eva, she still harbored hostile feelings toward her former husband, but was she angry enough to set fire to the workshop? Maybe, but she could hardly be responsible for Kristoffer's injures. He had been subjected to a frenzied attack, with real power behind the kicks and blows. It was sheer luck that the boy hadn't died.

No, Carina couldn't have assaulted him herself, but that didn't mean she wasn't somehow involved in the terrible events at Breidablick. They couldn't rule out the possibility that she'd paid someone else to carry out the crime.

After several attempts, Embla managed to contact her by phone. Carina tried hard to get out of setting up a meeting on the basis that she and Olof hadn't spoken since the divorce, but Embla stuck to her guns, pointing out that they still had one thing in common: Evelina. At the mention of their daughter, Carina went quiet, then snapped that she could spare fifteen minutes at eleven-thirty. Which gave Embla exactly thirty-six minutes to get to Strömstad.

HAMPUS DROPPED EMBLA off in the square. She passed the now-familiar police station and continued over the bridge, then turned left and headed toward Skeppsbro Square. Carina Sjöberg lived in one of the apartment blocks.

An elevator whisked Embla to the top floor. Nothing happened when she rang the doorbell next to the name SJÖBERG. It wasn't until the third ring that she heard footsteps in the hallway, and the door opened to reveal a tall woman. Her hair was dyed almost black, and cut into a neat bob. Her makeup was perhaps a little too thickly applied, as if she was going to a party, in spite of the fact that it was late morning on a gloomy Thursday in January. Her clothes reinforced the air of forthcoming festivities. She was wearing a bright-red lace dress and black high-heeled shoes. A pearl necklace gleamed at her throat, and one wrist was adorned with several gold bangles. Rings with stones the size of hazelnuts sparkled on both hands. Maybe she really was going to some kind of event?

"Come in," Carina said before Embla had time to introduce herself. She stepped inside and took off her jacket and boots, then followed Carina into the living room. As expected there was a spectacular view over the water from the west-facing window. A glass door led out onto a generous roof terrace that continued around the corner, overlooking the harbor and town center. She glanced around the apartment before taking a seat on one of the two enormous white sofas facing each other. Beneath the glass coffee table was a dark-blue patterned rug; even Embla realized it must be valuable. She wasn't usually interested in such things, but this one was exceptionally beautiful. Carina sat down opposite her. The light from the window revealed her age, in spite of her determined attempts to hide it. Embla knew that she and Olof had been the same age.

"I'm going out to lunch at twelve. I assume we'll be finished by then."

The voice was dry and hoarse, as if she smoked too much. The deep lines around her mouth and eyes told the same story. Embla could see through the bored expression she'd adopted right away. She'd been to drama school in Gothenburg and had learned quite a bit about body language. Arms folded, legs crossed, one foot constantly bobbing up and down. Carina was nervous.

"I hope so, but if not we can always continue the conversation down at the police station. That interview would be conducted by Chief Superintendent Roger Willén."

Embla kept her tone pleasant, but she could feel the tension around her mouth. Admittedly she'd left "acting" out of the chief superintendent's title, plus the fact that he was no longer in Strömstad and had gone back to Trollhättan, but there was no need for Carina to know that.

She looked as if she'd just bitten into something very sour, then swallowed it with a concerted effort. "Right."

Embla began by asking when Carina had last seen Olof or Kristoffer. Carina informed her that she never saw either of them; they had no contact whatsoever. How long had she and Olof been married? Twenty years, and it was twenty years since the divorce. Evelina was married with two children, and lived in Australia.

"Will she be coming home?"

"Yes. I think it's important for her to . . . protect her interests."

The response was grudging; she clearly thought it had nothing to do with the police.

Even though she already knew the answer, Embla asked, "Did she and Olof get along well?"

"No. He abandoned both of us for that . . . woman!"

In spite of the fact that the woman in question had

been dead for ten years, and now Olof was dead, too, Carina made no attempt to disguise the venom.

"Did he just kick you out? Leave you with nothing?" Embla tried to sound sympathetic.

The red flush on Carina's cheeks glowed through the makeup. Embla's question took her by surprise, and she mumbled something unintelligible.

"Sorry? I didn't hear what you said."

Carina took a deep breath. "He had to pay his dues! Evelina was still in school, and I didn't earn much at the gallery."

The gallery—that explained all the paintings on the walls. Embla glanced around the luxuriously furnished room. Three doors, so at least three more rooms.

"Did you have a falling-out?"

Carina glared at her. "What do you think! He let us down, both me and Evelina! After everything I'd done for him . . . I gave up my education to support him!"

Anger burned in her eyes, and the red flush had spread to her throat. *She's absolutely furious*, Embla thought. *But all this happened a very long time ago, and she certainly hasn't been short on money*.

As if she could read Embla's mind, Carina straightened up and took a couple of deep breaths. Her voice was much more controlled when she spoke. "This isn't about money. It's about betrayal. The way he walked all over me. Everything we'd built up together—none of it mattered. I'll never forgive him! Never!"

"Not even now that he's dead?" Embla asked quietly.

"No! Never!"

Implacable hatred. But had it been enough for her to hire someone to kill Olof and his son? Did she think her daughter was going to inherit a fortune? Embla remembered what Eva had said: the finances were tied up in the businesses Kristoffer would take over when he was eighteen. He and Evelina would receive "four or five million" each. That sounded like a lot to Embla—maybe worth killing for? Could Carina get her hands on the money? She might need it; her lifestyle was clearly expensive.

"Do you still own the gallery?"

"No, I sold it and invested in the stock market. And I got it right. Don't imagine Olof was generous when it came to the alimony. Okay, he fixed up this apartment, but that was mainly for Evelina's sake. He covered the rental and maintenance for her."

"But he's carried on paying your alimony since Evelina moved away?"

Carina pursed her lips. "It's only fair. The court said he had to go on paying until I die," she said eventually.

That sounded like an American divorce. Carina must have had a good lawyer, and Olof probably wasn't represented by Charlotta Stark back then. She never would have allowed her client to go along with such an unfavorable arrangement.

"So what happens now that he's dead?"

"It doesn't make a difference. I still get my money."

For the first time the hint of a smile played around that mean little mouth.

THE THAI RESTAURANT was past the Laholm Hotel, opposite the quay for the ferries to North and South Koster. The service was infrequent at this time of year. The only disturbance came from a group of gulls, screaming as they fought over something in the water.

Given what she knew about their eating habits, Embla was pretty sure she didn't want to find out what it was.

Even though it was well after lunchtime, they weren't alone in the small dining room. There were a number of guests, many of them speaking Norwegian. The food wasn't cheap, but it was well worth the price. It was easy to see why the place was so popular.

They had chosen a corner table, and spoke quietly. The tables were close together—it wouldn't be hard to eavesdrop. Their nearest neighbors were two elderly Norwegian couples. You had to admire their vitality; it was only just after two, and they were already more than a little tipsy. From the fragments of their conversation she picked up, Embla gathered that one couple owned an apartment in the town, and were trying to persuade their friends to buy one, too. Their lively debate and loud laughter provided excellent cover for the three detectives.

"The guys who checked out the CCTV cameras did a good job," Göran said. "Not only did they spot an SUV heading south on Uddevallavägen just before eleven on Sunday night, they found something even better."

He opened up his laptop and switched it on. He clicked on a video clip and turned the screen toward his colleagues. The black-and-white film, taken at a gas station, was jerky. In spite of the lack of color it was possible to see that the SUV was probably black or dark blue. A blond man in jeans and a leather jacket got out and walked around to the trunk. He opened it, took out a petrol can, and closed it again. Another man climbed out of the passenger seat. He was tall and skinny, wearing jeans and a thick padded jacket with a fur-trimmed hood. He turned and spoke to someone in the back seat. It was impossible to see whether there was more than one person in the vehicle. Then he wandered over to the kiosk; he seemed to be having some difficulty walking in a straight line. Meanwhile the blond guy filled the gas can and replaced it in the trunk. He got back in the car and waited for the tall man, who reappeared after a moment or two. He was about to open the passenger door when he dropped a cigarette packet. His clumsy movements as he attempted to pick it up showed just how drunk he was. He half-fell into the car, which sped away with a screech of tires. The time on the screen was 9:57.

"Ted Andersson and Johannes Holm," Hampus said.

"Are you sure?" Embla asked. She hadn't met Viggo's and Amelie's fathers.

"I spoke to both of them earlier today. It's definitely them."

Göran nodded. "Correct. Andersson owns a black Lexus RX 300, which is the one we can see in the video. You might have noticed that he filled the can with diesel, while his Lexus runs on gas."

"That's . . . Diesel is the accelerant most frequently used in arson attacks. It's not as volatile as ordinary gas." Hampus couldn't hide his anger.

"Exactly. And bearing in mind what you told me in the car about what Ted said and how he behaved . . ."

Göran broke off as the young waitress came over to clear their plates. All three of them said how much they'd enjoyed their meal, and she looked delighted.

"Two coffees, one white, one black, and a cup of green tea, please. And three truffles," Göran said.

"Truffles? Are we celebrating something?" Embla wanted to know when the waitress had gone.

"Absolutely. I've just had Andersson and Holm brought in. They're waiting for us in separate rooms at the station. And they can sit there and sweat a while longer. I'm convinced they were responsible for the fire at Breidablick and the attack on Kristoffer. We don't know if they were aware that Olof was in the workshop, but we'll find out."

The waitress returned and served their drinks with a practiced hand. The truffles looked delicious, topped with crushed licorice and a raspberry.

"Thank you so much," Göran said, smiling warmly at the young woman.

She gave him a radiant smile in return, and there was something of a glow about the superintendent as he focused on the matter at hand once more.

"Ted has two convictions for the possession of cannabis: the first at the age of sixteen, the second at eighteen. The quantity was relatively small in both cases, but too much to be regarded as for personal use only. He was referred to the local rehab team the first time, and given a community service sentence the second. He was on the fringes of a gang that dabbled in a variety of activities. The three leaders were caught breaking into a fancy house near the Svinesund Bridge. All three were from the Strömstad area, but none of them mentioned Ted when they were questioned."

"Are they still around?" Hampus asked.

"No—things didn't go too well for any of them. Two of them are in jail serving long sentences for dealing. The third was released almost a year ago and now lives in

Stockholm. Ted does appear twice more in the database; on both occasions he beat someone up while he was under the influence of alcohol."

"So he's aggressive," Embla said.

"Yes, especially when he's had a few drinks. However, the last time was almost seven years ago. Since he met Pernilla and Viggo came along, he's kept his nose clean. Got himself a house and a steady job. He's had two speeding fines, but he was lucky. Both times he was just under the limit for losing his license. Apart from that, nothing."

"Until now," Hampus said.

"Exactly."

"How old is he?" Embla asked.

"Thirty-five—the same age as Johannes Holm."

"Does Holm have a record?"

"He and a pal stole a moped when they were fifteen. The other kid got away, but Johannes refused to tell the cops who he was. Johannes was referred to social services because he was a juvenile. He was also involved in one of the fights when Ted was charged with assault. Apparently there was some beef between two gangs in a bar. Ted beat the crap out of one of the guys, but Johannes had his nose broken. That was seventeen years ago."

Hampus ran his fingers through his dark quiff several times, a sure sign that he was thinking hard. With his hair standing on end, he gazed thoughtfully at Göran through his Harry Potter glasses.

"Something tells me Ted was the pal who stole the moped. It sounds like the classic setup: the leader and his sidekick," he said.

"Yes—and we can exploit that."

They decided to start with Ted Andersson. He was probably the harder nut to crack, because he'd been questioned by the police before. He had made the most of his right to remain silent even as a teenager, but on a few occasions the interviewer had managed to make him lose his temper, and he'd blurted out things he hadn't meant to say. So the best strategy was good cop/bad cop, as long as the good cop wasn't too nice.

AN HOUR LATER Patrik Lind and Alice Åslund collected Ted Andersson and escorted him to Sven-Ove Berglund's office, which was free because the chief inspector was still sick. Göran and Hampus sat behind the desk, and opposite them was Andersson's defense attorney, a man in his thirties who'd introduced himself as Nadir Khadem. In the middle of the table lay a small tape recorder. Embla positioned herself by the door.

Ted Andersson's face was bright red when he was brought in. His lips were clamped together, and he glared at Göran and Hampus as he slumped down on the chair. He was slightly above medium height, and well-built. Judging by his belly, however, they could see he put away a fair amount of beer as well. His dirty curly hair was plastered to his sweaty forehead, but his eyes were bright blue, his features pleasingly regular. He turned and gave Embla a scornful smile and a meaningful look, licking his lips slowly. She unconsciously pursed her lips. Once upon a time he might have been an attractive guy, but now he was pretty repulsive in his smelly shirt and scruffy jeans. His upper lip was beaded with perspiration, too. There was something of the worn-out has-been about him. He had definitely lost his appeal.

His lawyer, on the other hand . . . A strong face with well-defined cheekbones and a firm chin, honey-brown eyes, and thick eyelashes. His dark hair was cut short. His best feature was his mouth. His smile reached his eyes. He was wearing a black jacket, pale-blue shirt without a tie, and dark-blue designer jeans. No doubt his shoes were also some exclusive brand; they were super smart. To her surprise, Embla felt a little pull in her lower belly that spread downward. Nothing like this had happened since that fatal moose hunt last year, when she had been seriously assaulted by a man. Men and sex had held no attraction since then, but now she was turned on by a total stranger she hadn't even spoken to. She'd experienced something similar from time to time over the years, but never in circumstances like this.

Hampus went through the formalities for the tape, while Göran kept his gaze fixed on Ted's face. Ted stared back defiantly, his eyes burning with suppressed rage. Or was it fear?

"So, Ted. You're not exactly unfamiliar with police interviews, but this time we're dealing with considerably more serious matters than in the past," Göran began.

No response. He was asked where he'd been Sunday evening: silence. Who he had spent time with on Sunday evening: nothing.

"The fact that you're refusing to answer our questions isn't a point in your favor, especially as we know where you were and what you were doing," Göran said.

"Where's your evidence?" Nadir Khadem interjected.

Hampus clicked on his laptop. "We have CCTV footage." He turned the computer to face Ted and his lawyer.

"Please note that the can is being filled with diesel. Your Lexus runs on ordinary gas," Göran pointed out.

Ted began to shuffle uncomfortably as he watched. When the final image appeared, he leaped to his feet. At first it looked as if he was intending to grab the laptop, but he changed his mind and spun around. He narrowed his eyes and yelled at Embla, "Out of the way, you fucking cunt!" He hurled himself at the door, but she was ready for him. A well-aimed kick between his legs stopped him dead. He let out a muffled groan and doubled over. The uppercut with her right fist came from below. It wasn't too hard, but it landed perfectly on his chin. He collapsed on the floor and lay there moaning.

Patrik Lind, who was stationed in the corridor, flung open the door. "What the hell . . . ?" He fell silent when he saw Ted.

"Handcuffs please," Embla said, holding out her hand.

Patrik gave them to her without another word. He couldn't take his eyes off Ted, who started cursing and threatening Embla as she secured his wrists.

"That was . . . I mean . . . Wow!" the lawyer exclaimed. He couldn't hide the admiration in his voice, which made him even more attractive. However, Embla wasn't entirely happy with the course of events.

"That was a tactical error, Ted. You just tried to force your way past the reigning Nordic light welterweight champion. Didn't go too well, did it?" Hampus kept his tone neutral, but the corners of his mouth were twitching.

"Police . . . police violence!" Ted spat.

"Go ahead and try that—the interview is being filmed." Göran sounded bored.

Embla was surprised—was the interview really being filmed? Where was the camera?

"We'll take a break—my client needs time to recover," Khadem stated firmly.

As Ted Andersson was led back to the custody suite by Patrik Lind and Alice Åslund, Khadem turned to Göran.

"I'd appreciate if this . . . incident . . . wasn't blown out of proportion. Ted is very agitated, off balance. His young son is still missing, and of course the little girl's disappearance is always in the back of his mind. I'll have a word with him."

His smile included all three officers in the room. Embla's stomach did a somersault. This guy had her hormones popping.

"Is the interview being filmed?" she asked when the door had closed behind him.

"No, there are no cameras in here. I just said that to cool him down," Göran replied with a smirk.

BEFORE THEY QUESTIONED Johannes Holm, Embla went out into the corridor and googled Nadir Khadem. Iranian parents, all three of their children were born in Sweden. Nadir was the eldest. His mother was a well-known Persian poet, and his father was a doctor. They'd lived in Gothenburg since the late 1970s. After qualifying as a lawyer, Nadir had pursued his career with single-minded determination. He was currently employed by a large law firm in Gothenburg. Aged thirty-two, married to Soraya. One daughter, Jila, almost three years old.

It was unfortunate that he was married, but not a disaster. Quite the reverse: Embla wasn't looking for a long-term relationship. A little no-strings sex with handsome Nadir would suit her very well.

JOHANNES HOLM RADIATED as much energy as a wrung-out dishcloth. The dark circles around his eyes looked like bruises on his sallow skin. *We don't need to worry about any violence or escape attempts*, Embla thought. *This guy's already broken.* As if in response to her unspoken assessment, he began to weep quietly.

His lawyer was a young woman by the name of Jasmin Carell. Embla had checked her out, too, and knew she was half African American and had grown up in Sweden with her Swedish mother. She worked for one of the biggest law firms in Uddevalla. She was certainly beautiful, with long dark hair and perfectly chiseled features. She was tall and slim, and wore her discreet navy-blue skirt suit in a way that would grace any catwalk. Her heritage seemed like a quirk of fate; her skin color was very similar to Amelie's. And Elliot's. Embla smiled to herself when she thought of him.

The two of them had decided to go up and see Uncle Nisse during the February break. Even if there wasn't a hint of snow along the coast, there would be plenty in Dalsland. Only two weeks to go, and she was really looking forward to it. So was Elliot—he called or texted almost every day. When you're nine years old, two weeks is an eternity. He was the best thing to come out of Embla's year-long relationship with his father, Jason Abbot.

Elliot's mom had died before his first birthday, and he had no memories of her. Embla's role in his life was never that of a mother. She was his friend, and she provided a sense of security. Together they came up with fun things to do, and he often stayed with her when his dad was on tour. In recent years Jason had become increasingly well-known as one of Europe's best jazz musicians. His choice of instrument was one of the reasons their relationship hadn't worked: the sax sounded harsh and old-fashioned to Embla's ears. When she had come out with her opinion during one of their quarrels, Jason had gone crazy. He had never forgiven her. Another reason for their breakup was Jason's notorious inability to remain faithful. However, Embla's bond with his son was strong, and as a single parent Jason was wise enough to see the value of another adult in Elliot's life. His family was split between Jamaica and Miami, which wasn't much help when he needed someone to watch the kid on short notice.

Embla was brought back to the present by Jasmin's deep, warm voice.

"Johannes isn't feeling too well. He's innocent of all the accusations against him, and in view of the trauma his family is currently experiencing, I'm requesting his immediate release."

"He claims he's innocent, but I'm afraid he still has a great deal of explaining to do." Göran shifted his attention from Jasmin to her client. "Let's start with what you were doing last Sunday evening just before ten."

Johannes's eyes darted all over the place, and he cleared his throat several times before he managed to speak.

"I . . . I was home."

"Can anyone vouch for that?"

"Er . . . my wife. But she'd gone to bed. She was asleep."

Göran allowed the silence to seep into every corner of the room. Johannes lowered his head, eyes fixed on the table.

"Okay, let's take a look at some CCTV footage."

He turned the laptop so that Johannes and Jasmin could see. As before, he pointed out that the gas can had been filled with diesel rather than ordinary gas.

The expression on Jasmin's face grew more and more rigid, while Johannes dissolved into tears once more. By the time the sequence came to an end, he was in pieces. Hampus handed him a wad of tissues, and they waited for him to calm down. When that didn't happen, Göran made a decision.

"Okay, we'll leave it there and let you rest until tomorrow." He stood up and placed a hand on Johannes's shoulder as he walked by. "Tell us what happened. It'll make you feel much better."

Johannes gave a start and turned his tear-stained face up to Göran. Fear shined in his wide-open eyes as he slowly shook his head.

"WE'LL TRY TED Andersson again first thing tomorrow. Johannes is already on the edge. We need to play them off against each other," Göran said.

"There's no doubt it was them," Embla said.

"None whatsoever."

Göran was absolutely sure of his ground, and his colleagues agreed with him. All they had to do now was work out exactly what had gone on.

"I'd like you two to go and see Pernilla Andersson, talk to her about Sunday evening. She probably doesn't know much, but it might be a good idea to check out the house and garage—and the car. Bring in the gas can if you find it. If there's a drop left we can send it to the fire specialists at forensics for analysis. They should be able to tell if it came from the same pump as the diesel that was used as an accelerant at Breidablick."

"Do we have a warrant to search the house?"

"Yes, the prosecutor's already given the go-ahead, but I'm going to wait at least an hour before I send Paula Nilsson and Lars Engman over there. They'll arrive about the same time as the CSIs. You don't need to mention the search to Pernilla Andersson until you're about to leave."

"Okay. When do you want to meet up again?" Hampus asked.

"In a couple of hours—three at the most."

IT WAS QUITE some time before the door opened. An overweight middle-aged woman nearly filled the doorway. It was clear she wasn't pleased to see them, and she stuck out her chin aggressively.

"What do you want?" she barked before Embla and Hampus had the chance to introduce themselves.

They showed her their IDs, which she examined carefully before once again demanding to know what they wanted. When they asked if they could come in and have a chat with Pernilla, the woman's chin shot out even further.

"My daughter's not feeling too good. Viggo . . ." She fell silent and her lower lip began to tremble, but she stood her ground.

"We'd just like to ask her a few simple questions. We thought if we came here it would save her from coming to the station because we assumed that would be too much for her," Embla said, trying to inject as much empathy as possible into her voice and expression.

It seemed to work; the woman was clearly hesitating. After a moment she stepped aside. "Okay, but only for a couple of minutes. I'll call her down."

They found themselves in a cramped hallway with an

overloaded coatrack and a cracked mirror on the wall. The floor was strewn with shoes, clothes, and toys.

Pernilla's mother went over to the narrow staircase and shouted, "Pernilla! The police want to talk to you!" She turned back and jerked her head toward an open door. "You can go and sit in the kitchen."

Embla discreetly scanned the hallway. Just inside the door was a large metal flashlight. Viggo had been out in the garden playing with a flashlight when he disappeared. Was this the one he'd been using? Embla hadn't taken off her woolen gloves—good, no fingerprints. She quickly bent down and picked it up. She noticed how light it was as she slipped it into her pocket: no batteries. Her pockets were pretty roomy, but it only just fit.

The kitchen was also a mess, with dirty dishes, sticky pizza boxes, and empty beer cans on the counters.

"I came over today . . . Pernilla called when you arrested Ted. I haven't had time to clean up yet," said the woman, whose name they still didn't know.

"Do you live nearby?" Hampus asked in a pleasant tone, eyes warm behind those round-rimmed glasses. It hardly ever failed; older ladies fell for the polite young man who looked like a reassuring doctor rather than a highly competent detective.

"No, Uddevalla. And I don't have a car, so I have to take the train or the bus. I have a bad hip, so it's difficult to sit for long periods, but when your grandson disappears and his father's accused of a crime . . . Poor Pernilla—she's devastated!" Her voice was trembling by the end.

Hampus tilted his head to one side and nodded sympathetically. "She's under a tremendous strain. We all feel for her," he said gravely.

"Thank you. Viggo means . . . everything."

In the silence that followed they heard slow footsteps on the stairs that turned into a shuffle as Pernilla reached the bottom and began to make her way to the kitchen.

She stopped in the doorway and stared at the two officers with swollen, red-rimmed eyes. She was wearing a black T-shirt and tights with a hole in one knee and had draped a grubby pink fleece robe over her shoulders. On her feet were a pair of trodden-down fluffy slippers with eyes on the front. Presumably they were supposed to represent some kind of animal—possibly piglets, judging by the color.

"Have you . . . found him?" she whispered.

"Hi, Pernilla. My name is Embla—you've already met Hampus. No, unfortunately we haven't found Viggo, but hundreds of people are out there looking, along with dog teams and a helicopter with a thermal-imaging camera. The chances of locating him are very good."

Embla tried to sound more optimistic than she was feeling.

Pernilla let out a sob. "That's what you said about Amelie, too. And she's still missing!"

There was no mistaking the accusatory tone. Her mother placed a hand on Pernilla's arm, but she shook it off and slumped down on a chair.

"We just wanted to have a chat with you about Sunday evening," Hampus began.

There was no indication that Pernilla had heard what he said; she stared blankly into space.

"Did anyone visit during the evening?"

Slowly she turned her head and looked at him, as if

she'd only just realized he was still there. Almost inaudibly she whispered, "No."

"What time did Ted leave the house?"

"I don't know. I was lying on the bed . . . I didn't hear him leave."

"Do you remember when he got back?"

Nervously, she licked her dry lips, clearly on guard now. "No . . . around ten, maybe."

Since the CCTV images from the gas station were taken a few minutes before ten, they knew she was lying.

His voice still gentle, Hampus said, "Are you sure? We have proof that he was in the center of Strömstad at that particular time."

Pernilla gave a start. Embla could see the fear in her eyes.

"Sure . . . I don't really remember. I was . . . I mean, Viggo was missing! You don't understand what it's like!"

The last sentence was more of a hysterical scream. Before either Hampus or Embla could do anything, she leaped to her feet, her face bright red and distorted. Her entire body was shaking with anger.

"Ted had to do something—you're all so fucking incompetent! First it was Amelie—why the fuck didn't you arrest that lunatic when it was obvious he'd murdered her? And now he's taken Viggo!"

Embla got up and went over to Pernilla. Calmly she put her arms around her and simply held her. At first Pernilla stiffened and made a vague attempt to free herself from Embla's embrace, then suddenly she seemed to give up. She collapsed against Embla's shoulder, sobbing with despair and bottomless grief. Neither Hampus nor her mother moved or spoke.

After a while the sobs began to subside. Embla stroked Pernilla's tangled hair and said, "We're doing everything we can to find Viggo, but we have witness statements from five people confirming that Kristoffer was in his workshop at Breidablick on Saturday afternoon. He has a watertight alibi."

Pernilla stayed where she was for a few seconds, then pushed Embla away. "That's not true! Ted said . . ." She stopped and clamped her lips together.

Hampus cleared his throat. "It is true—Kristoffer had nothing whatsoever to do with Viggo's disappearance. So what did Ted say?"

Pernilla remained silent, refusing to look at any of them.

Hampus waited a moment before continuing. "We have to check out times and so on—it's essential if we're going to find out what's happened to your son."

Embla and Hampus allowed the silence to do its work, but when Pernilla showed no sign of cooperating, Hampus said:

"You told us Ted went out on Sunday evening to help search for Viggo. What time was that?"

Pernilla merely shrugged. Once again Embla could see the fear in her eyes. It was her husband she was afraid of.

"We're not trying to get you to testify against Ted. We're absolutely certain he was in the town center just before ten. But what did he do before that? Did he meet up with anyone else?" Embla asked, her tone deliberately gentle.

"I . . . I don't remember. He didn't mention anyone else . . ."

Pernilla's eyes were darting all over the place; it was obvious she was lying.

"Did he take the car?"

Pernilla hesitated. "Yes." She began to move toward the door. "I can't do this . . ."

Hampus got to his feet. "Before you go upstairs I must inform you that this house will be searched shortly," he said.

Pernilla spun around with surprising speed and yelled, "We're not criminals—our son is missing because you can't do your fucking job!"

Hampus didn't allow himself to be provoked. "Ted is suspected of extremely serious crimes. Olof Sjöberg died in the arson attack, and his son, Kristoffer, was badly beaten. In fact he almost died, too. In such cases we always carry out a house search as a matter of routine. There are no exceptions."

Pernilla looked as if he'd slapped her across the face, as if she had only just realized how much trouble Ted was in. The tears began to flow once more.

"Mom! They're coming here!"

She ran into the hallway and straight up the stairs. One of the pink piglet slippers came off, but she didn't stop to put it back on. Her mother stayed in her chair. When she glanced up at Embla and Hampus, resignation was written all over her face.

Shortly afterward Paula Nilsson, Lars Engman, and the CSIs from Trollhättan arrived. Embla warned them about Pernilla's volatile state. Paula understood perfectly because she'd already met Viggo's mother. They agreed that she would go up to the bedroom, partly to keep Pernilla company, partly to see what she was doing.

Before leaving the house Embla and Hampus decided to check out the garage, but the door was locked. Hampus went back inside and asked Pernilla's mother for the key. Without a word she took it from the hook inside one of the kitchen cupboards, handed it over, then began to make her way laboriously up the stairs.

The garage door slid up with a rattle. They switched on their flashlights and shined the beams over the interior and the car. Embla found a switch, and two powerful fluorescent lights flooded the space with a harsh glare.

The Lexus was black, and looked pretty new. The windows were heavily tinted. Embla tried the trunk, and to her surprise it opened. It was clean and empty—apart from a red gas can.

"Yes! We'll take that with us," Hampus said. He went over to a workbench cluttered with wood and rubbish. There was a roll of garbage bags at the side; he ripped one off and put the roll back. Carefully, so as to avoid smudging any fingerprints or leaving any fresh ones, he managed to ease the can into the bag.

"There you go! Back to the station for analysis," he said.

Instinctively Embla patted her pocket. The flashlight she'd picked up in the hallway was still there. Why had she taken it? Maybe because she'd felt it could be important, since Viggo had been playing out in the garden with a flashlight when he went missing. Then again, this was old-fashioned rather than modern. It wasn't really suitable for a little boy; it was bulky and would be heavy with the batteries in it. But if Viggo had been playing with this flashlight, there were a number of questions that needed answering. Why hadn't the boy taken it with him when he disappeared? Or had the perpetrator taken it off him and thrown it down in the garden? And why were there no batteries in it?

OUTSIDE THE ICA grocery store, they saw the headlines on the newspaper placards: DOES HE KNOW WHERE AMELIE AND VIGGO ARE? and PARENTS IN DESPAIR WHILE MAIN SUSPECT KEPT SEDATED.

"Where the hell do they get this stuff from?" Embla exclaimed.

"Social media," Hampus informed her dryly.

His words were confirmed by Göran when they arrived back at the Shore House. He was sitting in the armchair with his laptop on his knee, his injured foot resting comfortably on the footstool. There was an almost empty packet of Ballerina cookies on the coffee table, along with a large cup of coffee. That was the typical scene when the chief inspector was working.

Hampus left the sack containing the gas can in the hallway. Before handing over the flashlight, Embla put on a pair of latex gloves and slipped it into a plastic bag she found in a kitchen drawer. Then the two of them reported back on their encounter with Pernilla Andersson and her mother.

Göran took the last cookie and washed it down with the remaining few drops of his coffee. "I'm glad you brought the most important things away with you," he said. "I'll take a look at the flashlight shortly. Is there anything left in the can?"

"A little."

"Great—and the flashlight could be interesting. Did

you ask Pernilla if it was the one Viggo was playing with on Saturday?"

"No, I didn't really get the chance. And there are no batteries in it, by the way."

Göran shook the crumbs out of the packet into the palm of his hand and tossed them into his mouth. He picked up his cup and seemed surprised to find it empty.

"Shall I make some more?" Embla asked.

He shook his head. "We'll be eating soon, but thanks for the offer."

"We saw some pretty annoying headlines on our way back," Hampus told him.

"I know. I've checked out the newspapers online. The trolls are having a field day, and the venom directed at Kristoffer is unlike anything I've ever seen. I've called Paula Nilsson and asked her to bring me Ted's computer. Something tells me a lot of the hate mail has come from him. I recognize his choice of words."

"Kristoffer was a target when Amelie disappeared—are you saying it's gotten worse?" Embla said.

"Much worse. There's a torrent of abuse flowing through every online forum. It started on Saturday night. One person posted a battery of abuse directed at both the police and Kristoffer across all social media platforms. It carried on all day Sunday, and now all the trolls who've jumped on board have made it a thousand times worse."

Hampus looked pensively at his chief. "What security do we have in place around Kristoffer?"

"I've just spoken to Willén, and he promised to post a guard outside his hospital room around the clock. He wants another team meeting first thing tomorrow. He's booked the same room at the town hall, so we can all brief one another and see where we are in each investigation."

Hampus nodded. "There's a lot going on."

"You could say that." Göran gave a theatrical sigh, then clapped his hands together. "Okay, let's go have dinner. I've booked a table at that spa hotel over in Kebalviken."

THE COMPARATIVELY NEW hotel was attractive and luxurious. The foyer was busy with smartly dressed Norwegians, presumably there for the oil industry conference. Embla's heart leaped when she noticed Nadir Khadem emerging from the elevator with two women who looked as though they were heading for a party. They were chatting with him and laughed at something he said before going off to join a larger group.

Embla glanced around, then said to Göran and Hampus, "I'm just going to the ladies' room. I'll join you in a minute."

"We'll be in the bar," Göran replied.

Embla headed toward the elevator; fortunately there was a sign for the restrooms right next to it. She was just a few feet away from Nadir, and as she passed him she caught his eye and smiled.

"Hi. It's pretty crowded around here."

He returned her smile, and she thought she saw a glint in his eye. "Hi—yes, I think there's some kind of conference on."

Embla continued to the ladies' room. She waited a few minutes, and when she came out she saw that he was still hovering nearby. To be fair, he was in line at the bar and might not have been waiting for her. But on the bright side, he was chatting with Göran and Hampus. So far everything seemed to be going well.

Göran spotted her just as it was his turn to order. "What would you like?"

"Orange juice."

He asked for two beers and an orange juice. When he'd paid they went in search of a table, but had to give up. They ended up standing by one of the huge windows, toasting the fact that they were a team once more.

Embla thought she could hear someone calling Göran's name above the hum of conversation. She looked around and saw Nadir perched on a barstool. He beckoned them over and said:

"You seem to be limping—take a seat."

He slid off the stool, and Göran didn't need asking twice. He heaved himself up with some difficulty, and the stool protested beneath his weight but didn't collapse.

"Thank you!" he said, raising his glass. The other three politely followed suit, and Embla saw that Nadir was also drinking orange juice. It might be spiked with vodka, of course, but she didn't think so.

They chatted about everything except the reason why they were in Strömstad—for obvious reasons. After a while the foyer bar began to empty as people moved into the restaurant.

"I'm hungry—shall we join them?" Hampus asked.

"No."

Both Hampus and Embla looked at their boss in surprise.

"No?" Hampus said eventually.

Göran gave a cunning smile. "The dining room is fully

booked, which is why I've reserved a table here in the foyer."

"Clever!" Embla said.

"I know!"

"Damn—I wasn't that clever," Nadir said.

"You're welcome to join us," Göran assured him. With a certain amount of grunting and groaning he managed to clamber down from the stool, and the four of them made their way over to a table with a *Reserved* sign on it.

The menu looked promising, and Embla chose a seafood salad with homemade bread and aioli. Göran and Hampus opted for the roast beef with potato salad, and after some thought Nadir went for a jumbo prawn sandwich.

They ate and talked, still without mentioning Ted Andersson or anyone else involved in the case. To her relief Embla discovered that Nadir was pleasant and laidback. Her colleagues seemed to like him, too, and for some reason, that was important to her. Neither of them was intending to go to bed with him, something she was increasingly determined to do. Her body was making its intentions very clear; this guy was hot. At last—she had almost begun to fear that she'd never feel that way again.

"So you're staying overnight," she said casually.

"Yes, Ted Andersson is being interviewed first thing in the morning. The hotel had a cancellation at the last minute. I've got plenty of paperwork to do," he replied with a faint smile.

I guess it's nice to have some peace and quiet when you're the father of small children, Embla thought without allowing her mask to slip.

As the meal progressed she flirted a little with Nadir,

and could see that he was interested, although he was trying to hide it from Göran and Hampus. Not that Hampus would have noticed if they'd thrown themselves on the table and started making out. He was in a world of his own most of the time, tapping away distractedly on his cell phone. Göran raised his eyebrows at one point, but said nothing.

She knew what he was thinking: it wasn't exactly best practice to embark on an intimate relationship with a suspect's lawyer. But Embla was far from naïve; she had no intention of discussing the investigation with him. She just wanted to get laid.

After a while they heard music from the hotel's nightclub. They'd seen a poster by the entrance: DISCO TIME! NOSTALGIA EVENING 10:00. Since Göran was the only one who'd been alive when disco was at its peak, a discussion broke out about music past and present. His view was that nothing decent had been written since the seventies; house and techno were synthetic crap, while rap wasn't music at all, "just noise." These opinions evoked howls of protest from the others, and they had a lively and entertaining conversation.

"Maybe we should go and see what it's like to dance to those old tracks?" Nadir suggested.

"I've sprained my ankle."

"And I couldn't think of anything worse," Hampus said without looking up from his phone.

Embla was a little concerned. She was the designated driver because she hadn't consumed any alcohol, which meant she couldn't stay behind with Nadir. She tried to swallow her disappointment, but that didn't go well.

At that moment Göran's phone rang. He glanced at

the display before answering. "Hi, Paula." He nodded and made various noises of agreement, then said, "Good. Can you pick me and Hampus up from the spa hotel in Kebalviken? Great."

Me and Hampus? Embla was confused, but a little seed of hope began to grow. Was she going to be able to stay after all?

"I asked Paula to pick up Ted Andersson's laptop. She's got it in the car, and she's coming to collect the two of us. She'll drive us back to Sandgrav."

He got to his feet with some difficulty, and he and Hampus said their goodbyes before heading for the door.

When they'd disappeared into the darkness, Nadir looked at Embla. There was definitely a glint in his eyes now, and she could feel her heart racing.

"Would you like to come up and see my etchings? I'm sure there must be at least one in my room," he said with a little smile.

At that moment Embla couldn't think of anything she'd like more.

THE 176 WAS deserted. The full moon appeared intermittently between the dark clouds scudding across the sky. The car radio was playing quietly, and Embla hummed along to Darin's "Nobody Knows." An appropriate song, but she could tell Göran wasn't fooled.

She felt as if a whole lot of internal knots had been untied. It was actually easier to breathe. A quiet, harmonious glow had spread through her body, and for the first time in months she was completely at ease with herself. The recollection of her encounter with Nadir made her smile into the darkness.

They had hardly gotten through the door of his hotel room before they started to undress—or rather rip each other's clothes off. She had been slightly surprised to discover that he was just as horny as she was, but only for a fraction of a second until lust swept everything from her mind.

They were like two perfectly matched dancers, each knowing instinctively what the other wanted.

Afterward they lay together for a while, her head resting on his chest. He stroked her hair, allowing the strands to run through his fingers.

"Embla . . ." He fell silent.

This is where he tells me he's married and this was a one-off, Embla thought, with an unexpected pang of disappointment. However, he didn't say anything else for a while; he just carried on stroking her back and her hair. When he cleared his throat, she unconsciously braced herself.

"We can . . . get together again. If you want to."

She couldn't hide her relief. "Absolutely."

"Tomorrow night?"

"Will you still be here?"

"Yes."

One more evening. She was more than grateful for what had just happened; another was a welcome bonus.

"I bought something in the spa shop," he said suddenly. Gently he moved her head and got out of bed. He walked over to the desk and picked up a small white paper bag as Embla admired his muscular legs. His running gear was draped over the chair, with his sneakers underneath it. He'd told her he'd done two marathons, Stockholm and Minneapolis. Apparently he had relatives both there and in New York. He reached into the bag and took out a little bottle.

"Massage oil."

He came and sat on the end of the bed. He tipped a few drops of oil into the palm of his hand, then began to massage her with firm, caressing movements.

Friday's early meeting took place in the town hall, in the same room as last Wednesday's briefing. This time there were significantly more officers in attendance; reinforcements had been brought in from the National Crime Unit in Stockholm in the hunt for Viktor Jansson's killer. Embla noticed that Sven-Ove Berglund was still out sick. It must have been something serious—a heart problem, rumor suggested—which meant a heavier responsibility lay on the shoulders of Acting Chief Superintendent Roger Willén. He stood there straight-backed in his impeccable uniform, his blue shirt freshly ironed. Who took care of that kind of thing? Did he have a wife or someone else at home, or did he do it himself? Embla realized she didn't know a thing about his personal life, which was a little strange given how closely they'd worked together during the events of the previous fall. Then again, maybe not. VGM had never been part of the regular team, but had always worked as a separate external resource.

Willén began by informing everyone that he'd spoken to the doctors responsible for treating Kristoffer Sjöberg at the hospital. They had reluctantly agreed to bring their patient out of his induced coma.

"His aunt, Eva Sjöberg, will be there. She's his next of kin and a trained nurse. I've also asked for a police presence, and I'd like VGM to take care of that. Okay?"

He looked at Göran, who nodded.

"Good. They'll be bringing him around this morning. I don't think it will be possible to question him right away, but maybe in a few hours?"

Willén moved on to the CCTV footage from the gas station, which elicited a murmur of approval. Ted Andersson wasn't going to get away with this. But why was Johannes Holm with him? He wasn't known as a bad guy. And who else was in the car? Willén asked the locally based officers to try to come up with possible names. They were probably looking at one or more associates of Andersson, possibly Holm as well.

Patrik Lind was sitting not far down the table from Embla, whispering to an older colleague from Strömstad. The other man was speaking a little more loudly, and she heard him say that he could understand the fathers' frustration and that he didn't know how he would have acted under the circumstances.

"That Sjöberg kid has always been weird. My daughter went to junior high with him. Like I said, weird. I bet he took Amelie, and it wouldn't surprise me if he took Viggo, too," he said.

The online trolls and the gutter press have done a good job, Embla thought.

The hunt for Viggo was still ongoing, it was day five now, and no trace of the boy had been found. There was an air of resignation about the team responsible for organizing the search. The parallels with Amelie's disappearance were all too evident. The theory that both children had been abducted and were no longer in the area had been put forward on a number of occasions, but online investigations and contact with other police regions had produced nothing, apart from the fact that Oslo had uncovered a new pedophile ring previously unknown to them, with branches in Bergen, Gothenburg, Trondheim, and Copenhagen.

The team looking into the murder of Viktor Jansson also seemed somewhat disheartened. They had been unable to secure leads at the scene of the crime because the dogs and their owners had trampled over everything in sight. The pouring rain had also helped to destroy any possible footprints or tire tracks in the thin layer of earth and gravel covering the tarmac in the tiny parking lot. Nor was there any sign of the murder weapon. The forensic pathologist had said they were looking for a blunt, heavy object; the force of the blows had killed Viktor.

Willén was about to summarize the situation when there was a loud knock on the impressive double doors, and a very stylish gray-haired lady wearing a pale-gray skirt suit and black boots came in. She looked straight at the chief superintendent through the thick lenses of her glasses, which made her eyes look unnaturally large.

"Sorry to interrupt, but there's a call for you. You all have your cell phones switched off in here . . . I was asked to get a hold of Chief Superintendent Willén as quickly as possible—it's extremely urgent!" she said, stressing the last two words.

"Okay, thanks."

For a moment he seemed unsure what to do, then he made up his mind.

"Stay here—I'll go and see what it's about."

He hurried out of the room and everyone started talking at once, speculating about what might have happened. Had one of the children been found? Or maybe both?

Göran leaned over to Embla and Hampus. "The three of us will have a chat with Ted and Johannes again before you go to the hospital," he said.

Just then Willén returned. His cheeks were flushed, his expression tense. "That was the head of the fire investigation unit at Breidablick," he said once the conversation had died down. "They found an old toolbox in the trunk of one of the cars outside the workshop. One of the technicians decided to open it this morning, and inside he found a small battery-powered candle. The kind children carry in the Lucia procession."

At first there was a deathly silence, then the chatter broke out again.

"I knew it! It was that weirdo Sjöberg!" the older colleague from Strömstad shouted. He underlined his words by raising his hand to high-five Patrik Lind.

THEY DECIDED TO start with Johannes Holm. Jasmin Carell, his lawyer, arrived an hour after she'd been contacted. She was wearing the same skirt suit as the previous day, but had added a pair of elegant black boots. As she walked by leaving a faint trail of fresh perfume, Embla suddenly felt short and dumpy. She measured five foot eight in her stocking feet, so she knew perfectly well that she wasn't, but there was something about the slender woman in high heels that made her feel that way.

Someone who appeared to have shrunk noticeably during the night was Johannes Holm. He was stooping and his head was down as Alice Åslund brought him into the room. He was still in the same clothes he'd been wearing when he was arrested—jeans and a long-sleeved gray cotton top. The dark circles around his puffy eyes indicated that he hadn't slept much, if at all. As soon as he sank down on the chair, Embla knew he wouldn't be able to stand up to any pressure. The arrangement was the same as before: Göran and Hampus opposite Johannes and his lawyer, with Embla standing by the door.

After going through the formalities for the tape, Göran said, "Johannes, you're not known for being a violent guy. I've spoken to a number of local officers, and they can't understand why you're on the CCTV footage from the gas station. What actually happened on Sunday evening?"

Johannes kept his head down and made no attempt to answer.

Göran leaned across the table and said slowly and clearly, "Olof Sjöberg died in that fire, and his son was lucky to survive. Arson with intent to endanger life, assault, possibly attempted homicide in Kristoffer's case. Extremely serious crimes."

Jasmin Carell looked as if she was about to say something, but Johannes preempted her by half-getting to his feet.

"You don't understand! If I say anything . . ."

His voice broke and he began to sob uncontrollably. Slowly he sank back down onto the chair and buried his face in his hands. His bony shoulders shook. Göran and Hampus exchanged a quick glance. Hampus nodded almost imperceptibly, then turned to Johannes.

"Are you scared of Ted?"

At first it seemed as if Johannes hadn't heard the question, but after a moment he looked up. Jasmin quickly produced a packet of tissues, which Johannes took, his gaze still fixed on Hampus. He wiped his eyes and blew his nose. Hampus's expression was sympathetic behind those round glasses.

"Ted is used to interviews like this. He knows if he blames you, he'll get a lighter sentence. But these crimes are so serious that you'll both go down for at least ten years if you refuse to tell the truth," he said.

At that moment Johannes's face cleared and he

appeared to be more present. When he spoke, the words came out as a hoarse whisper. "But . . . it wasn't me."

"In that case you need to tell us what really happened, otherwise it's your word against his."

Hampus was good, there was no doubt about it. He made it sound as if Ted had already started blaming the whole thing on Johannes.

"I can't go to jail and leave Maria alone with Julien! And then there's Amelie . . ." His voice failed him again, but he struggled to regain his composure. He blew his nose once more, then swallowed hard. "Me and Ted . . . we hung out together in school, and he always got his way."

Hampus nodded, his face conveying nothing but warmth and understanding. "I get it—he's always been a leader."

Johannes nodded and mumbled a barely audible "Yes."

"And is that still the case? He takes the lead and no one dares to go against him?"

"It's not quite the same—he's less aggressive these days. Except when he's had a drink. Then he can go kind of crazy."

Jasmin Carell leaned back, making no attempt to interrupt her client. *I guess this is exactly what she wants*, Embla thought. *Johannes is telling the truth—that's the only thing that can help him*.

Hampus gazed calmly at the man opposite. "So what about Sunday? Did Ted . . . go kind of crazy?"

The direct question took Johannes by surprise, but after a deep breath he answered. "Yes."

And there it was.

He spoke hesitantly at first, searching for the right words, but after a while the whole story came spilling out.

It was as if he needed to lance an abscess that had been festering inside him.

Ted had called him at around seven on Sunday evening and insisted that they meet up. They were both in the same boat now—they both had a missing kid. As always when his friend made a suggestion, Johannes went along with it. Maria tried to persuade him to stay home, but when Ted came to pick him up an hour later, she had to let him go.

They drove off toward the town center in Ted's Lexus. He parked outside a bar and they went in. One of Ted's other pals was there, and they joined him. Hampus asked for the man's name, but Johannes insisted he didn't know. His eyes were darting all over the place, but Hampus chose to let it go. If he pushed too hard, there was a risk that Johannes would clam up. It was obvious that he was very frightened, even though he wanted to tell them as much as he dared.

Hampus managed to get Johannes back on track. Ted had bought a round of beers in the pub, and the three of them had chatted about this and that. The atmosphere had been relaxed. Johannes thought he'd only had two beers, but it must have been more because his memories were very hazy. Suddenly they were in the car, he and Ted in the front and the other guy in the back. He remembered Ted saying over and over again: "We're going to get the fucking truth! We're going to find out what's happened to Amelie and Viggo!"

They had stopped at a gas station and Johannes had gone inside to use the toilet. The CCTV footage brought it all back to him, but he had no recollection of Ted filling a can with diesel.

When they arrived at Breidablick there were lights showing in several windows. The barn, or rather the workshop, was in darkness. The only source of illumination was an external lamp on the gable; he did recall that. Before they had a chance to discuss what they were going to do, the other guy had jumped out of the car, grabbed the can of diesel, and run over to the workshop. In no time at all flames were licking the wooden walls.

When he came back to the car, Ted yelled, "Those fuckers are gonna get exactly what they deserve!" He headed for the house. Johannes saw him yank open the double doors and disappear inside. By the time he reached the hallway, Ted had already started on Kristoffer. The boy was lying on the floor, trying to shield himself from the kicks and blows raining down on him. Ted was completely out of control.

"What have you done with our kids, you fucker?" he yelled.

At first Johannes had stood there, completely at a loss as he watched the brutal assault. The man who had set fire to the barn came in, and eventually the two of them managed to drag Ted away from Kristoffer. They had to keep a firm grip on him; he was like a thing possessed. Together they pushed him out of the house, and suddenly he stopped resisting. It was as if someone had pulled the plug on his rage.

Johannes had been deeply shocked, and hadn't been able to utter a word. Ted had been excited, and kept saying things like: "Look at those flames! I've taught that little shit a lesson—he'll never fucking do it again!"

They had dropped off Johannes in front of his house. He had staggered in without waking either Maria or Julien. His wife was in a deep slumber. She'd been taking sleeping pills ever since Amelie's disappearance. Strangely enough Johannes had gone out like a light as soon as his head hit the pillow. The following morning he'd had a crippling headache.

"Could you have been drugged?" Hampus asked.

Johannes hesitated, then mumbled, "Don't know."

"Who was the other guy? What's his name?"

Johannes's face closed down and his mouth became a thin line. It was obvious that he didn't want to answer.

"He'll be able to confirm your story."

The look Johannes gave him was difficult to interpret. Hampus tried again, this time injecting a mild reproach into his voice. "Why won't you tell us his name?"

"I don't remember it. Or maybe I don't know it. I don't think I heard it."

It was obvious that he didn't intend to say any more. Hampus announced that the interview was over, and Johannes was led away.

Nadir Khadem entered the room with his client. He smiled and greeted everyone. His eyes lingered for a fraction of a second too long on Embla, but that was it. She made an equal effort not to show how she felt about the man with whom she'd enjoyed a night of passion just a few hours earlier.

Ted Andersson's face was beaded with sweat when he sat down on the chair that Johannes had warmed for him. His hands were twitching, and at regular intervals his whole body jerked uncontrollably.

Göran and Hampus took turns asking questions, which were met with absolute silence. That was clearly the strategy for the day.

The two detectives also fell silent after a while. Hampus leaned back and fixed his gaze on Ted through those round glasses.

"The doctors are bringing Kristoffer out of his induced coma this morning. In fact they've already begun. What do you think he's going to say?" he asked, keeping his tone neutral.

Ted gave a start, and there was a dangerous glint in his eyes. A direct hit. Embla braced herself in case he decided to make a run for it again.

Suddenly he slammed his fist down on the table. "That slimy little shit—he's sick in the head!"

You could have heard a pin drop after his outburst. Neither Göran nor Hampus moved a muscle.

Hampus stared at him for a while, then said, "We have reason to believe that a friend of yours set fire to Olof Sjöberg's workshop. Is that correct?"

"It was Johannes."

"Who assaulted Kristoffer?"

"Johannes."

"That's not what we've heard."

The color rose in Ted's face, and he looked as if he was going to jump to his feet, but after a couple of deep breaths he managed to calm himself.

"Listen, this is what happened. I called Johannes for a chat—I mean we're in the same situation, with both our kids missing. He wanted to go somewhere—a bar. I drove over and picked him up and we went into town."

"What time was this?"

"Around eight. Anyway, we went to Rocky's. Johannes was putting it away, knocking back the booze like there was no tomorrow. I was driving, so I took it easy. Then he wanted to get back in the car. He asked if there was any gas in the can I always carry. I said no, and he told me to drive to a gas station. When we got there he asked if he could borrow the can—said he needed some gas for his car or something. Then he decided he needed to go and pee. He told me to fill up the can, so that's what I did while he was gone. We headed home, but as we got close he changed his mind and told me to keep going. He insisted on going over to the Sjöberg place to talk to the boy. That was all he kept saying, talk to the boy. I did as he said, and . . . you know the rest."

Hampus stared searchingly at Ted's face. His cheeks were bright red, his upper lip and forehead beaded with sweat. Giving nothing away, he asked, "Who was the guy you met in the bar?"

"We met plenty of guys in the bar. This place is a shit hole in the winter—everybody knows everybody else."

"I mean the one who came with you to Breidablick in the car."

Ted raised his eyebrows, the epitome of total surprise.

"Came with us . . . There was nobody else in the car, just me and Johannes. He was drunk and crazy. If I hadn't been there he would have killed the little fucker!"

Göran had been tapping away on his laptop while Hampus conducted the interview. He looked up and said quietly, "I've just been checking the vehicle register. Johannes Holm drives an eight-year-old Mazda. Runs on gas. Why would he need a can of diesel?"

"To set fire to the fucking workshop, Einstein!"

With that Ted clamped his lips firmly shut and refused to say another word.

"We've got time to go and have a chat with Maria Holm before lunch," Hampus said as they emerged from the police station.

It had started raining again, and a cold wind swept across the deserted square. In a few months the place would be swarming with tourists, and the market would be in full swing. Right now that seemed a long way off.

Embla and Hampus set off to speak to Amelie's mother; Göran had decided to work from the station and wait for them to come back for lunch. They'd all voted for a return visit to the Thai restaurant.

Hampus had to ring the bell several times before there was any response. The door edged open and Maria's face appeared in the narrow gap. When she let them in, they could see she'd been crying.

"Is Julien home?" Embla asked.

Maria shook her head. "Preschool."

She showed them into an airy living room with modern furniture: black armchairs and a pale-gray leather sofa. Nice. A large rug in shades of blue and several colorful, exotic pictures on the walls, probably painted by an artist from Maria's homeland of Guadeloupe. The large windows and glass door overlooked a south-facing patio. There wasn't much of a view, thanks to a tall cypress hedge just a few feet away. It was covered with a net of LED lights, which looked very pretty. In spite of the fact that it was almost lunchtime, there wasn't much daylight out there.

Embla and Hampus each took an armchair and Maria sank down on the sofa.

"Can I get you a coffee or something?" she asked in a flat voice.

"No thanks."

Hampus smiled warmly at her. She tried to return his smile, but managed only a grimace. A single tear trickled down her cheek, and she dashed it away with the back of her hand.

"I don't understand why . . . why he went with Ted!"

She sounded angry, but they realized it was Johannes she was mad at, not them. When they began to ask about Sunday, Maria confirmed her husband's story. Ted had picked him up around eight, saying they were going out to search for the children. He'd had an idea or been given a tip-off, she couldn't remember exactly what he'd said. Maria had gone to bed at about ten o'clock after taking a pill. She had to get some sleep for Julien's sake. She didn't know when Johannes had come home, but he'd been as sick as a dog the following morning. At first she'd thought it served him right, but then she'd gotten worried. It took him almost the whole day to recover.

"Has Johannes ever said he believes Kristoffer is responsible for Amelie's disappearance?" Hampus asked.

Maria stiffened and gave him a suspicious look. Maybe she thought he was trying to get her to say Johannes had attacked the boy.

"I guess we both thought that—at first . . ."

"But not now?"

She turned her head and gazed out the rain-spattered window. "Maybe . . . Who else could it be? But I don't know . . ."

"What makes you unsure?"

She took a deep breath and met his eyes once more. "Kristoffer is related to Amelie's best friend, Tuva. He's never . . . how shall I put it . . . tried to get close to the girls. He lives in his own world of engines and cars."

"You've never heard anyone say he was violent? Prone to outbursts of rage?"

"Never—quite the reverse. Apparently he doesn't defend himself against bullies—that's what Tuva's always said. It drives her crazy. She looks up to him. I think she sees him as a kind of older brother. She's an only child and would have loved an older sibling, and Kristoffer . . ."

She broke off, eyes shining with tears as she stared at a framed photograph on the wall: Amelie and Julien on a sun-drenched beach. They were in their swimming gear, grinning straight at the camera, each clutching an enormous ice cream. The palm trees in the background suggested the picture might have been taken on Guadeloupe.

Embla was struck by a terrible thought. *Julien probably doesn't have a big sister anymore. Now he's an only child, too.*

Even though hope is the last thing to leave a human being, Embla was pretty sure that Amelie was no longer alive. And if they didn't find Viggo very soon, there was every chance that he was dead, too.

A MALE NURSE in his thirties whose name badge informed them that he was called Ahmed showed them the way. At first glance he reminded Embla of Nadir. He greeted the police officer on duty in the corridor, then accompanied them into Kristoffer's room. Eva Sjöberg got up from the chair beside the bed and came toward them, smiling.

"He's come around, but he's not fully awake yet. He keeps drifting in and out of sleep. Hassan—Kristoffer's doctor—says he probably should have been kept sedated for another twenty-four hours," she told them quietly.

"How is he otherwise?" Embla asked.

Eva shook her head.

"His life is no longer in danger, but it's going to take quite some time for his injuries to heal. His whole body is black and blue. They've replaced the shattered cheekbone with a titanium insert, and they've set his jawbone, which was broken in two places. He can't chew, so he'll be fed through a tube for a while. He has three broken ribs, plus a fractured ulna and wrist. They've removed his spleen, because it was ruptured, so the dressing on that wound will need to be changed regularly. He's going to need strong pain relief, and they'll be keeping him in for the foreseeable future."

She paused to catch her breath after the detailed report on her nephew's condition. Kristoffer's physical injuries would heal in time. The question was what kind of scars the mental trauma would leave.

"Does he know about his father?" Embla whispered.

"No. He hasn't been awake for long enough yet . . ."

A faint whimper came from the bed. Eva immediately turned and hurried back to the boy. She spoke softly, gently stroking the arm that wasn't in plaster. He fell silent, but moved restlessly beneath the covers.

"Are you in pain?" Eva asked.

The response was a low groan. Eva stood up and pressed a red button on the edge of the bedside cabinet. Embla and Hampus edged a little closer.

Half of Kristoffer's face was bandaged, while the other half displayed all the colors of the rainbow. His eye was closed, but the eyelid was twitching. His features were so swollen that Embla didn't even recognize the gangly teenager she'd met at Breidablick. His left arm was plastered up to the elbow. The sleeve of his hospital gown had ridden up the uninjured arm, which looked heartbreakingly pale. However, his forearm was muscular, and his large hands were callused. *He must be pretty strong, given the work he does*, Embla thought.

The door opened and Ahmed came in carrying a syringe. He checked on Kristoffer, then attached the syringe to the IV catheter just below the boy's throat, and slowly injected the contents. He adjusted the intravenous drip and had a word with Eva before leaving the room. Eva gave Embla a wink.

"He's good," she said, sounding satisfied. She was certainly in a position to judge his competence.

"Are you going to tell Kristoffer we're here, or shall we do it ourselves?" Embla asked quietly.

"I'll do it."

Gently Eva stroked the back of Kristoffer's hand and said softly, "Kristoffer, honey? There are two police officers here who want to have a little chat with you. They need to know what happened when you got . . . hurt."

His eyelid began to twitch again, and he managed to open it a sliver. They could see his eye darting from side to side; he was clearly finding it difficult to focus. Embla leaned over the bed, trying to put herself in his line of sight.

"Hi, Kristoffer. My name's Embla."

Hampus followed suit.

Kristoffer groaned and closed his eye.

"Do you think you might be able to answer a couple of questions?" Embla continued.

She decided to interpret the ensuing grunt as a yes.

"What happened on that evening when you got beaten up?" Might as well get straight to the point.

A small furrow between his eyebrows showed that he was making a real effort to think. The eye flew open, and he stared in terror at the three faces around his bed.

"Do you remember anything?" Eva asked anxiously.

"No," he mumbled, almost inaudibly. It was bordering on a sob, and there was panic in that wide-open eye.

"It's okay, sweetheart. You've had a blow to the head. Your memory will come back soon," his aunt reassured him.

The look she gave Embla and Hampus didn't reflect the same conviction.

However, her words seemed to have the desired effect. Kristoffer relaxed, although that worried little furrow remained. Before any of them could ask another question, he looked straight at his aunt.

"Dad . . . where's . . . ?" he managed to force out, in spite of his damaged jawbone.

Eva went pale and held his hand tightly. "You remember he was out there in the workshop? Which was on fire?"

He grunted, keeping his eye fixed on her face. Eva lifted his hand and placed it against her cheek, then she broke the news that Olof had died in the flames. Kristoffer didn't show his feelings, but Embla saw the light die in his eye as Eva went on talking. When she had finished he withdrew his hand and closed his eye.

They tried speaking to him again, but there was no reaction. They weren't even sure if he could hear their voices.

Eva stood up and signaled to Embla and Hampus to follow her. She stopped by the door and said quietly, "This is how he reacts when the world is too much for him. He'll come back to us, but it will take time. They're going to put an extra bed in here for me, and I've also been given a room in the patients' hotel. I'll call you when he starts communicating, Embla."

She looked a little embarrassed, and added, "Do you have a card with your cell phone number? I know you gave me one already, but I left it at home."

Embla took out her card and handed it over.

"I'll put it in my phone right now," Eva said, digging her cell out of her pocket.

They agreed that she would call the next day and let

them know if it was okay to come back and talk to Kristoffer again.

They passed reception on the way out. Ahmed was chatting to some of the other nurses, and beamed at Embla and Hampus as they went by. Well, he actually beamed at Hampus, who as usual didn't notice. Embla did—she found it very funny.

They had almost reached the main door when Embla's phone rang. She glanced at the display and was surprised to see Eva's name.

"That was quick," Hampus said.

Before Embla had time to speak she heard a hoarse whisper:

"Hurry! He's . . ."

Then came a gasp, followed by a loud scream. Even Hampus heard it.

"What the hell . . ."

They both broke into a run. Embla was faster and led the way. The foyer was crowded, but everyone moved aside when she yelled at the top of her voice, "Police! Out of the way!"

They were in luck: one of the elevators had just emptied and she dashed inside. Impatiently she held open the door as she waited for Hampus. He ran in and leaned against the wall to catch his breath, while at the same time calling for backup on his cell phone.

When they reached the right floor Embla shot out as soon as the door began to open. Short distances had always suited her best, and she sprinted down the corridor. The deafening screech of an alarm sliced through the air. She could see three nurses racing toward Kristoffer's room. They stopped at the door; the police officer who had been on guard was lying motionless on the floor. Embla could see his legs, but his upper body was hidden by a cleaning cart that was parked beside him. The nurses didn't quite know what to do. They looked from the officer on the floor to the closed door and back again. Ahmed knelt down and checked for a pulse, and one of the others reached for the door handle.

"No! Wait!" Embla yelled.

The nurse immediately stepped back. Embla paused for a fraction of a second. Should she fling the door open? What was on the other side? Neither she nor Hampus was armed. From inside the room she could hear Eva screaming and people moving around. A thud. Someone else was screaming—or rather yelling. A man. Kristoffer? Hardly—this voice was too loud, too deep. Then she heard rapid footsteps approaching the door from the other side. Heavy footsteps, not Eva's. Shallow breathing. Embla moved back silently and positioned herself so that whoever was trying to assess the situation couldn't see her. A shaven head appeared as the door opened; Embla noticed a cauliflower ear and a tattooed neck. He paused when he saw the nurses, staring at him in horror.

At that moment Embla kicked the handle with all her strength. The man didn't even have time to react as the door slammed shut, trapping his head against the frame with a horrible sound, like a coconut being smashed with a hammer. He sank to the floor without a sound. Something flashed as an object fell from his hand, and Embla quickly bent down and picked it up. She immediately recognized what it was because she owned a similar one: a broad-bladed hunting knife, a lethal weapon. It was an expensive item. She'd received hers as a birthday present from the hunting club when she turned twenty-five.

In the other hand he was clutching something that looked a bit like a cell phone. When Embla pried his fingers apart, she realized it was a Taser.

The man was wearing a typical hospital uniform—a white tunic and white trousers. On his feet, however, were sturdy military boots. Definitely not standard hospital issue.

Embla straightened up and flung the door wide open. Still screaming, Eva staggered toward her brandishing a toilet cleaning brush. She was bleeding from her mouth, and she had an angry red mark below one eye.

"It's me, Eva. It's Embla."

When Eva registered that it was indeed Embla, she stopped yelling.

The shaven-headed man was moving now, attempting to get to his feet. *Talk about having a thick skull*, Embla thought before she heard a familiar voice bellow:

"Police! Stay right where you are or I'll shoot!"

Shoot? Where had Hampus found a gun? Not that it mattered—the man by the door sank back down.

"Eva, how are you and Kristoffer?"

"He didn't . . . he didn't get to Kristoffer. I screamed and hit him with the brush. But I think he cut my . . . my hand. And he punched me in the face."

Eva held out her left hand; she was still clutching the toilet brush in her right. Blood was dripping from her palm, and she stared at it uncomprehendingly. Then her legs gave way, and Embla just managed to grab her before she went down.

Reinforcements arrived within minutes and handcuffed the man with the cauliflower ear. A doctor had already examined him to see if he sustained a concussion from his encounter with the door, and he was pronounced fit to be transported to a holding cell in Trollhättan, where the chief superintendent and his team would question him. The custody officer would be asked to keep a close eye on him; there are always risks associated with head trauma, as Embla knew from personal experience.

It was high time they called Roger Willén to tell him what had happened at the hospital. At that second Embla's phone began to vibrate in her pocket. The display told her it was Willén. Since calls weren't allowed on the ward, she answered quickly before he had time to say anything.

"Hi, I'm on the ward. I'll go outside and call you back."

She ran down the stairs and through the foyer. It was visiting time, so there were people everywhere. She stopped outside the glass doors and took a couple of deep breaths. The air was cold and crisp. Her brain cleared, and she was ready for a conversation with the chief superintendent.

"Apparently there's been some kind of incident at the hospital. I believe you and Hampus were there. Update please," he said, getting straight to the point.

Embla went through everything from the start of their visit. Willén grunted when he heard about Kristoffer's memory loss, but apart from that he kept quiet.

"How's the officer who was on guard duty?" he asked when she was done.

"He's being taken care of. I checked to see if he'd been stabbed, but he hadn't—just Tasered. The wound in Eva

Sjöberg's hand was quite deep and is being sutured now. She's also in shock, of course."

"Was there any sign that the boy had been hurt?"

"No. According to Eva, the guy didn't get near the bed. She defended herself and Kristoffer with a toilet brush."

There was a brief silence as the chief superintendent digested this snippet.

"A toilet brush?"

"Yes. I gave her my card just before she left, and she added my number to her contacts list while she was sitting on the toilet. The door wasn't completely closed, so she saw the guy sneak in. She called my number, pressed the alarm button, then ran out screaming at the top of her voice and attacked him with the only weapon she could find. The perp couldn't focus on Kristoffer and defend himself against Eva; she really went for him with that brush. She's a strong woman, in spite of her age. And of course she wasn't part of his plan; he was after Kristoffer. He probably wasn't expecting her to be there, maybe he couldn't work out what to do when things went wrong. He was running out of time . . ."

Embla realized to her surprise that Willén was laughing. He was actually laughing. At first she was angry because her adrenaline was still pumping. What was so fucking funny? But when she thought about it, perhaps there was a little humor in the situation. And she hadn't even gotten to the really amusing part yet. Ignoring the chief superintendent's muffled chuckles, she went on.

"He must have an unusually thick skull because only a minute or so after I'd slammed the door on his head, he started moving, but then Hampus yelled that he'd shoot if the guy didn't stay down. I came out into the corridor and saw Hampus pointing something that looked a bit like a weapon at the guy on the floor. He must still have been groggy, otherwise he would have realized it wasn't a gun."

Embla deliberately paused. As expected Willén quickly grew impatient.

"So what was it?"

"A rectoscope."

"A what?"

"A rectoscope. Doctors use it to look up a patient's rectum. He found it on a cart and grabbed it. Fortunately it was clean."

That was too much for Willén. He guffawed with laughter, and she found herself grinning in response. A good laugh was exactly what they needed during this difficult and upsetting investigation.

Someone else who had a good laugh was Göran Krantz. They were having a meal in the Thai restaurant, which was definitely their favorite place in Strömstad, enjoying a spicy stew. It was delicious, and Embla was starving. All three agreed that Eva was the best guardian angel Kristoffer could wish for. If she hadn't been there, the man with the cauliflower ear would almost certainly have achieved his aim.

"But where did he get a hold of the clothes?" Göran asked, serious once more.

"He stole them from a linen room down in the basement. He was lucky to find a uniform that fit—he's a big guy. He also came across an ID card and hung it around his neck. He took the cleaning cart from the cleaners' storage closet, so he looked totally authentic as long as no one wanted to examine his ID. The staff soon realized both doors had been broken open, but of course they didn't know where he'd gone," Hampus explained.

"And we still don't know who he is?"

"No, he's refusing to talk."

Göran nodded and raised his eyebrows.

"Okay, so this seems like a classic case. The killer disguises himself and tries to kill someone who's lying in a hospital with a guard outside the door of his room. It often happens in crime shows on TV. And it's always pretty creepy."

"Creepy! Too fucking right it was creepy!" Embla snapped.

She didn't like Göran talking about the incident as if it were some movie! And it definitely hadn't been a comedy—it had been deadly serious. Someone wanted to kill Kristoffer.

"I'm sorry, Embla. I didn't mean to play it down—of course I realize it was a serious situation. The guy was armed, and the two of you did a great job. With the assistance of the lady with the toilet brush."

He couldn't help smiling again, but Embla appreciated his apology.

After their meal they walked the short distance back to the square where the Volvo was parked, and Göran asked Embla to drive them to Olof Sjöberg's car showroom. Apparently he'd arranged a car rental.

It wasn't unusual for VMG to need an additional vehicle when they were out on an assignment. Given how isolated their current base was, a second car wasn't a bad idea.

The showroom was located on Uddevallavägen, not far from Ted Andersson's house.

Göran had rented a small white Nissan. When he got in, it dipped noticeably on the driver's side. He gave Embla and Hampus a cheery wave and set off toward Sandgrav, leaving the Volvo in his wake.

It was dark by the time they pulled up to the Shore House. The wind whipped their faces, and Embla buried her chin in her scarf as she scurried across the yard. The cold air made it hard to breathe, but at least it wasn't raining any longer. The sound of the waves crashing against the rocks was somehow threatening. Far away in the distance she could see a huge ship moving slowly north; no doubt it was going to Norway to pick up oil. She longed to be indoors, sitting in front of the fire with a cup of tea and discussing the day's events with her colleagues. That meant a lot to her.

Göran set up the computer and his papers, Hampus got the fire going, Embla made tea and coffee. She found a packet of Ballerina cookies in the larder—Göran's favorite. Personally she avoided sweet things, although she did reward herself with a small piece of dark chocolate occasionally. She always had a bar with a cocoa content of at least seventy percent around somewhere. Göran had yet to work out where she hid them, but it was only a matter of time. He didn't usually like dark chocolate, but if there was nothing else, that wouldn't stop him. Which was why she slipped a bar inside a pack of sanitary pads. Foolproof, surely, or was it? Göran's intuition was almost supernatural when it came to candy and cookies.

To be fair, he looked good with his thick dark-blond hair, just beginning to turn gray at the temples, and his warm blue eyes. It was unfortunate that he'd put on so much weight after the divorce almost ten years ago. Even though he was quite tall, he was beginning to look fat. Before his marriage broke up his weight had been normal, according to the colleagues who'd known him back then. The divorce had been traumatic: his wife had fallen in love with a Spaniard ten years younger than Göran and moved down to Spain. Both their teenage sons had chosen to stay with their father and were now at college in Luleå and Lund. Göran must have felt lonely when they moved out, and as far as Embla was aware he hadn't found a new partner.

She arranged the cookies on a plate and placed it on a tray. It was his business if he got even fatter, but it would be a shame; he was only just over fifty.

The wind was hurling itself at the windows, but inside the house it was warm and cozy. The fire crackled behind the glass doors of the stove. The three of them settled down to talk over the day's events.

Göran had contacted the hospital and received reassuring news about Eva Sjöberg. The stab wound in her hand hadn't damaged any tendons, and was expected to heal without complications. Thanks to the injection he'd been given, Kristoffer didn't seem to have noticed the fracas. Security had been increased, and there were now two police officers stationed outside his door.

A call to Trollhättan had revealed that the guy with the cauliflower ear still hadn't said a word. They were running his prints against the database, since it seemed likely that he had a criminal record, but no luck so far.

When they had topped off their drinks and Göran had eaten what he swore would be his last cookie, he said, "Coming back to Amelie and Viggo, we have to consider the possibility that the two cases aren't connected at all, and that we might not even be looking at a criminal act. However, the likelihood of two children vanishing without a trace from Strömstad within six weeks is pretty small."

"And in the winter. There are lots of people here in summer, which means more children and a greater chance of something happening," Embla said.

"Agreed. I don't think Amelie drowned; the area where she went missing is well over a mile from the sea. As far as Viggo is concerned, it's not impossible. It's only a few hundred yards from his house to the quayside where the ferries dock. As I said, we need to keep an open mind: we could be dealing with two completely separate crimes or accidents. I'll come back to that."

"This investigation is going to take a long time," Hampus stated gloomily. Embla had a strong feeling that he wanted to clear things up as quickly as possible and go home. He really wasn't himself, but she couldn't work out why.

"You're right—it's complicated. But if we assume the children's disappearances are connected, then there are various hypotheses. The first is they were kidnapped but are alive and being kept hidden. That means they were taken away by car. The area in and around Strömstad has been searched so thoroughly that I'd have to conclude they're some distance away. In which case the perpetrator is probably a pedophile."

An uncomfortable silence descended on the room. That hypothesis had been put forward shortly after Amelie went missing and unfortunately couldn't be ruled out.

"Or there could be several pedophiles involved," Embla commented grimly.

"You're thinking of the pedophile ring our colleagues in Oslo uncovered. Yes, that's a possibility. But we've checked out all known pedophiles within a three-hundred-mile radius in both Sweden and Norway: nothing. And so we come to the next hypothesis: they're both dead."

Silence once more. Embla felt a chill run from the nape of her neck and down her spine. Crimes against children were always the hardest to deal with. *They're completely defenseless in this evil world.*

Göran stared down into his empty cup; Embla took it and went into the kitchen to refill it. She didn't bother asking Hampus because she knew he didn't like to drink too much coffee in the evenings. She was getting a little impatient. She wanted to move things along because Nadir would be waiting for her in his hotel room. She'd told him she wouldn't be there before ten at the earliest, but right now it was looking as if it could be later.

Göran gave her a grateful smile when she handed him a fresh coffee.

"If both children have been murdered, then there are two possibilities. Firstly, most children are murdered by those closest to them. People do kill children they don't know, but it's very rare. Secondly, we could be dealing with an unusually dangerous type of pedophile: a sadistic child killer. The few we have and know about in Sweden are all behind bars, and the same applies in Norway. If this is the correct scenario, then as I said the children must have been taken away by car, otherwise we'd have found them," he said.

"Unless they're incredibly well hidden," Embla pointed out.

"Good point."

He opened up his laptop.

"I've listed the similarities between the two disappearances. Number one: they both went missing outdoors and close to home. Comments?"

"No one saw or heard anything when they were taken," Hampus said.

"It was dark," Embla added.

"Good—factors that were in the perpetrator's favor. But another common denominator is that they vanished straight after darkness fell, late in the afternoon. In Amelie's case it was between three and four, Viggo around a quarter to five. Any thoughts on that?"

Göran looked encouragingly at his colleagues.

"As Hampus said—it's strange that no one noticed anything," Embla said. She had found this puzzling from the start. The children hadn't gone missing in the middle of some wilderness, but in residential areas with plenty of people around.

"That suggests to me that the children didn't resist, didn't scream or fight back. Which could mean they weren't scared of the perpetrator," Hampus said reflectively.

"So they knew the person?"

"It's not impossible."

Göran nodded. "So who knows both children?"

Embla and Hampus thought for a moment.

"Their parents know one another," Embla said. "Johannes Holm and Ted Andersson were childhood friends and often travel home together from their jobs in Norway."

"I thought about that and checked with their employers. Both Johannes and Ted were working on the Thursday when Amelie went missing. Neither of them could have been involved," Göran said.

"What about the mothers?" Hampus asked.

"Maria Holm was at work until four-thirty. Pernilla was free, but had an emergency dental appointment in the center of Strömstad on that Thursday afternoon. She'd been suffering from a bad toothache, and the dentist made a start on root canal treatment. According to the nurse at reception she arrived at three-fifteen and left at four. The preschool staff confirm that she picked up Viggo a quarter of an hour later, so she has an alibi.

Hampus frowned. "And what about the day Viggo disappeared?"

Göran picked up a sheet of paper from the table. "Johannes and Maria were home. Both of them were still off sick. Their younger son and Johannes's mother, Iris Holm, were also there. Pernilla Andersson was on the afternoon and evening shift at the Co-op supermarket from midday until eight. Ted was home with Viggo."

"So it doesn't look as if the parents are involved—but there's something very shady about Ted," Embla said.

"Absolutely. I've spent several hours going through his computer, which Paula picked up for me. Ted has tried to cover his tracks, but he's no hacker. I had no difficulty following his activities. He's the one behind most of the hate mail that's flooded social media since Viggo disappeared. He's decided that Kristoffer is the perp."

"But Kristoffer has a watertight alibi," Embla said.

Göran took a sip of his coffee, then nodded. "Yes. Olof may be dead, but there are still four people who can confirm that he and Kristoffer were at Breidablick with them at the relevant time. One of those witnesses has no connection with the family; he's just a client, the owner of an American car that Kristoffer's been working on. I checked him out particularly carefully, and there's absolutely no personal link between him and the Sjöberg family. The other three are Eva Sjöberg and Kristoffer's friends, Anton and Gabriel."

Hampus's eyes narrowed behind the round glasses. "So what about that battery-powered candle?"

Göran leaned forward and brought up the image of a plastic candle in a red holder on the screen. The battery was concealed in the holder. "Found in a toolbox in one of the cars parked a short distance away from the workshop. There are no fingerprints on the candle—it's been wiped. We think it's Amelie's, but we can't be sure."

"It could have been planted there after the fire," Embla pointed out.

"Absolutely, by someone who wanted to put the blame on Kristoffer. But one important detail is that the candle was wiped with an oily rag. If you look closely at the picture, you'll see the surface is dirty."

He was right; there was a brownish film on the white plastic in places.

"Could the rag have been in the workshop?" Hampus asked.

"It seems likely."

"We can ask Kristoffer about the candle when we see him tomorrow," Embla said.

"Have we found anything on Amelie's cell phone?" Hampus asked. "And did Viggo have a phone?"

"There's nothing of note on the girl's phone, and Viggo didn't have one. Neither of them was on Facebook or any kind of forum. They haven't had contact with anyone online."

The fire crackled and Embla gazed into the dancing flames, watching the sparks swirl. The house was lovely and cozy, but soon she would venture out into the darkness. To Nadir. She was brought back to the moment by Göran's voice.

"I've been in touch with Sven-Ove Berglund's wife. Apparently he's had a heart attack. He's in the hospital and will be off work for some time. And Willén called to tell me that we might be getting additional resources from Stockholm to help investigate the Viktor Jansson homicide."

"Nothing new there?" Embla said.

"Not a thing."

"Strange—that also happened late in the afternoon, but of course no one saw anything," Hampus said.

"To be fair, that stretch of road is pretty isolated. There are no houses overlooking the parking lot. Although you'd think the odd vehicle would have driven by."

Göran shut down the computer and stood up, smiling. "It's Friday night and it's almost ten o'clock. I'm going to get in my new little car and drive into Strömstad. Are you going to keep me company, Hampus?"

Embla felt herself blush. He'd assumed she would be going into town in the Volvo. Hampus glanced up from his phone and shook his head.

"No. I've got things to do."

Now or never, Embla thought.

"What are you searching for? You're always online these days."

Hampus looked up at her, a weary expression in his brown eyes. He pushed his glasses up his nose. "Property ads."

"Are you and Filippa thinking of moving already? But it's only . . ."

She was going to say it was only two years since they'd bought their house, but something in his face made her break off.

"I'm moving. We're splitting up."

Silence filled the room. Embla could see that Göran wasn't completely taken by surprise, but that his suspicions hadn't been confirmed until now. After a moment he cleared his throat.

"Maybe that's exactly why you ought to come with me. I'm happy to drive."

"No thanks. I'm not in the mood."

"Sure?"

"Sure."

"Do you want me to stay? It might be better if you're not alone . . ."

"No, I'm fine." Hampus took a deep breath, then continued: "This is nothing new. We've been fighting for a long time, and now we've made up our minds. Filippa and the girls will stay in the house, and I'll find an apartment nearby. Don't you worry about me—I've got plenty to do." He waved his phone in the air, determined to stick to his plan.

Embla and Göran exchanged glances, then went off to their rooms to get ready for the evening.

THEY LEFT THE house at the same time, Embla in the Volvo and Göran in his Nissan. Neither had suggested traveling together.

Fifteen minutes later Embla hurried in through the glass doors of the spa hotel. In her peripheral vision she noticed someone who seemed familiar, but when she turned her head, she realized it was her colleague Paula Nilsson, sitting at a table in the foyer bar. It was a table for two, and her jacket was draped over the empty chair. She was obviously waiting for someone. When she saw Embla she nodded and raised a hand in greeting. She looked slightly embarrassed, as if she'd been caught out. And suddenly Embla knew who that chair was for.

She pressed the call button for the elevator, keeping

an eye on the main door. Seconds later her boss walked into the hotel. A date. Göran had a date. At long last!

IT WAS ALMOST three in the morning by the time Embla parked outside the Shore House. There was no sign of the white Nissan. So he was still out on the town! She giggled to herself. That was nothing compared to what she'd been doing. Wonderful, steamy, uninhibited sex. Fantastic! It was pure therapy as far as she was concerned, she felt better than she had in a long time, and Nadir seemed equally happy. He'd kept on saying that they must see each other again, that he adored her, that she was so beautiful. There had been no need for him to say any of it; what he did was more than enough.

But he still hadn't mentioned his wife and daughter.

THE ALARM ON her phone sounded its peremptory signal. Still half-asleep, Embla struggled to turn it off. When she finally managed to, she discovered it was set for nine o'clock. Nine! Suddenly she was wide awake. Talk about oversleeping . . . And why hadn't Göran or Hampus . . . Only then did she realize it was Saturday. A chance to sleep in, but they weren't taking the whole day off. Best to make a move.

Trying to sound livelier than she felt, she burst into the kitchen with a cheerful, "Good morning!"

Eggs were bubbling away in a pan on the stove. Hampus had made coffee and boiled some water for tea and set out bread, jelly, and yogurt on the table. He really had made an effort to produce a good breakfast for the three of them.

"Would you like an egg?" he asked.

"Please."

Embla glanced over at Göran's closed bedroom door. "Any sign of life?" she whispered.

With a conspiratorial smile, Hampus shook his head. "I'm sure he'll appear when he smells the coffee. I guess he's had a hard night."

He's not the only one, Embla thought.

GÖRAN WAS IN an excellent mood when he ambled into the kitchen. None of them mentioned the previous night; instead they discussed the plan for the day. It was decided that Embla and Hampus would go to the hospital to ask Kristoffer about the candle in the toolbox, while Göran would continue to follow up on the forensic leads on the fire. He also wanted to take a closer look at Johannes Holm and Ted Andersson.

"They're being transferred to a holding cell in Trollhättan today. They've had an easy time of it in the custody suite in Strömstad, where their relatives and legal representatives have been able to come and go as they wished, but that's over now," he said, sounding pleased with himself.

Which meant that Nadir would no longer be able to stay at the spa hotel. Embla felt a stab of disappointment. But the best things in life are brief, as her mother used to say. Maybe it was better if it ended here and now. Or not. She really didn't know how she felt about the guy.

"Willén has booked a hotel room for Paula Nilsson over the weekend so that she can support me . . . us. I'm going to drive over and catch up with her later. Or she might come here."

Göran delivered this information without a trace of embarrassment. Embla and Hampus tried not to look at each other and managed to maintain an air of professional detachment. Kind of.

THEY DIDN'T SAY much during the trip to the hospital; they were both lost in their own thoughts. Hampus was driving, so Embla was able to relax, which was nice. She was beginning to feel the lack of sleep over the past couple of days. Hampus broke the silence as the yellow hospital buildings came into view above the treetops.

"I've been wondering about the guy with the cauliflower ear. Do you think he intended to kill Kristoffer, or did he just want to scare him into keeping quiet?"

Embla's mind had been on something quite different, but she pulled herself together and tried to concentrate. The knife . . . Suddenly she realized what had been floating around in her subconscious.

"Shit! The knife! I need to call . . ."

She grabbed her phone, called Göran, and switched to speakerphone so that Hampus would be able to hear. Göran's voice sounded muffled when he answered; no doubt he was eating as usual.

"Listen, the knife the guy used at the hospital—I just thought of something. It's a perfect match for the blade the forensic pathologist said had caused Halvorsen's stomach wounds! I have one myself—it's a hunting knife, really expensive. Mine was a present, but I know they cost around fifteen hundred kronor. It's a Buck Vanguard. The blade is four inches long and about an inch wide and—"

"Wait!"

They heard slurping and swallowing. *I guess it's coffee time again*, Embla thought irritably.

"So let me get this straight: you think there's a connection between the stabbing of Robert Halvorsen and the attack on Kristoffer."

"It might be a long shot, but . . . yes. The knife fits."

After a brief silence, Göran said, "Paula brought some news. The guy you caught at the hospital could be linked to the gang who came here to party on New Year's. His name is David Hagen, and he's thirty-seven years old.

His father's Norwegian, and his mother's a Swede from Strömstad; she moved back after the divorce. David was five at the time. When he was a teenager, he went to live with his father in Oslo, but his mother and sister are still in Strömstad. He doesn't have a criminal record in Sweden, but the Oslo police found him in their database. He's served several years for narcotics offenses, assault, and armed robbery. We should get more details during the course of the day, although I think I'll call Gilstrup right away. This business with the knife is interesting. Catch you later."

Embla felt a rising sense of excitement. Had the knife provided a missing piece of the puzzle, or was it in fact a piece from a completely different puzzle, not part of the same picture at all?

"Who's Gilstrup?" she asked.

Hampus braked gently as a bus signaled that it was pulling out. Without taking his eyes off the road he explained. "He's an inspector with the Oslo narcotics unit. He's working with their violent crimes unit on the investigation into Halvorsen's death."

"Okay. So this David Hagen is obviously a real piece of work. What's he doing caught up in the arson attack and the assault on Kristoffer? Why was he trying to intimidate or kill the boy with a knife? I don't get it."

"A knife is a silent weapon . . ." Hampus said thoughtfully, then paused as he negotiated the heavy traffic on the approach to the hospital. When they were almost there he went on:

"What if Hagen was the guy in the back of Ted Andersson's Lexus when they went to Breidablick? What if he was there when the fire was set and Kristoffer was beaten up?"

Embla realized he had a point. "That would explain why Johannes Holm daren't tell us who was in the car—he knows how dangerous Hagen is," she said.

"Or he never knew his name."

"And Hagen came to the hospital because there's a risk that the boy could have seen him at Breidablick."

"It's possible."

But the mystery remained: What was the connection between the fatal stabbing of a Norwegian gangster and the events at Breidablick? Andersson and Holm had allegedly gone out there because they believed Kristoffer was responsible for the abduction of their children. Embla suddenly had an idea.

"Could Hagen have had something to do with Amelie and Viggo's disappearance?"

"I don't know, but I guess Göran's had the same thought. He'll be taking a close look at that guy."

Hampus flipped the signal on, ready to turn into the parking lot. Just as before it was visiting time, and there were no spaces. However, they were in luck: a car began to pull out right in front of them. A woman in a Golf had also noticed what was happening and tried to nip in first, but when Hampus revved the Volvo's engine and turned the wheel, the middle-aged woman driving the Golf had to slam on the brakes. She glared at Hampus through the windshield, before resuming her hunt for a space.

"Sometimes size does matter," Hampus announced with a grin.

THEY GREETED THE two uniformed officers outside Kristoffer's room and showed their IDs, just to be on the safe side. A young woman in white who was sitting by the bed immediately got to her feet.

"Who are you?" Her voice was trembling slightly.

They introduced themselves and showed their IDs. She looked relieved and told them her name was Carolin and that she was a junior nurse.

"Eva's having lunch. She'll be back soon," she explained.

"You can go—we'll wait here for her," Hampus said.

Carolin hesitated for a second. Presumably she'd been told not to leave Kristoffer alone under any circumstances. To reassure her they held up their IDs one more time; she gave an embarrassed smile and left the room.

A second bed had been brought in for Eva to use when she wasn't at the patients' hotel.

Kristoffer was snoring gently. The swelling on his face had begun to subside, and the angry tones of red and purple had faded to bluish-yellow. His mouth was half-open, exposing the metal and plastic that held his broken jaw together. He was on two different drips, and there was a glass of water with a bendy straw on the bedside table, so he'd obviously started to drink a little. The fingers visible below the plaster on his arm were also swollen and discolored. *He must be in pain all over his body*, Embla thought. *And he's just lost his father. He's lucky to have his aunt, and thank God she managed to save him from David Hagen*. At that moment the door opened and Eva Sjöberg came in. Her face lit up when she saw them.

"Hi," she said quietly, raising her injured hand in greeting. Apart from the bandage and a reddish knot under one eye, she seemed like her normal self. As she came closer Embla could see that she also had a split lip.

She was wearing jeans and a loose top in shades of purple and cerise. Strong colors suited her.

"Hi, Eva—how's your hand?"

"Fine. Seven stitches and antibiotics."

She looked at her sleeping nephew. As if he sensed her presence, he opened his eye. When he turned his head and saw the two police officers he gave a start, clearly frightened.

"It's okay, Kristoffer. It's only Embla and Hampus from the police—you already know them," Eva reassured him.

She went over and stroked his cheek. He nodded and mumbled something inaudible. His eyelid flickered, and Embla hoped he wasn't going to go back to sleep. She stepped forward and positioned herself next to Eva.

"Hi, Kristoffer—good to see you're on the mend, and that you've started drinking."

She nodded in the direction of the glass. He didn't respond; she hadn't expected him to. It was just a matter of keeping him awake.

"Have you been able to get out of bed yet?" she continued briskly.

"He was allowed to sit on the edge, and that went well," Eva said.

She hadn't given the boy time to answer, but he probably wouldn't have anyway.

"I'm so pleased you're making progress. Listen, we'd like to ask you a couple more questions, Kristoffer. Is that okay?"

At first she thought he hadn't grasped what she'd said, but just as she was about to ask again, he whispered yes.

Encouraged by his reaction, she decided to get straight to the point.

"Do you remember anything else from the evening when you were beaten up?"

"No."

The answer was flat and devoid of any emotion. He was staring at the wall opposite the bed.

"You don't have the faintest recollection of what the men who attacked you looked like? Or what kind of car they drove?"

At the mention of a car, his eyelid twitched.

"An . . . an SUV."

Embla's heart beat a little faster.

"Any idea what make?" she ventured hopefully.

"No."

"Color?"

"Dark."

He was weary and distant, as if the events had nothing to do with him.

"And you don't remember who was in the car?"

"No."

"Do you recall anything that happened?"

Kristoffer lay motionless, his eye fixed on the wall. After a second, tears began to run down his cheek.

"The workshop . . . it's on fire," he sniveled.

Eva went over to the sink by the door and dampened some paper towels. Tenderly she wiped his cheek, then patted it dry.

"Oh dear, your bandage is a little wet, but it doesn't matter. Are you okay to carry on talking?" she asked softly.

Shit, we haven't even gotten to the reason we're here, Embla thought. Casually she said, "Actually we just need to check on one more thing."

"What's that?"

Eva frowned, but Kristoffer showed no reaction. He had stopped crying, but was still sniffing quietly.

"Two days ago the CSIs found Amelie's battery-powered candle in the trunk of one of the cars parked outside the workshop. It was hidden in a toolbox. The car wasn't damaged in the fire, and . . ."

"The Plymouth?" Kristoffer croaked.

Embla raised an eyebrow at Hampus.

"Yes, it was a Plymouth," he confirmed.

A flash of something that might have been surprise passed across the visible part of Kristoffer's face. Then he shook his head and clamped his lips together.

"A battery-powered candle?" Eva was still frowning, and there was a certain sharpness in her voice. Patiently Embla explained that Swedish schoolchildren were no longer allowed to carry real candles in the Lucia procession, or on other occasions when they were moving or standing close together. There had been many serious accidents over the years.

When Embla turned back to Kristoffer, she could see that he wasn't remotely interested in what they were talking about. His good eye was half-closed, and he looked as if he was falling asleep. She leaned forward and tried to re-establish contact with him, but it was no good.

He was back inside his bubble.

THE TWO BOYS were waiting for them outside the café in the square. Both were wearing low-slung ripped jeans and black hoodies with a T-shirt underneath. Totally inadequate for such a damp and chilly day; the thermometer in the Volvo showed that the temperature was just above freezing. The boys were hunched against the bitter wind, hands pushed deep into their pockets.

Anton Borg was almost as tall as his friend Kristoffer, but more powerfully built. His eyes were blue, but Embla couldn't tell what color his hair was, as his hood was drawn tightly around his face. He was smoking a hand-rolled cigarette. Gabriel Garcia was shorter, with lively brown eyes. His hair hung down to his shoulders beneath his baseball cap. The look he gave Embla was both openly appreciative and speculative. His attitude clearly showed that at seventeen he was no longer a little boy, but a young man with a young man's needs. She recognized that look, but had been unprepared for it. Several people had described Kristoffer as more or less asexual, and somehow she had expected his friends to be the same, with nothing in their heads but cars and engines. This obviously didn't apply to Gabriel.

"Hi—shall we go inside and get a snack?" Hampus suggested.

The boys muttered their agreement. The place was crowded, but they managed to grab a table right at the back. Whoever was responsible for the décor had gone for beige and brown in a big way. It wasn't exactly cheerful, yet the overall impression was cozy and homey. Both Anton and Gabriel opted for a Coke and a donut, while Embla and Hampus chose a hot drink and a prawn sandwich.

"Late lunch," Embla explained when their order arrived. The boys nodded; they seemed perfectly happy with their donuts.

After some small talk about what it was like living in Strömstad as a teenager—they both agreed that summer was fantastic and winter was the pits—and their motor vehicle engineering courses, the conversation turned to Kristoffer and everything that had happened to him.

"Do you know what Kristoffer was doing on the afternoon when Amelie Holm went missing?" Embla asked.

The boys exchanged a glance, and Anton answered.

"He dropped her outside her house and drove home. He was like totally stressed about the Pontiac Firebird—the owner was picking it up the following day."

He sounded absolutely certain, and Gabriel nodded in agreement. Embla couldn't see any indication that they were lying.

"Did either of you have any contact with Kristoffer that day?"

"I called him at like two-thirty and asked if he was coming into town, but he said he'd already been in, and was heading home to finish the Pontiac," Anton said.

Now it was Embla and Hampus's turn to exchange a glance. This was new information.

"Did you arrange to meet up later?"

"Yes, over at his place."

"What time?"

"Between four and five."

"And when did you get there?"

"Around four-thirty."

Anton looked inquiringly at Gabriel, who nodded.

"And how long did you stay?"

Gabriel leaned forward and gave Embla a dazzling smile.

"We left at eleven. There was no point in staying—no girls!"

This was followed by a wink. Embla was a little taken aback. *He's flirting with me*. She didn't know whether to feel flattered or annoyed. She decided to pretend she hadn't noticed.

"Was Kristoffer's dad home when you arrived?"

"We didn't go into the house. We were in the workshop the whole time," Anton informed her.

"You didn't go in for something to eat?"

"No, we'd brought pizza."

"Did you see Olof during the evening?"

"He came in and said he'd been testing the Plymouth Fury. The brakes were like completely shot, and the engine was misfiring. Then he said he was going to some Christmas party."

Hadn't Olof said he'd gone straight out to join Kristoffer in the workshop when he got home? And that he'd stayed there and helped him with the Pontiac until it was time to leave for the party?

"When did Olof come into the workshop?"

The boys looked uncertain.

"A while before six. Definitely not after six," Anton said eventually.

Hampus was playing with his coffee spoon; it clinked against the cup as if he was about to give a speech. He came straight out and asked the boys, "Do you think Kristoffer had anything to do with Amelie's disappearance?"

"No way!"

They both spoke simultaneously, both equally convinced that the idea of their friend harming Amelie was ridiculous.

"He's not interested in little girls. And he's kind of . . . weak!" Anton said firmly.

"He won't fight back, never has. I don't think he even knows how," Gabriel said, catching Embla's eye and taking the opportunity to wink at her again.

"All that crap on Facebook and Twitter is fucking garbage!" Anton exclaimed.

Hampus nodded to show that he understood and agreed. "And he's never hurt anyone younger than him? Or a girl?"

The response came in unison: "Never!"

Embla considered what the boys had said. They had no doubt that their friend was innocent. Something occurred to her.

"Do you think he might know something he hasn't told us?"

Anton met her gaze. "Kristoffer doesn't know how to lie."

"Never has," Gabriel concurred.

Anton leaned forward and almost whispered, "But he does know how to keep quiet if he doesn't want to tell you something."

That was exactly the feeling Embla had had. They needed to go back and have another conversation with Kristoffer the next morning.

SHE WAS STANDING by the bed. Sheer blue fabric was draped around her slender body. Her blonde hair wafted gently around her pale face as if there were a breeze; it was hard to make out her features. She held out her transparent hand and said:

"Don't look for me. Find the girl."

Slowly she turned toward the window and faded away. Embla tried to shout out, to tell her to stay, but she couldn't make a sound. Her heart was pounding as if it were trying to break out of her chest. *Don't disappear again, Lollo! Stay!*

When she woke, she sat up in bed. Her mouth was bone dry and there was a rough coating on her tongue. She knew she'd screamed out loud; it happened sometimes, but it had been a while. Lollo, Lollo! It felt like she'd really been there!

Embla switched on the bedside lamp and glanced around the room. She realized she was looking for damp footprints on the floor. Hampus was in the room next door. He must have heard her yelling, but both he and Göran had gotten used to it. At first Göran had anxiously asked why she had such terrible dreams, but she had brushed off his concern, said she'd had nightmares ever since she was a child and there was nothing to be done about it. The truth was that they'd started haunting her after Lollo had disappeared. That was fourteen and a half years ago, when Embla had just turned fourteen.

At the end of August her best friend, Louise—Lollo—went missing. Embla felt she was to blame for the fact that those responsible had never been brought to justice and forced to reveal what they had done with her. She had carried the guilt ever since.

The memories of the night Lollo had gone missing were hazy for Embla. She had been drunk—really drunk—for the first time in her life. At the club, she and Lollo had gotten separated, and Embla had looked around in despair and caught a glimpse of Lollo's blue dress before it disappeared through a door marked STAFF ONLY. Somehow she had managed to fight her way across the room, and that was where her recurring nightmare began.

Cautiously she pushed open the door and peeped inside. A bare bulb glowed faintly at the end of a dark corridor. She slipped through the door and tried to close it as quietly as possible. Her heartbeat was pounding in her ears and it was difficult to work out what was going on around her. She knew she had to get to the light; that was where Lollo was. And the others, too, presumably. Although she didn't want to think about them right now; it was Lollo who mattered. She had to get her out of this place. The corridor went on and on. The floor was no longer solid; her feet sank deeper and deeper with each step. Keep going, keep going! You need to hurry! The light came closer and she thought she could hear voices through the thudding in her ears. There were three big shadows up ahead, bending over a tiny, hunched figure. She knew it was

Lollo. She tried to yell; her lips moved, but no sound emerged. One of the shadows suddenly straightened up and she realized she'd been discovered. At first she went rigid with fear, then she turned to run. But she had paused for a fraction of a second, and that was enough. She felt as if her feet were stuck to the floor. The threatening shadow was approaching at speed. He reached her and grabbed her by the throat.

"If you say one word to anyone, you're dead! We know who you are and where you live!" he hissed.

Shaking with terror, she managed to say: "Lollo, Lol . . ."

"Forget about her!"

He threw her down. The walls around her collapsed and she sank down into ice-cold slime; her nostrils and mouth became blocked in seconds. Breathe . . . she couldn't breathe!

Always the same nightmare. Always exactly the same inexorable conclusion. Because that was what the confused images in Embla's memory looked like.

Somehow she had managed to get out of the club and catch the tram back to Högsbo and Axel Dahlström Square, where Lollo's mother's apartment was. Fortunately Lollo had given her a spare key.

"In case we don't come home together," she'd giggled.

Almost as if she knew what was going to happen, Embla had thought many times over the years.

From then on, Embla had done everything wrong. She hadn't dared tell the truth, not to her parents, Lollo's mother, or the police. Instead she'd lied and said they'd had an argument on the way into town, and Lollo had gone off on her own to meet some guy. Embla had sulked and headed back to the apartment to wait for her.

There were witnesses who'd seen Lollo and another girl on the tram, but no one could remember what Lollo's companion looked like. Embla's striking hair had been hidden under her mom's turquoise silk scarf. She'd been wearing a white top, black tights, and white sneakers. Next to Lollo, who was an ethereal vision in blue, she had faded into the background.

Two witnesses claimed to have seen Lollo walk straight past the line at the nightclub, with another girl trailing along behind her. However, they weren't sure if the two girls had even known each other because neither of them had seen the girls together inside the club.

At that point Embla had been hugely relieved that no one could describe her or prove she'd lied. However, as an adult she knew that was why the search for Lollo had gotten nowhere. If she had been forced to tell the police what had gone on that night, they could have conducted a much more productive investigation and brought the Stavic brothers in for questioning.

Due partly to Embla's cowardice, Lollo had never been found. The feelings of angst and shame were still just as strong, which was why she couldn't shake off the nightmare. During the fourteen and a half years that had passed, it had never changed. Until last night, when Lollo had been standing by her bed. She had told Embla not to look for her, but to find the girl. She must have been referring to Amelie.

What did the dream mean? Did it mean anything? And what about the terrifying question that always came into her mind after the nightmare: Was Lollo dead? Probably, in which case, it must be her spirit that had visited Embla last night. What a stupid idea! Embla didn't believe in ghosts, but that thin, cold, transparent figure had felt very real. It was as if a chill still lingered in the room. Impossible. But she'd heard her speak; it had sounded exactly like Lollo's voice.

What had happened on that August night? What had the Stavic brothers done with Lollo? Would it be possible to reopen the case? Embla was old enough and experienced enough to start investigating Lollo's disappearance now. She had to know, if only to put a stop to those nightmares.

HAMPUS GAVE HER a searching look at the breakfast table, but Embla simply made a comment about the weather.

Their boss wandered into the kitchen, his whole face contorted in a yawn. "Coffee—terrific!" he exclaimed, rubbing his hands together with delight. He had found a large floral-patterned breakfast cup in one of the cupboards. Judging by the size, it was meant for porridge, but he filled it to the rim with coffee and four lumps of sugar.

Embla poured natural yogurt into a bowl, then added a few spoonfuls of the muesli she'd brought with her. Göran peered at her breakfast.

"I don't understand why you insist on eating rabbit food and slop. There's everything you could possibly need for a good, nutritious breakfast on this table!" He waved his arm expansively. He liked to joke about Embla's eating habits, but she ignored him and simply smiled.

"So are you going to accept the Norwegian's challenge?" Hampus asked.

It wasn't really something she wanted to discuss at the breakfast table, but as he'd asked a direct question, she didn't have much choice.

"Not the way things are looking at the moment. The

doctors have advised me against competing. I suffered a serious concussion."

"And you're going to follow their advice?" Hampus raised his eyebrows, clearly unconvinced.

"Right now I can't put in the kind of training necessary to defend my title," Embla said with a sigh.

Göran swilled down the last of his toast and marmalade with a big gulp of coffee. "No title is worth permanent brain damage. You're the reigning Nordic light welterweight champion. You have nothing to prove."

She knew he was right, but it still hurt. She was training almost as regularly as before, but she had to be a lot more careful. It was frustrating.

Time to change the subject. She found it hard to discuss her uncertain future in the world of boxing. She decided to bring up something that had occurred to her as she lay awake the previous night.

"I've been thinking about Ted Andersson and David Hagen. It seems likely that Hagen was the guy who was waiting inside the bar, and who then went with Ted and Johannes to Breidablick. He's lived in Strömstad, so he and Ted could well be old friends. Maybe he knows Johannes, too. What if we contact Oslo, see if Ted's popped up in any of their investigations in the past? Something narcotics-related, probably, even if it's been a few years since he did anything like that around here."

Göran frowned, weighing what she'd said. The two men had both grown up in Strömstad and now spent a lot of their time in Oslo, so a connection wasn't too much of a stretch. And it could well be worth checking out what Ted might have been up to across the border in Norway.

"Great idea," he said.

"Absolutely," Hampus agreed. "It's difficult to get a handle on Ted; one minute he's the heartbroken, grieving daddy, the next he's going crazy, accusing Kristoffer and Johannes and yelling at us."

"I'll call Oslo later. I know it's Sunday, but there ought to be someone there who can help," Göran said.

Hampus's cell phone pinged. He picked it up and quickly read what was on the screen. A huge smile spread across his face, and he punched the air.

"Yes! I got it!"

For the first time since the three of them were reunited almost a week ago, he looked really happy.

"What did you get?" Embla asked.

"The apartment—my bid was the highest."

"Congratulations—where is it?"

"Just over a mile from the house. It'll be perfect for us."

Göran and Embla were puzzled. It was Göran who asked the question.

"Us? Are you moving in with a new partner?"

"What? No, no—Filippa and I will be co-parenting. She and the girls will carry on living in the house, and the kids will come and stay with me every other week. It's a two-bedroom apartment."

It sounded like a good arrangement from the children's point of view; there wouldn't be any problem with preschool or their friends.

They cleared the breakfast table, ready to start work. The sky had begun to brighten; it had stopped raining, and the sea rolled slowly toward the shore. The gulls were circling down by the jetty. In her mind, Embla saw a thin body in a pale-blue summer dress, carried by the waves. So cold. So horribly cold.

"Daydreaming?"

Göran's voice brought her back to reality. She gave him a little smile to show she was definitely in the moment, then she ran upstairs to get ready for another trip to the hospital.

Eva was sitting in the green armchair by the window, reading the morning paper. She peered at them over the top of her glasses when they walked in; when she saw who it was, she smiled and stood up to greet them. Kristoffer was resting on the bed, his iPhone earbuds firmly in place. For the first time he wasn't wearing pajamas, but clothing supplied by the hospital for its patients. It wasn't particularly flattering, but it was still a sign that he was feeling better.

"As you can see, we're making progress!" Eva said cheerfully.

Kristoffer glanced at them with his one visible eye, but quickly looked away. At least he'd noticed their arrival, which meant he'd emerged from his bubble. Embla went and stood at the foot of the bed.

"Hi, Kristoffer! How are you feeling today?"

She tried in vain to catch his eye, but she was beginning to understand that this wasn't necessarily a bad sign. It was just the way he handled encounters with other people.

"Better," he muttered.

The pins and wires holding his broken jaw in place made it difficult for him to talk, but at least he removed his earbuds. The faint sound of Wilson Pickett's version of "Mustang Sally" seeped out into the room. Embla recognized the music and felt the need to show off, but admitted it was because her friend Tobias in Dalsland was also a fan of rockabilly, and often played it on his car stereo. On the subject of cars, she mentioned that she was having some problems with her 1990 Volvo 245. Could he possibly take a look at it for her when he was back at work? Something resembling a faint smile passed across Kristoffer's face as he nodded.

Cautiously, Embla broached the key question, the real reason for their visit.

"Kristoffer, have you had any more thoughts about the battery-powered candle that forensics found in a toolbox in the trunk of . . . was it a Pontiac?"

"Plymouth Fury."

"Okay, a Plymouth Fury. Do you have any idea how the candle could have ended up there?"

He met her gaze for a second, then immediately looked away. She realized he had tears in his eyes. Eva noticed, too, and handed him a tissue without a word. He blew his nose, then slowly and laboriously began to speak.

"Amelie . . . was . . ."

Embla held her breath. What was he trying to say? He wiped his nose with his shirtsleeve and tried again.

"Dad . . . ran over . . . Amelie."

"Kristoffer, what are you saying? Olof ran over the child?"

Eva stared at him, and her hand flew to her mouth as her expression shifted from pure horror to certainty.

Kristoffer's only response was a nod.

"What makes you think your father ran over Amelie?" Embla asked.

Somehow Kristoffer managed to tell his story. With a lot of help from Eva, who seemed to understand him almost intuitively, he explained what he had realized when he first heard about the discovery of the candle. It took quite some time, but the course of events was finally clear.

Around fifteen minutes after Kristoffer arrived home, Olof drove into the yard. He'd stuck his head into the kitchen, where Kristoffer was eating a sandwich and drinking a glass of milk. The boy immediately noticed that his father was drunk and very agitated. Olof had told him he'd had a few things to take care of in Strömstad, so he'd decided he might as well test-drive a 1967 Buick Electra that was in for repair. On the way home he'd hit a deer; the windshield had been damaged and one of the headlights was broken. He'd asked Kristoffer to carry out the repairs as quickly as possible. Kristoffer was about to fix the starter motor on a '68 Pontiac Firebird that was due to be collected the next day, so he promised to deal with the Buick as soon as he was finished with the Pontiac. Olof had gotten angry at first, but after a while he'd conceded that his son was right; the Pontiac had to be ready for the following day. Kristoffer had repeated his promise that the Buick would be his next job, and Olof had left the house. Kristoffer had gone to the bathroom, and while he was in there, he'd heard the sound of a car starting up and driving away. He was worried, because he knew Olof was far from sober.

When he went out to the workshop, he saw that the

Plymouth Fury was missing—the car in which Amelie's candle was later found.

The Plymouth was due for a respray, but it wasn't urgent. The owner was on an extended vacation in Thailand, and they'd agreed that the car would be ready by the beginning of March.

Needless to say, Kristoffer wondered why his father had taken the Plymouth rather than his own Mercedes, but couldn't come up with a sensible explanation.

Olof was gone for exactly one and a half hours. When he returned he didn't go straight into the workshop to join Kristoffer and his friends, which he usually did. He came in a while later to say hi to Anton and Gabriel, and said he was off to the Lions' Christmas party.

The following day Kristoffer had been questioned about Amelie's disappearance. Before the interview Olof had made it clear that he and his lawyer would do the talking; all Kristoffer had to do was nod and agree with whatever they said. Even at that point Kristoffer had thought his father was behaving strangely, but he assumed that he and Charlotta Stark knew how to handle a conversation with the police.

So when Olof stated that he'd been in the workshop with his son from the time he got home until he went to get ready for the party, Kristoffer had simply done as he'd been told, and agreed.

Kristoffer had spent the Christmas holiday fixing the Buick's damaged windshield. The workshop had a well-stocked store of original parts imported directly from the United States, and fortunately there was a suitable replacement. The broken windshield was removed and thrown in a dumpster outside the workshop.

A truck came along on the first Thursday of each month to take away the dumpster and replace it with an empty one. However, because of the Christmas and New Year's break, the company responsible had skipped the January collection, and the truck wasn't due until the beginning of February.

Kristoffer turned his head and looked out the window as he whispered, "The windshield's . . . still in there."

He and Olof had worked together on the final repairs before the Buick was resprayed its original color, a pale bluish-green. The owner had been delighted when he picked up the car on Saturday—the day before the fire. He was one of the witnesses—along with Olof, Eva, Anton, and Gabriel—who'd provided Kristoffer with an alibi for the time of Viggo's disappearance.

"Lucky he came then. Otherwise people would have thought . . . I took the little boy," Kristoffer said with difficulty.

When he found out that Amelie's candle had been found in the Plymouth, the pieces began to fall into place. His father hadn't hit a deer; it must have been Amelie, running along the dark road. Olof had been too drunk to see her.

"Dad's . . . dead. I want . . . the parents . . . to know."

Kristoffer's gaze was fixed on his tearful aunt.

"Why do you think the candle ended up in the toolbox?" Hampus asked gently.

Back to the key question. Kristoffer's eye darted from side to side before he answered.

"Dad must have found it after . . . after he . . ."

He couldn't go on, and Eva stepped in.

"You mean after he'd hidden Amelie somewhere."

He nodded and continued in a monotone, "No time . . . Christmas party. Panicked . . . hid it . . . in the toolbox. Must have meant . . . to get rid of it . . . forgot . . ."

Could Olof have forgotten? Very likely, Embla thought. He'd been under extreme stress, plus he was in the middle of one of his drinking bouts.

Both Amelie's cell phone and the candle must have fallen out in the trunk of the Plymouth, but he hadn't noticed until after he'd hidden the body. He probably got mad when her phone kept ringing, which was why he threw it into the recycling container.

These were all hypotheses based on circumstantial evidence and guesswork; they would never be able to prove what had actually happened.

By this time Kristoffer was exhausted. His eyelid flickered, and within a minute or so he was fast asleep. Embla and Hampus signaled to Eva to come with them. They left the room quietly, nodded to the officers on duty outside the door, and moved over to the area by the elevators. It wasn't the ideal place for a chat, but luckily no one was around to overhear them.

Eva spoke first.

"I'm devastated, but I think Kristoffer's drawn the right conclusion."

"It does sound credible, but we'll need to check out a few things," Embla said.

The elevator stopped on their floor and the doors slid open. They fell silent, waiting to see who would appear. A porter pushing a whey-faced elderly man in a wheelchair emerged and headed down the corridor.

Embla turned back to Eva. "Where do you think Olof could have hidden Amelie?"

Eva shook her head, frowning as she thought hard. After a moment she stiffened, and the look she gave Embla was hard to interpret.

"Kristoffer is good with time. If he says Olof was gone for an hour and a half, then that's exactly right. Which means he didn't go very far. Could he have hidden her out at Sandgrav?"

EMBLA CALLED GÖRAN as soon as they left the hospital. He sounded cheerful, and she could hear voices and the clinking of crockery in the background.

"Hi—Paula and I are having coffee in that place where you met the two boys yesterday. It's great, and the cakes—"

She couldn't listen to any of that. "Kristoffer talked," she said, cutting him off. "We might have a breakthrough in Amelie's case."

That shut him up. He didn't interrupt once as she summarized what Kristoffer had told them.

"I'll see you at Breidablick," Göran said when she was done. "That dumpster needs to be emptied with great care. There's no point trying to get the CSIs over from Trollhättan today for a windshield that *might possibly* be of interest, but I want it in the lab in Gothenburg as soon as possible. I'll take it down there myself."

Before they drove back toward Strömstad, they stopped at a fast-food outlet. Hampus ordered the special, while Embla opted for a veggie burger—something she regretted after the first bite. Admittedly sawdust wasn't meat, but forming it into a circular patty and calling it a veggie burger had to be a false declaration under some government ruling. The bread and salad were edible, however, and she washed them down with a can of mineral water. Hampus was much happier with his lunch: in less than fifteen minutes he'd put away a large Coke, mashed potatoes, and two hot dogs with all the fixings. Anyone who didn't know him couldn't possibly imagine how much he ate based on his gangly body. *That guy must have worms*, Embla thought sourly. She was still hungry.

THE SUN WAS low in the sky by the time they reached Breidablick. It was trying to peep through the clouds, but with little success. Even if it did manage to break through, it wouldn't have long left to shine.

Göran and Paula had already arrived. They were sitting in the little white car, chatting and laughing away. When Paula saw the Volvo, she tried to adopt a more professional expression, but her sparkling eyes and flushed cheeks betrayed her. The contented look on Göran's face gave him away, too. *There's definitely something going on between those two*, Embla thought. Then again, it was nowhere near as weird as her liaison with Nadir. Neither Göran nor Paula were in a relationship. They were mature individuals who knew what they were getting into. All she could do was cross her fingers and wish them luck.

As soon as they got out of the cars, Göran started issuing directives: on with protective overalls, hairnets, gloves, and shoe covers. Embla thought the face mask was a little over the top, but Göran was very firm on that point.

"We need to ensure the least possible contamination," he insisted.

They set off toward the dumpster beside the blackened ruin. The gable closest to the house was in better shape than the rest of the workshop. Next to the wall was something resembling a carport, which was where the dumpster was. This meant it was protected from the snow and rain. Another plus was that it was open-topped, so it was easier to climb in and out. Göran had found a ladder in the boathouse. He propped it up against the dumpster, then they all put on their protective gear.

Without any discussion, Embla clambered up; she was definitely the most agile. She peered over the top and saw a chaotic heap of old car parts, cables, rags, empty tins and oil cans, along with a whole load of other crap. This was going to take a while.

"I need to get in there—I can't reach," she informed her colleagues.

"I brought this," Göran said with a cunning smile as he held up a long litter picker.

"It's actually a disability aid, but I keep it in the car in case anything rolls under the seat," he explained.

He must have had it in the Volvo, but Embla had never seen it before.

"Okay."

Resolutely, she began the tedious task of removing objects one by one and passing them to Hampus at the bottom of the ladder. He then handed them to Paula and Göran, who checked them over. Embla would have to leave the larger items for the time being; they were too heavy for the tongs. At regular intervals Hampus gave her the camera so she could photograph the contents. Everything had to be meticulously documented. The work was time-consuming but vital. They mustn't miss a thing.

When darkness began to fall, Hampus fixed a small floodlight onto one of the posts holding up the roof. Embla had reached quite a way down now and was grateful for the light; it made things so much easier.

"I need to move some heavy stuff. I'm going in," she said.

Cautiously she lowered herself down. Fragments of metal and glass crunched beneath her feet. Now it was Hampus's turn to climb the ladder. He shined the beam of a powerful flashlight into the bottom of the dumpster. The floodlight helped, but Embla needed to be able to see every detail. Methodically, she began to shift the bulkier items, which gave her more space.

Suddenly she caught the flash of broken glass.

"I can see a windshield!"

She didn't even try to conceal her excitement. If it belonged to the Buick, it could mean a major breakthrough in Amelie's case.

"Can you reach it?" Göran asked.

"I'm not sure—there's a car seat on top of it."

She began to edge toward it, holding a sterile plastic sack supplied by Göran. Most of the windshield was hidden by the broken seat. Little by little she managed to move the heavy seat, then she took more photographs before easing the windshield into the sack and passing it to Hampus. The broken headlight was there, too, and around what remained of the shattered glass she saw reddish-brown marks that could well be blood. Her heart leaped when she spotted red fibers stuck to the glass. Amelie had been wearing a red jacket when she went missing.

"Okay, let's cover the whole lot. I'll call Trollhättan

and they can get the CSIs over here in the morning," Göran said.

Hampus fetched a tarp from the trunk of the Volvo, and together they spread it over the remaining contents of the dumpster. It was essential to protect any traces of blood or other key evidence.

"I suggest we all drive to Gothenburg together. I'll go straight to the lab; I want this done by the book."

"You mean tonight?" Embla asked.

"Yes. If that's okay."

Embla was slightly surprised, but it would be useful to go home, check out her mail and her two pot plants. They were a particularly hardy variety called Zanzibar Gem, which was apparently capable of surviving in challenging conditions. Hers had certainly lived up to their reputation during the year they'd spent on her windowsill; they were still alive despite the fact that they were badly neglected. The thought of spending a night in her own bed was also appealing, even though the one in the guest room at the Shore House was comfortable.

"We'll meet back at the house at ten tomorrow morning. I'll call Willén right away and ask him to send a team to search the area around Sandgrav. We'll need the dogs, too."

Paula went with Göran in the little white car. She lived in Trollhättan, so it was obvious she was planning to spend the night with him. Embla and Hampus exchanged a meaningful glance, but neither of them said a word.

THEY STOPPED BY the Shore House to pick up anything they needed to take with them. As far as Embla was concerned that was her iPad, her toiletries, and her dirty laundry. When she emerged from her room Hampus was on his cell phone. He had lowered his voice, but she could still hear every word.

". . . you can park across the street . . . No, don't do that. She'll see you . . . Behind the house would be better."

What was he up to? Was he meeting someone he didn't want Filippa to see? Interesting. Never try to keep a secret from a cop because that arouses her interest. Hampus ought to know that. He mustn't suspect that she'd overheard a fragment of his conversation.

THE APARTMENT SMELLED familiar when she opened the door: slightly stuffy, a hint of her perfume, a whiff of the liniment she'd used after her latest training session, and dry dust, of course. There was a pile of mail on the mat, mostly junk and the odd bill. She read her newspapers online.

The first thing she did was go into the bathroom and load the washing machine. It was a little late, but it would be fine. The guy in the apartment below was in his first year at the Chalmers Institute of Technology. When he wasn't studying for exams he liked to stay up late partying—a common reaction to moving away from home and escaping the watchful eye of one's parents. He could hardly complain about her washing; he had disturbed her plenty of times.

She decided to make herself a sandwich: sliced hard-boiled egg with fish roe. She went into the kitchen and put on a pan of water and filled the kettle. A cup of herbal green tea with lavender would help her sleep.

A short while later she was sitting on the leather sofa she'd inherited from her brother Atle—or rather his wife, Sanna, who was the one with an eye for décor—eating her supper and thinking about Hampus.

He was up to something, and it wasn't just the new apartment. He was constantly fiddling with his cell phone, there was the conversation she'd overheard, plus his peculiar behavior earlier that evening.

Embla had offered to drive. They hadn't chatted much during the journey, but as they drew closer to the tower blocks that housed the police station, the custody suite, the courts, and a number of other organizations associated with the law, Hampus had glanced up from his phone.

"You can drop me outside the station."

Without even trying to hide her surprise, Embla had said, "You're not going home?"

"No. I need to pick up something."

She had pulled over outside the police station without another word, and he'd jumped out.

"See you here tomorrow morning at seven-thirty," he'd said.

Then he closed the door and practically ran to the main doors. He went inside, swiped his pass card, and disappeared down the security corridor. Okay, so he didn't want her to pick him up outside the house in Björkekärr as usual. Strange! Then again, maybe the atmosphere between him and Filippa wasn't so great after all. But in that case, where was he going to spend the night?

She had decided to hang around, and had walked to the 7-Eleven store on the corner. She bought milk, eggs, and whole-grain rolls, then hurried back to the illegally parked car. She kept the bag containing her purchases in plain sight; she didn't want him to realize she was spying on him. She took her time placing the bag between the seats while keeping a watchful eye on the main entrance to the police station. People came and went, but there was no sign of Hampus. She took out her phone and held it to her ear, faking a call. The minutes crawled by, and one or two of her colleagues glanced at the car on passing. She couldn't stay here, it was too embarrassing. And she couldn't possibly tail him; if there was one car he was bound to recognize, it was the great big black Volvo. Plus there were plenty of other exits from the building. If he thought she suspected something, he'd choose a different way out.

Her curiosity still piqued, she'd given up and driven home.

Her thoughts were interrupted by the sound of her phone. Her heart leaped when she saw NADIR on the display, and her blood suddenly began to fizz. The reaction surprised her, but it was far from unpleasant.

"Hi, Nadir."

"Hi. Embla, I . . . where are you?"

She could hear tension in his voice.

"At home, sitting on my sofa, drinking tea, and . . ."

"So you're in Gothenburg."

It was hard to interpret his tone. He sounded surprised, but there was a sharpness there, too.

"Yes. We found something and wanted to drop it off at the lab tonight. It has to do with Amelie's case. But we'll be back in Strömstad at ten o'clock tomorrow morning."

There was a brief silence then, "Listen, can we meet up? I . . . we need to talk."

SHE TOOK A quick shower, brushed her teeth, put on clean clothes, a couple of dabs of mascara, and a few sprays of Chanel Chance. She wound her hair into a messy bun on top of her head and secured it with a barrette. That would have to do. But why was she feeling so nervous? Or maybe it was anticipation? It wasn't just the sex; Nadir was a great guy in every way. *Shit!* She didn't want to get tangled up in a relationship with a married man. One of her best friends, Malin, had made that mistake and it had broken her. In the end the guy had naturally decided to stay with his wife and their two small kids. Embla had frequently tried to warn Malin; when you were standing on the sidelines, it was easy to see where things were heading. After the breakup it had taken almost a year before Malin even began to recover. Two years had passed now, and she was still brooding over what had happened. Embla had tried to listen and offer words of consolation, and she had promised herself that she would never get involved with a married man.

And now here she was, dangerously close to walking into the same trap with her eyes wide open. But it takes two to tango! He had a responsibility, too . . . At that moment the doorbell rang. Her heart rate increased and her head began to spin.

AFTERWARD THEY LAY in her bed, holding each other.

I want to stay in this moment. But soon he'll leave, and go home to his family. To his wife and daughter.

It was as if the cold shock of reality sobered her up. She moved away a fraction.

"Time to talk, Nadir."

He gave an involuntary start and immediately tried to hide it with a smile. "Why? This is lovely."

Embla sat up and stared at him. "Is it?"

Before he could respond she swung her legs over the side of the bed. She stood up and put her hands on her hips.

"Get dressed and come into the living room."

On her way into the bathroom, she wondered if she was about to scupper the whole thing. Possibly, but it was a sexual adventure with no long-term prospects, she reminded herself. And it was built on one partner's dishonesty. She washed up in the bathroom, then went back to the bedroom to get dressed. Nadir had already gone into the other room.

She grabbed a bottle of mineral water and two glasses from the kitchen. She poured them both a drink; neither said a word until she was done. Embla curled up in one corner of the sofa, leaning on the armrest. Nadir got the message and took the red floral-patterned armchair, bought for a hundred kronor at an auction in Dalsland. It was as good as new, and very comfortable. A real bargain. However, Nadir looked anything but comfortable.

Embla broke the silence, totally in control and determined not to sound bitter.

"I know you're married. When were you planning on telling me?"

To her surprise, he smiled.

"When I called you earlier and asked if we could meet up. It's true. But something got in the way . . ."

Okay, so he was blaming their sexual encounter. She realized to her surprise that he was starting to annoy her.

"So what were you going to say?" Her tone was brusque, and it was exactly what he deserved.

"I understand if you feel I've deceived you. But you never asked. And I . . . I couldn't resist."

That little smile was playing around the corners of his mouth again. *Smug bastard!*

"You couldn't resist the chance of getting laid. Me neither. It was only meant to be a one-night stand. Then it turned into two. And just now . . ."

A glance at his face silenced her; his expression was deadly serious.

"That's not how it was for me. The minute I saw you in Strömstad . . . I felt something so powerful. Here!"

He gently placed his hand on his heart and looked her in the eyes. She was dumbstruck, but at the same time a voice in her head snapped: *Pull yourself together! He's only saying what he knows will make you melt.*

"Even though you're married."

He grimaced, resignation etched on his face. He slumped in the armchair and seemed to shrink.

Here we go with the usual litany, my-wife-doesn't-understand-me. So predictable! She didn't say a word, just carried on staring at him. After a little while he cleared his throat a couple of times.

"My parents and Soraya's parents fled from Iran together. Our fathers were colleagues, and politically active. They finished up here in Gothenburg, and always said their children should marry each other. I have two younger sisters and Soraya's an only child. Our marriage was arranged many, many years ago."

He fell silent and looked down at his hands, which were linked together in his lap. Embla didn't move.

"Neither Soraya nor I gave it much thought when we were kids, but when I was a teenager I started to worry. I fell in love with other girls, but my mom and dad were implacable: Soraya and I were meant for each other, and that was the end of the matter."

He glanced up at her, not a trace of a smile there now.

"I have to tell you that Soraya was . . . *is* beautiful. Very beautiful. There were plenty of boys who envied me, but I was never in love with her. She was like a sister, and she felt the same way about me. We've never put it into words, but that's still true today."

He took a sip of his water, then continued. "I started to study law, while she read archaeology and Arabic history. The pressure from our parents increased. They kept telling us it was time for the wedding. I managed to postpone it for a while, blamed my studies, but once I was qualified, there was no escape. We got married. But I've longed for love . . . and then there you were."

He stood up and walked over to her. Hesitantly he held out his hand. She took it and got to her feet. He gently drew her close.

"I want to be with you."

All her good intentions and convincing arguments disappeared in an instant, leaving nothing but this moment. They shared a deep, intense kiss, as if they were determined never to give each other up.

At 7:35 on Monday morning Embla pulled up outside the main door of the police station. Hampus was waiting for her, the collar of his jacket turned up as he shivered in the bitter wind. The temperature was around freezing, and lead-gray clouds pressed down on the city. His face brightened when he saw her. She hadn't seen him smile like that since they embarked on the investigation in Strömstad; he looked both happy and relaxed. They'd always started the day with the same question when they were a permanent team:

"Hi—did you sleep well?"

His smile grew even broader. "I did. But not for very long."

It took a few seconds for the penny to drop. So she wasn't the only one who'd had a good night! But who had Hampus . . . ? Best not to ask. He might draw the same conclusions about her, and if he decided to ask questions, things could get tricky. Instead they simply chatted all the way to Strömstad, and he glanced down at his phone only a couple of times.

When they reached the Shore House and got out of the car, it was immediately clear that the whole team,

Paula included, had had a great night. She and Göran were standing close together by the Nissan. In spite of the drizzle and the strong wind, they didn't look cold at all. They were smiling at each other, and were surrounded by a kind of aura. They tried to adopt a more professional air as Embla and Hampus approached, but their sparkling eyes gave them away.

"Morning—we just arrived," Göran said. "The CSIs from Trollhättan called; they're on their way, and the dogs will be here any minute. A team from Strömstad will help with the search, too, but not until after eleven."

They unlocked the door and switched off the alarm.

As Göran was hanging up his jacket in the hallway, he said over his shoulder, "I can confirm that the blood on the windshield was human, and the same blood group as Amelie's. They're running DNA tests right now. The quantity was so minute that I didn't dare do them myself; one of the girls in the lab is an expert in that kind of thing. I suspect the shield has been wiped, but not very thoroughly. Fortunately. The fibers have been secured."

He looked tired but satisfied.

"Coffee!" he demanded.

Paula and Embla exchanged a glance and went into the kitchen to fulfill his order, while the men headed for the living room to get the fire going. The standard allocation of tasks between the sexes since the Stone Age . . .

A while later they were all gathered around the table in front of a crackling blaze. As expected Göran complained that no one had remembered to buy cookies, but Paula quietly pointed out that he'd had breakfast less than two and a half hours ago.

Hampus asked the obvious question:

"So where do we start searching?"

"This is a big area, and he could have thrown her in the sea," Göran pointed out.

"Wouldn't she have drifted ashore somewhere by now?" Embla asked.

Göran shook his head. "Not necessarily. The temperature of the water is very low at the moment, which slows down the process of decay, so less gas is formed. I assume there are strong currents offshore, so she could be a long, long way from here."

They sat in silence for a moment, all visualizing that little body being carried out to sea by the current.

"But is that a reasonable assumption?" Embla wasn't convinced. "If Olof threw her in here and she was found nearby, he would have immediately become a person of interest. Who else comes here in the winter? By road, I mean."

Göran nodded as he held out his cup for a refill.

"There's something to what you say, but remember he'd been drinking, and no doubt he was in a panic. He might not have been thinking clearly."

"We need to search without any preconceptions," Paula said.

"So where do we start?" Hampus repeated.

Buoyed up by the sweet coffee, Göran set out his plan. "The CSIs are going to Breidablick first to examine the dumpster. The dog team will come straight here. I want them to search the area, moving outward from the house. The four of us will split up. Paula and I will take the house, the shed, and the boathouse. You two start over at the store. It's closed for the season, but I spoke to Eva this morning, and she said the key is in the cupboard in the hallway. The alarm code is the same as for this house, but with an extra six on the end. And don't forget your gloves and shoe protectors."

They got to their feet and prepared to set to work.

There were several keys in the pale-blue cupboard with white flying gulls painted on the door. In the bottom right corner were the initials A. S. Maybe Ann Sjöberg was the artist, Embla thought. She rummaged around and found a small bunch of keys labeled *Store + shed*. They were underneath a stubby key marked *Lobster trap*.

"Must fit the padlock Göran tripped over," she said.

"Is his foot okay now?" Hampus asked.

"Seems to be."

She replaced the stubby key and followed Hampus out into the rain.

THE AIR IN the shop was stale and damp, and there was a faint smell of sour milk. Hampus found the light switch. The place was divided into two rooms. In the smaller one were empty shelves and a substantial chill counter. Next to the chill counter was a freezer with a transparent lid. Hampus strode over. "Empty."

Everything was covered in a fine layer of dust. Embla looked carefully to see if there was any sign that someone had been in since the closure three months earlier, but she found nothing.

The same applied to the other room. A range of chandlery items was displayed on the walls and shelves, all neatly arranged and apparently untouched. Hampus immediately gravitated toward several outboard motors in one corner.

"Wow! A hundred and fifty horsepower! All I need now is the boat!" he exclaimed.

The mischievous look on his face when he turned back to Embla cheered her immensely; he was getting back to his old self. Whoever he'd spent the night with, she was exactly what he needed.

They conducted a thorough search but found nothing of interest. They moved on to the storage shed, which contained even more engines in different sizes, plus skiffs and dinghies in both wood and plastic. Everything the discerning boat owner could possibly need, in fact.

"The contents of this shed alone must be worth a fortune," Embla said.

"Absolutely."

Hampus's voice was slightly muted because he was rummaging among various fenders hanging in a corner. The smallest was about the size of a cola bottle, the largest bigger than a full-grown man. A notice on the wall informed customers that if anyone needed a larger fender, they should speak to a member of staff at the boatyard. Embla heard a huge sneeze from the corner. The shed was very dusty, which made it easier to see if anyone had been there. But once again, nothing.

They reset the alarm on their way out into the wind and sleet. Snow crystals stung their skin like tiny needles. The sound of exciting barking was coming from the direction of the Shore House; the dogs had arrived.

"Now what?" Embla asked.

"How about I take the boatyard and you go in the opposite direction? I don't think we need to stick together."

Without waiting for an answer, Hampus set off along

the jetty toward the boatyard, which was quiet at the moment. Presumably the men were on a break. Embla turned and slowly went back the way they'd come.

The high tide made it almost impossible to see anything in the water. The waves crashed against the rocks, making them treacherous. Under normal circumstances it would have been hard to make out whatever might be on the seabed; today there was no chance. Still she tried to peer down into the murky depths, even though she knew it was pointless. If Amelie had been thrown in around here over a month ago, she was long gone. Maybe the body had been carried out by the currents, as Göran had said. In which case they would never find her. The sea can be a good place to dispose of a body, especially if it's as small as Amelie's. Fish and other creatures would make short work of . . . Other creatures!

She stopped dead and almost slipped down into the icy water. Fortunately she managed to grab hold of a rusty ring embedded in the rock face; apparently larger vessels had anchored in this protected inlet during the war. The waves licked her boots, but her feet didn't get wet. If they had she wouldn't have noticed, though. Her focus was elsewhere.

As she approached the jetty down below the Shore House she could see that Göran and Paula were searching the shed. A wheelbarrow and some garden tools had been dumped outside, and she could hear their voices. Their words were carried away on the wind, but their laughter reached her. She went straight into the main house, opened the pale-blue cupboard, and took out the little key marked *Lobster trap*.

Down on the jetty she noticed that the lid of the

wood-fired hot tub was slightly askew; someone must have checked inside. She also caught the back view of one of the dog handlers, heading down the steps to the shore. She couldn't see the dog, which must have gone on ahead, but it was yapping excitedly, eager to start work.

The padlock Göran had tripped over was hard to open. The bitterly cold, damp air numbed her fingers, but after a while she managed it. The hinges creaked reluctantly as she pulled up the heavy hatch. She took out her flashlight. A steel wire ran into the water from each corner of the trap. On the edge of the hatch was something that looked like a switch with two small levers. One was in the "off" position, the other "down." She turned the first to "on" and heard an engine begin to throb beneath the jetty. She flicked the other switch to "up" and the wires began to move. Slowly they drew up the trap.

"Embla! What are you doing?" Paula was standing on the top step.

"Just checking out an idea!"

Paula said something over her shoulder to Göran, then came to join Embla.

The trap broke the surface of the water with an audible splash, before coming to a halt on a level with the underside of the jetty. The lid was held in place by a couple of simple clips. In spite of her stiff fingers, Embla managed to undo them. Her suspicions were confirmed as soon as she lifted the lid.

The trap contained a black plastic sack. And there was something inside it. The top was secured with a piece of rope that had been wound around several times and tied tightly. The knots appeared to be the work of someone who knew exactly what they were doing. Embla didn't touch anything else. She and Paula stared down at the contents of the trap, then looked at each other. It wasn't only the wind that brought tears to their eyes.

They called over Göran, who had his camera with him, and he began to take photographs. He was particularly interested in the knots, and took several close-ups.

"The CSIs are on their way from Breidablick. We'll wait for them before we open the sack."

IT WAS ESSENTIAL to keep the rope and the knots intact, so one of the CSI technicians simply slit the sack open.

The collar of the red jacket was torn. Her white Lucia costume peeked out of the top of a red-and-white ICA plastic bag. She was lying with her head turned to one side at an unnatural angle. The white hat was discolored by rusty-brown blood. Embla fought back the urge to lift her out of the icy water in the trap.

But Amelie could no longer feel the cold.

Maria Holm swayed and collapsed on the sofa when they told her they'd found Amelie. Embla and Hampus were with her in the family's living room. Julien was at a friend's house, which made it easier for them to talk to her.

After a while Maria stopped crying, and went to the bathroom to dry her eyes. When she came back she seemed surprisingly composed, although one hand was clutching a packet of paper tissues.

"Amelie has come to me in my dreams. She . . . she looked happy. She laughed and hugged me. But I knew she'd come . . . to console me." Her voice broke. She blew her nose and wiped her eyes with a sodden tissue. "At least I'll be able to bury my little girl," she whispered.

Embla's throat constricted, and she, too, had to blink away the tears. She went and sat beside Maria and put her arms around her. They sat like that for quite a while.

Göran and Paula went straight to the custody suite in Trollhättan to speak to Johannes Holm. They knew his mental state was fragile, and discussed the best way to tell him about Amelie. They had no idea if Johannes was religious, but Paula suggested contacting a priest, who might be able to help him either way since priests were used to comforting those who were grieving. Göran agreed, and Paula put in a call to the custody officer.

No spiritual mentor in the world could have handled the impact the news had on Johannes. He broke down completely and was taken by ambulance to the emergency psychiatric unit.

"So that leaves Viggo," Hampus said to Göran and Embla.

They were having a late dinner at the Laholm Hotel because none of them felt like cooking. Göran had given Paula a ride home earlier since it was her week to watch her children. When he returned, he insisted they needed a decent meal after the upsetting events of the day, but Embla didn't feel the least bit hungry. It was always hard to investigate crimes when the victims were children.

"We need to go over everything again. It's clear that there's no connection between the disappearance of Amelie and Viggo. Amelie was hit by Olof Sjöberg's car. He was drunk. Then he panicked and hid her in the lobster trap."

"You have to wonder what he was thinking—I mean she couldn't stay down there," Embla interjected.

Göran scraped up the remains of his red wine sauce and swallowed it with obvious pleasure before he answered. "No, she couldn't, but Olof was in the middle of one of his drinking bouts. I think he was intending to go back for her when things had calmed down. Take her far out to sea in his boat and dump the body."

The body. Little Amelie was just a body now. As a police officer, Embla knew perfectly well that this was a professional way of distancing oneself from people, reducing them to a body, a plaintiff, a witness, a victim. She had to try to suppress the grief she was feeling. Such emotions could cloud an investigator's judgment, meaning that he or she might miss vital details, become a less effective officer. Although she wasn't convinced that always applied. When you're working with people going through some form of crisis, it's important to pay attention to them and to listen to and follow your inner voice if need be.

IT WAS ALMOST eleven by the time they parked outside the Shore House. The wind was still strong, and it had started raining again. The only dots of light were provided by the external lamps on the gable ends. The place lay before them like a dark, solid mass. For the first time it felt threatening.

A brief flash in her peripheral vision as they walked toward the door made Embla realize why.

"There's someone in the house!" she hissed.

Both Göran and Hampus stopped dead beside her.

"Are you sure?" Göran whispered.

"Yes—I saw something at the hallway window, a flashlight maybe . . . There!"

A beam swept across the room and disappeared.

"There's definitely someone in there," Hampus agreed.

"But what about the alarm?" Embla was confused.

"Did you set it?"

She had to think for a moment. "No."

"Me neither. Göran?"

"No—the CSIs were still here. I gave them the spare key and the code, but they could have forgotten to set it."

Things had been a little chaotic earlier. The CSI team had still been on the jetty when Embla and her colleagues left. Once Amelie's body had been sent down to Gothenburg, the technicians had continued to examine the immediate area. They had found a gray pair of men's trousers and a thick blue lumber jacket at the bottom of the lobster trap, both marked with large stains that looked like blood. Meanwhile they had been given access to the Shore House so that they could make a hot drink and use the bathroom. They'd left about an hour ago.

"Look—whoever it is has moved to the living room," Hampus said quietly.

"Okay, you and I will take the front door while Embla goes around the back."

None of them was armed, but Embla understood Göran's tactic. If the intruder—or intruders—decided to make a run for it via the patio, she would be able to stop them. The blow would come as a complete surprise out of the darkness. It had worked before.

Did the interloper know they were out here? Possibly, but with a bit of luck the wind would have drowned out the sound of their engines.

The fact that they'd been staying in the house for a couple of days gave them the advantage; they knew the layout. Embla still had to be careful as she made her way around the back; the ground was uneven and slippery with the rain. She was planning to tiptoe through the gap between the shed and the garage, which would give her easy access to the patio. The plexiglass fencing and the glass doors leading onto the sun deck would enable her to see what was going on inside the living room.

The strategy was sound, until she found an SUV parked next to the garage. It had tinted glass, which made it difficult to see if anyone was sitting in the car. Moving as quietly as possible, she crept up behind the vehicle. She reached into her pocket for her powerful little flashlight and held it up to the back window.

Then she switched it on.

Nothing happened.

After a few seconds she looked up; the car was definitely empty. She shined the beam on the trunk: Lexus RX 300. She knew exactly who their uninvited visitor was.

PERNILLA ANDERSSON WAS in floods of tears. There was no point in trying to get anything sensible out of her. Göran was sitting beside her on the sofa with a roll of paper towels, ripping off sheets and handing them to her at regular intervals while trying to calm her down. It wasn't working; she just kept sobbing. Instinctively Embla went and sat on the other side of her. She gently put her arm around Pernilla's shoulders and drew her close. The floodgates opened, and she wept as if her heart was breaking. Embla could feel the dampness seeping through her top, but maintained her comforting embrace. Maybe it was the proximity to another person that made Pernilla let go completely, and maybe it was that same feeling that eventually enabled her to pull herself together. It took a while, but she managed to sit up and blow her nose. Her face was streaked with mascara yet again. *Why does she insist on putting on makeup when she can't be bothered to wash her hair or change her clothes?*

Embla wondered with a certain amount of admiration. Then again, Pernilla had a pretty face; maybe the habit of applying makeup was a desperate attempt to cling to some kind of normality in an existence that had been smashed to pieces.

Hampus appeared with a tray of tea and cardamom crisp rolls, which Göran had bought instead of the usual chocolate Florentines or Ballerina cookies.

They gave Pernilla a cup of tea with milk and sugar, then served themselves. Göran was the only one who took a crisp roll. After some inconsequential small talk he decided it was time to get serious.

"How did you get in? Even if the CSIs forgot to set the alarm, I'm sure they must have locked the door."

For a second Embla thought Pernilla wasn't going to answer, but then the other woman took a deep breath.

"The spare key."

"What spare key?"

"Under the pot."

Embla remembered the two concrete pots on either side of the door, containing spruce and heather.

"I used to clean this house, and I worked in the store during the summer—before I got the job at the Co-op two years ago."

"So you looked under the pot and the key was still there."

"Yes."

The three colleagues considered this revelation in silence. What was the point of locks and alarm systems if you hid a spare key under a pot by the front door? However, Embla wasn't particularly surprised. Uncle Nisse always kept a key on top of the door frame.

"What about the alarm? Do you know the code?"

The shadow of a smile passed across Pernilla's face.

"Of course, otherwise I wouldn't have been able to let myself in to do the cleaning. Olof never changed it."

So much for security measures.

Adopting his least threatening tone of voice, Göran asked, "So why are you here?"

Pernilla's expression stiffened, and Embla was afraid she might start crying again. Instead she pursed her lips and suddenly looked angry.

"You're making stuff up, trying to frame Ted!"

All three officers were equally taken aback by this outburst.

"Making stuff . . . ? What do you mean?" A furrow had appeared between Göran's eyebrows.

"Planting false evidence! He's done nothing! It's that stupid boy you're all pandering to! He . . ."

Her voice broke and the tears began to flow once more. Another collapse was imminent.

"Pernilla, listen to me. We're not trying to frame Ted for something he hasn't done, but we know he was at Breidablick when the fire was started. Olof Sjöberg died and his son was badly beaten. Those are very serious offenses. While we're investigating what happened, Ted and Johannes will remain in custody," Göran explained.

Pernilla had demonstratively turned her back on him; now her head jerked around and she stared at him, eyes blazing.

"Kristoffer Sjöberg abducted both Amelie and our Viggo! He's the one who should be in a cell!"

The media still didn't know about the discovery of Amelie's body.

Göran held Pernilla's gaze and said slowly and clearly, "We found Amelie today. She's dead. We know how she died. Kristoffer is not under any suspicion whatsoever. He had absolutely nothing to do with her death."

Her eyes widened as she grasped what he'd said. Before she jumped to the conclusion that Viggo must have been murdered, Göran continued.

"The person responsible for Amelie's death cannot possibly have had anything to do with Viggo's disappearance. It's out of the question. And as we told you before, Kristoffer has an alibi for the time when Viggo went missing. Five people can confirm that he was at Breidablick."

The anger in Pernilla's eyes was just as fierce.

"They're lying!"

"No. Their statements have been meticulously checked. One of the witnesses has no connection with the Sjöberg family. He's simply a customer who was picking up his car."

Pernilla continued to glare at him but didn't say any more. After a moment Göran went back to his original point.

"So what are you doing here? What did Ted ask you to look for?"

Her lower lip began to quiver, but she remained silent.

"I can see that you've switched on my laptop, but it's password protected. What did he ask you to look for?"

Pernilla's voice was barely audible when, much to Embla's surprise, she replied, "He told me to search for false evidence . . . He said you're all lying, that you're determined to bring him down."

Something began to stir in Embla's subconscious. The sweating, the shaking, the explosive temperament. And now the paranoia.

"Does Ted take drugs?" she asked quietly.

Pernilla reacted as if she'd been slapped across the face. The color drained from her cheeks, and her eyes widened with fear. Embla had seen that same expression when they'd talked to her about Ted back at home. Pernilla turned away and didn't answer.

"I know you're scared. He's notorious for his temper. Long-term drug dependency leads to increasingly extreme mood swings."

Embla paused to see if Pernilla would respond but got nothing back. Calmly and with as much empathy as she could muster, she said, "I'm sure he's taken out his anger on you from time to time. Has he ever hit Viggo?"

Without looking at any of them, Pernilla slowly shook her head. "No," she whispered.

"But he has hit you."

Pernilla straightened her back, but after a couple of seconds it was as if all the strength had drained out of her. Her shoulders slumped, and she stared down at the floor. "You can't tell him I've said anything!" she said, suddenly getting to her feet.

She was terrified. Hampus cleared his throat, signaling that he'd like to take over.

"We won't, but it's important for us to know how much he's using."

Pernilla looked at him with her swollen, red-rimmed eyes, then flopped back down on the sofa. Her voice sounded thick and she was mumbling; it was hard to make out what she was saying.

"Sometimes . . . when he comes home . . . I can tell . . . more often these days . . ."

"Are you saying he's using drugs more frequently now than in the past?"

A weary nod.

"What does he take?"

The lead interrogator with the narcotics unit had stepped in, but Pernilla merely shook her head, exhaustion showing in every line of her body. Hampus pushed his glasses up his nose and gazed at her with his kind brown eyes. He lowered his voice, inviting her to confide in him.

"Cocaine? Amphetamines?"

Her lips trembled and Embla thought she wasn't going to respond.

"Powder," she whispered.

"You don't know what kind of powder?"

Another shake of the head.

"Does he ever use a syringe? Does he inject himself?"

"A syringe? Never! He's terrified of needles—blood tests, anything like that."

That was all they needed to know. Given Ted's appearance and behavior during his interviews, he could well be suffering from cocaine withdrawal.

Göran took over. "We're not going to charge you with illegal entry into this house, Pernilla. We know Ted forced you to do it. This conversation has been very helpful, but Ted won't find out that you told us about his drug problem." He got to his feet. "Embla, could you give Pernilla a ride home? Pernilla, is your mother still staying with you?"

"Yes."

"Good—it's best if you're not alone."

Pernilla looked up and pointed to Hampus. "Can . . . can he follow us in my car?"

"Unfortunately both he and I have had a couple of beers, so I'm afraid we can't drive tonight. We'll bring it over tomorrow," Göran assured her.

They'd all drunk mineral water with dinner, but Embla realized that Göran was interested in the Lexus. He wanted to take a look at it while he had the chance.

NEITHER OF THE two women spoke on the drive to Strömstad. Pernilla was slumped on the passenger seat like a sack of potatoes, staring out the windshield. When the Volvo pulled up at her gate, she opened the door and stumbled out without saying either thank you for the ride or goodbye.

As she headed back to Sandgrav, it struck Embla that Pernilla hadn't once mentioned Amelie, or asked where and how the child had been found. Strange. But maybe it was because she was totally focused on her own problems. A missing six-year-old son and a husband on remand under suspicion of arson and serious assault could seriously reduce anyone's ability to empathize.

When she parked outside the Shore House there was a light on in the garage. Göran had driven the Lexus inside and was busy checking it over. His legs and butt were sticking out the door on the driver's side as he examined the floor and seat.

"Need any help?"

There was a dull thud and a muttered curse before he

straightened up, rubbing the top of his head. He forced a smile.

"No, it's fine. You go to bed."

Without waiting for a response he returned to the task in hand.

THE LAST FEW days had been intense with too little sleep—for a variety of reasons. It was no excuse for oversleeping but it was an explanation, as Göran pointed out when he was woken by a phone call from Chief Superintendent Roger Willén at exactly 8:15 on Tuesday morning.

"I understand, and I'm very pleased you found Amelie. I've just been to the hospital to see her father. I wanted to get the lowdown on his condition. I'm calling from the car—Paula Nilsson and Lars Engman are with me."

"Is Johannes feeling better?"

"He was pretty calm. He's now saying he must have been drugged when he was in the bar, presumably by Ted Andersson. He remembers Ted calling the other guy 'David' several times. Johannes described his shaved head and the tattoos on his neck; he also said he had a misshapen ear. We now know that David Hagen is a former wrestler, and we've seen his cauliflower ear."

Willén paused, and Göran interjected. "The description and the name certainly fit David Hagen, who's now being held in Trollhättan for the attempted murder of Kristoffer Sjöberg in his hospital room. Remarkable, to say the least."

"Exactly. And that's not all. The weapon Hagen was carrying is a particularly fine hunting knife, according to Embla. Expensive. She's an expert in these matters, and made the connection with Robert Halvorsen's stab wounds. Gilstrup contacted me from Oslo first thing this morning; forensics have confirmed the match. He thanked us for the tip, and is checking to see if there's any evidence that David Hagen was at that New Year's party. If so, he becomes a person of considerable interest in that homicide inquiry, too."

Göran was wide awake now. Things were really starting to move, on several fronts at the same time. "So we got one over on our colleagues in Oslo," he said with a brief laugh.

"You could say that, but Gilstrup did tell me something I didn't know. Hans Joffsén, the owner of the house where the New Year's party was held, said a number of items were missing, including a hunting rifle, plus—and I quote—'a few other bits and pieces related to hunting.' When he was asked for specific details he became evasive, claimed he couldn't remember exactly. I'll make sure we speak to him today. If a hunting knife was taken, that could well be the murder weapon used on Halvorsen. In which case we'll take a closer look at the knife Hagen was carrying in the hospital."

It only took a second for Göran to process the implications. "Jeez!" he exclaimed.

"Indeed. Going back to Johannes Holm, he's still saying there are huge gaps in his memory of that night—what happened in the bar, and the drive to Breidablick. He insists it was Hagen who set fire to the workshop, and that Ted Andersson beat up Kristoffer, until he and Hagen managed to stop him."

Göran quickly thought about what this new information might mean for the investigation into the arson attack. He decided to tell Willén what he'd been up to last night.

"We've actually made some progress in the case against Ted Andersson. I've gone through his car and made some interesting discoveries. I found an Alvedon tube in the glove compartment containing small white tablets—definitely not Alvedon. I also found a removable tow bar in the space where the spare tire should be, and—"

"Removable? I thought they were always fixed," Willén said, interrupting him.

"Not on the Lexus RX 300."

"You learn something new every day." Willén sounded slightly embarrassed over the gaps in his knowledge when it came to cars.

Göran chuckled. "I'll go down to Gothenburg today, ask forensics to take a look at the tow bar."

"So why is it of interest?"

"The shape matches the description of the object used in the attack on Viktor Jansson."

"Viktor Jansson!"

Willén was completely taken aback. He almost yelled out the name. He took a moment to compose himself. "That investigation has gotten nowhere, even though we brought in extra resources. So a tow bar like that could be the murder weapon—but do you really think it was the one you found in the Lexus?"

"I don't know; I don't want to examine it myself, even

though I've got the equipment here. We could be talking about microscopic traces of blood or brain tissue. There's a girl at the lab who's brilliant, and the equipment at her disposal is much more sophisticated. She's currently working on the windshield we found in the dumpster at Breidablick."

There was silence on the other end of the line, but Göran thought he could hear the cogs turning in Willén's brain.

Eventually he said, "I've just remembered a call that came in from a member of the public at the end of last week, an elderly man who lives in Mellerud. He and his wife had been visiting relatives in Strömstad. They were on their way home on Saturday afternoon—the day Jansson was murdered. At first he wasn't too sure of the time or where he saw the car, which was why he didn't contact us right away. He says they passed the spot where Viktor was murdered between three-thirty and four—he couldn't be any more precise. It was already dark, but he caught a glimpse of a car in the beam of his headlights for just a few seconds. It was a large dark vehicle, possibly a van or an SUV, in the small parking lot. He also saw two people standing there talking—he's in no doubt about that. They didn't appear to be quarreling; in fact one patted the other on the shoulder. He got the impression they were friends, which was why he didn't immediately make the connection with Viktor Jansson's death."

"A dark vehicle, possibly a van or an SUV . . . I'm taking that tow bar to the lab in Gothenburg right now!"

Göran ended the call and swung his legs over the side of the bed.

HE USUALLY ALLOWED himself a leisurely and substantial breakfast; he was convinced it laid the foundations for all the energy a person needed during the course of the day. However, this morning Göran grabbed a couple of sandwiches and washed them down with plenty of coffee. He was in such a hurry he forgot his vow to cut back on the sugar. Between bites he told Embla and Hampus about his conversation with Roger Willén, and about what he'd found in Ted's car.

Embla had been half-asleep when she staggered down the stairs, but she was wide awake now.

"Wow—what if it really is the knife that was used to stab Halvorsen?"

"But seriously—would David Hagen have kept it if he'd killed a man with it? Surely he knows it's essential to get rid of a murder weapon as quickly as possible," Hampus objected.

He'd been at least as tired as his colleagues, but he'd still gotten up first and made breakfast, and now his eyes were bright behind those strong glasses. The three officers around the table were firing on all cylinders, their investigative instincts aroused as they got closer to the truth—and not only in one case. Strangely enough, all the threads seemed to be coming together. Hampus pointed out how vital it was not to miss any key details in the flood of fresh leads and information.

"My thoughts exactly," Göran agreed. "Which is why I'd like you two to go and talk to David Hagen. And ask him more questions about what happened at Breidablick; I want him to realize we know he was there. The murder of Robert Halvorsen, arson, serious assault, and attempted murder—all major crimes that will carry a heavy sentence. He has to understand that he's going to be behind bars for a very, very long time. He needs to start talking."

As he got up from the table, his cell phone rang.

"Göran Krantz . . . Hi, Roger."

Embla and Hampus couldn't hear what Willén was saying, but he was speaking very quickly, and they saw a contented expression spread across Göran's face. When the call was over he flashed a triumphant smile.

"We've got the bastard! Willén's just spoken to Oslo. They'd gone through pictures from the New Year's party that some of the guests had taken on their phones, and David Hagen is definitely in one of them. They've been looking for him, but haven't managed to track him down. Which is perfectly understandable, as he's safely locked up in Trollhättan. Willén's sending me the photograph right away."

He went and fetched his laptop. He had several unopened messages in his inbox, and immediately clicked on the one from Willén. A picture filled the screen, a large group of people raising their glasses to the photographer. Lopsided grins and slightly dazed expressions suggested that it had been taken pretty late. The date and time were given in the bottom left-hand corner: 1 JANUARY 01:53. Less than thirty minutes later Robert Halvorsen was stabbed and never regained consciousness.

Göran, Hampus, and Embla huddled closer together to examine the image. Hagen's profile could be seen clearly, his shaven head, tattooed neck, and cauliflower ear slightly above the celebratory group.

"He's standing on some kind of step," Hampus said.

There were two tall glass doors next to him. He seemed to be talking to another man who'd stuck his head through one half-open door. Göran zoomed in. The face wasn't clear, but they saw tousled curly hair and the collar of a black jacket.

"Ted Andersson!" Embla and Hampus exclaimed in unison.

All three looked at one another.

"This puts things in a completely different light," Göran said. "We need to talk it through."

ON THE WAY to Trollhättan, Embla and Hampus discussed the best way to handle the interview with David Hagen. Willén had been informed they were coming and had immediately offered to question Hagen himself. After some consideration they had agreed. It was unlikely that Hagen would be particularly cooperative with the officers who'd arrested him after his attempt on Kristoffer's life.

Paula Nilsson was already waiting in Willén's light and pleasant office. A faint odor of paint in the air gave away the fact that it had recently been renovated.

"Okay, so Paula and I will talk to Hagen if you can fill us in on what you've found out about him," Willén said, settling down in his modern office chair, a symphony of chrome and black leather. There wasn't a speck of dust on the shining surface of his desk; it was clinically clean. He had a computer desk at the side within easy reach; all he had to do was turn his chair. The smell of new leather reached Embla's nostrils. Willén seemed unaware of the small farting noises that could be heard every time he shifted in the chair. He was, however, noticeably embarrassed when she told him they'd managed to identify Ted Andersson in the photograph from the party. He had focused on Hagen, and hadn't recognized the man in the doorway.

"Then again, I only glanced at the picture; I sent it straight over to Göran," he said by way of explanation.

As expected, David Hagen refused to answer any questions. The first reaction of any kind came when Willén informed him that the knife he'd been carrying in the hospital was now being examined by the Oslo police in order to see if there was a match with Robert Halvorsen's injuries.

"We have photographic proof that you were at the party. If that knife was used on Halvorsen, you have some explaining to do."

The only response was a quick glance. Hagen's expression was difficult to interpret, but Willén thought he saw both surprise and uncertainty.

"These are new accusations relating to a completely different case from the one for which my client has been remanded in custody. I demand that they be struck from the record on the grounds of irrelevance!" Hagen's lawyer piped up.

Fred Lindström was a big man. He wiped his face with a brick-red handkerchief that toned perfectly with his tie and socks. His chocolate-brown tailor-made jacket strained over his substantial belly. He tugged at his tie in an attempt to undo the top button of his shirt and ease the pressure around his neck. With a bit of luck, that might bring down the color of his face.

Paula Nilsson was sitting next to her boss but chose to keep a low profile and allow him to run things.

The contrast between the three men was striking. Hagen, the tattooed thug, wore a faded T-shirt with the words FUCK YOU on the front. He drummed his fingers on the table the whole time—very quietly, but loud enough to be a distraction. Which was the point, of course. Lindström's clothes were definitely expensive, but that wasn't enough to make him look elegant. The acting area chief superintendent was the one who epitomized style, even though he was in uniform. The pale-blue shirt with the police emblem on the sleeve and breast pocket was freshly ironed, the crowns and stripes on his epaulettes glinted in the light, the creases in his dark-blue trousers were razor-sharp, and his shoes shined as if he were going dancing straight after work. There wasn't the slightest hint of perspiration on his brow, no sweat marks under his arms. He was completely focused on Hagen and his lawyer, neither of whom seemed entirely comfortable under his gimlet eye.

The interview was being filmed. Embla and Hampus were sitting in front of a screen in the room next door, carefully observing. No one was expecting Hagen to hold up his hands and start confessing, but there was no doubt that the mention of the knife in connection with the stabbing of Halvorsen had shaken him.

"It knocked him off balance," Embla said quietly.

At that moment Paula asked a question. "How well do you know Ted Andersson?"

Another noticeable reaction. He stopped drumming his fingers and froze. He didn't say a word, but his body language spoke volumes. He didn't want to acknowledge that particular relationship.

AFTERWARD THEY GATHERED in Willén's office once more.

"The link to the knife and Ted Andersson came as a nasty shock. He can sit and sweat for a while before we talk to him again."

Willén seemed satisfied, even though they hadn't gotten any answers out of Hagen. He looked at Embla and Hampus. "Were you thinking of speaking to Ted Andersson today?"

"No—we're going to wait and see what Göran gets from the lab. Ted can stew until then."

"Absolutely! How about some lunch?"

The chief superintendent rose from his leather chair with a brief farting noise before either Embla or Hampus had time to answer.

After lunch Embla and Hampus returned to Strömstad. Embla was driving and Hampus was busy replying to a text he'd received just before they set off. Once he was done, he turned and looked at her.

"I was wondering . . . Your brother Frej . . . How did he come out? What . . . what did he say?"

Embla was completely taken aback. Her middle brother, Frej, was nine years older, and a well-known actor. He'd never hidden his sexuality—quite the reverse. He and his husband, Viktor, who was a news anchor, were often referred to as Sweden's gay icons. They were always out and about and featured in the gossip magazines. They'd lived in Stockholm for years, mainly because Frej had been offered wonderful theater roles there, but also because he felt the attitude toward the gay community was more positive in the capital.

Playing for time, she countered, "What do you mean?"

"How did he tell the family he was gay?"

Embla burst out laughing. "He didn't need to tell us—we've always known! Mom said he used to totter around in her high-heeled shoes and ask her to make up his face when he was four years old. Plenty of kids do that and don't turn out to be gay, but he also adored nail polish, and wore it to school every single day right from the start. He fell in love with boys, and told everybody about it. I wasn't born then, of course, but that's what I've heard."

"Was he bullied?"

"Maybe in junior high, but I was only little, so he never talked to me about it. People have always loved Frej, though. He's funny, charming, and loves to mess around. And he's a fantastic singer, too. A born entertainer, in fact."

Hampus sat in silence for a little while.

"When did you realize . . ."

"Like I said, I've always known because he was always open about it. No big deal. He's just my big brother who loves to tease me and never had time for me. Neither did my other two brothers, to be honest."

"How old were they when you were born?"

"Atle was twelve and Kolbjörn was seven. And Frej was nine. Why are you asking about him, anyway?"

Hampus stared out the windshield. Eventually he mumbled, "Because I'm . . . gay."

Suddenly everything became clear. He'd obviously been texting his new partner. That also explained the glow when she'd picked him up outside the police station. She remembered the way Ahmed the nurse had looked at him the first time they went to the hospital to speak to Kristoffer. This threw a different light on the divorce from Filippa.

"And?"

"I don't quite know how to deal with it."

She gave him a sideways glance. His expression was verging on pleading. "What's the problem?"

"Everything. How people will react, gossip at work, Filippa, the girls. My parents and siblings—they're Free Church, instead of belonging to the Church of Sweden. From Småland. Need I say more?"

"I think you just give an honest answer if anyone asks, but you don't have to walk around the station waving the rainbow flag. Just don't try to pretend that nothing's changed, because it has. And that can only be a good thing." She gave him an encouraging smile, and he managed a pale imitation in return.

"You're right. Lasse is the best thing that's ever happened to me."

"So tell me about him."

At last he broke into a grin. "You're not going to believe me, but he's a firefighter!"

Embla burst out laughing and couldn't stop. The car swerved as she attempted to pull herself together, but at least she managed to stay on the right side of the road.

"A firefighter! You're joking!" she howled.

"I know. Total gay cliché," he muttered, still grinning.

Embla regained control of both herself and the car. "So how long have you been together?"

"September."

That surprised her. They'd still been working together back then; she hadn't noticed a thing.

"Is he your first?"

"No."

The brief response made it clear that this was an area he didn't want to discuss.

"So am I the only person you've told?"

"Yes."

Hampus had never been particularly open with

colleagues about his private life; Embla now understood why. It wasn't just his personality; he'd been carrying secrets.

"I'm honored that you chose to confide in me, and I won't say a word. That's up to you," she said.

"I know. But it's not easy."

"How about Lasse? Does his family know about you?"

"Yes."

"Has he been in straight relationships in the past?"

"No, never."

"Do his coworkers know?"

"No. The whole environment, the language they use is so . . . macho. That's another thing I find difficult."

"I get it, but like I said, you don't need to flag up your sex life at work. Just lie low for a while. And I'm sure you know there's an association for homosexual police officers. Well, there is in Stockholm, and I think there's one in Gothenburg, too."

"I'm aware of that, but I'm not there yet. Far from it."

They turned off onto the narrow track leading down to Sandgrav and dropped the subject by tacit agreement. It was already dark, and Embla had to concentrate on her driving. The countless potholes were filled with water, and the car bumped and jolted along. For any with a tendency to car sickness, this was a nightmare route.

THEY HAD BEEN in the house for no more than fifteen minutes when Hampus's phone rang. It was Göran, so he switched to speakerphone.

"I've just heard—there's blood on the tow-bar mount. And"—he paused for effect, and they heard him inhale—"the blood is Viktor Jansson's!"

Embla and Hampus exchanged a startled glance. It had certainly seemed like a breakthrough when Göran had come up with the idea that the killer could have used the removable tow bar, but none of them had dared hope for concrete evidence.

Before they had time to come up with a sensible response, Göran continued.

"And the blood on the windshield is Amelie Holm's. Not a shadow of doubt."

"So there's our proof!" Hampus exclaimed.

"Yes, Olof Sjöberg ran into her in the Buick. Linda in the DNA lab is brilliant. While she was testing those tiny drops of blood, I decided to take a closer look at the flashlight Embla found at Ted Andersson's house. As you know, there were no batteries in it, but when I ran my finger along the battery compartment, I could feel a thin layer of powder. Because of what we now know about Andersson and his habits, I thought it was worth checking out. As I suspected, it tested positive for cocaine."

The surprises were coming thick and fast.

"That's just . . . sick!" Embla said.

"To say the least. I'm still in Gothenburg, but I'm heading straight back to Strömstad. In the meantime I want you two to go and talk to Pernilla Andersson again. I've been thinking about the witness from Mellerud who said he saw a large dark vehicle in the parking lot around the time of Viktor Jansson's murder, and the two men standing there chatting. As the murder weapon is linked to Ted Andersson, we believe he wasn't at home with Viggo when he claims he was. I think Ted killed Viktor Jansson, but what was he doing outside Skee? And why did he attack Viktor?"

"And where was Viggo then? Where is he now?" Embla added.

"Exactly. We have to make Ted tell us. Finding the children was our aim from the get-go. We've found Amelie and we know how she died, but we're no further with Viggo."

"Because the boy's father has lied to us from day one," Hampus commented dryly.

PERNILLA'S MOTHER OPENED the door. She looked tired and disheartened, which was understandable. The last week had been horrendous for both her and her daughter.

"She's asleep," she said.

"Would you like to go and wake her, or shall I do it?" Embla said in a friendly tone of voice.

"She needs her rest . . ."

"And we need to talk to her. We have a possible new lead on Viggo," Embla said firmly.

With a sigh Pernilla's mother embarked on her laborious ascent of the stairs, wheezing with every step. She sounded as if she were climbing Kebnekaise with a full kit. *I hope she doesn't collapse*, Embla thought with a tinge of anxiety.

After a while Hampus and Embla heard the murmur of voices, followed by a familiar shuffling sound. The first they saw of Pernilla was the grubby pink piglet slippers. She made her way down with surprising speed.

"Have you found him?"

Her eyes were darting between the two officers. Her hair was still unwashed, and she was wearing black tights and a faded yellow T-shirt under her old bathrobe.

Judging by her body odor, she hadn't showered for several days. Embla's heart contracted with sympathy for her. They definitely hadn't brought good news.

They went into the kitchen and sat down at the scruffy table. Most of the furniture in the house was well past its heyday. The kitchen showed signs of a renovation at some point in the 1970s, with pine cupboard doors and orange tiles above the sink and stove. The only indication that Ted and Pernilla were intending to put their own stamp on the place by adding a patio was the pile of building material under tarps in the yard. Otherwise it was as if time had stood still for at least a couple of decades. Which was odd, given their comparative youth. *Then again, it's expensive to renovate a house; maybe they can't afford it,* Embla thought.

Pernilla's mother slumped down next to her daughter. The resemblance was unmistakable.

Hampus began by asking how Pernilla was feeling. A listless shake of the head was her only response. He leaned forward and caught her eye.

"Pernilla, we have witnesses who saw Ted in a parking lot outside Skee last Friday. The time was around three forty-five, which means his assertion that he was at home with Viggo can't be true. The question is where he was going—and where Viggo was at that point."

Every scrap of color drained from Pernilla's face and her eyes widened. Her mother inhaled sharply and clutched at her chest; she looked equally terrified.

"I can see that you both have some idea of where he was heading," Hampus added quietly without losing eye contact with Pernilla for a second.

Through stiff lips that refused to work properly she whispered: "Vasseröd."

It took a while to elicit the details, but eventually they learned that Ted had inherited not only this house, but also an old cottage. Pernilla wasn't sure exactly when his father had died because she and Ted hadn't been together back then. Ted's parents had split up when he was little, and his mother had moved to Henån with her new husband. When his father died, the cottage by the lake in Vasseröd was left to him. Ted wasn't remotely interested in the property, but occasionally he and Pernilla would drive over to check on the place. They had no friends or relatives in the area, which was another reason why they didn't go there very often.

According to Pernilla, the cottage was pretty rundown, and was surrounded by dense forest. It was at least a hundred years old and lay at the end of a track. There was an even more dilapidated cabin nearby, and nobody seemed to know who the owner was. It was quite a long walk to the lake if you wanted to swim. Ted had put the cottage up for sale a few years earlier, but no one had been interested. Pernilla had nothing positive to say about any of it.

"But why would he go there? Do you think he . . . and Viggo . . ." Her voice trailed away.

Hampus was still holding her gaze, and he saw her eyes fill with tears.

"Has he taken . . . has he taken my Viggo there? Has he . . ." She shot to her feet, arms flailing as she tried to get the words out. "You have to . . . go and get him!" she managed at last.

Embla got up and stood beside the trembling woman. Gently she placed a hand on her shoulder.

"We will. If he's there. I promise."

It was another thirty minutes before they were able to leave. Pernilla wanted to drive up to Vasseröd immediately, but they convinced her that this wasn't a good idea. It was late, and pitch dark outside. It would be better if the police went there first thing in the morning, when they'd had time to organize a search party. Daylight would also make things easier.

Pernilla calmed down and gave them a rough idea of how to get there. They promised to keep her informed of developments.

Back in the car Embla took a deep breath. "Pernilla didn't make the connection between the parking lot outside Skee and the time of Viktor Jansson's murder," she said.

Hampus nodded. "I noticed that, too. Jansson's death has been big news—as big as Viggo's disappearance, but I guess she's blocked it out. She's had more than enough to deal with."

"Absolutely. Both she and her mother immediately jumped to the conclusion that Ted had taken Viggo. Neither of them had any problem accepting that idea."

"Which makes me think the boy could well be in Vasseröd."

Embla started the car. "So what do we do now? It's almost ten o'clock."

"First of all I'm going to call Göran, bring him up to date. Then I'll call the pizzeria and order three pizzas—we'll pick them up on the way."

ALL THE LIGHTS were on when they got back to the Shore House. Göran was on the phone, sitting in front of the fire.

". . . and I've spoken to the guy in charge of the local Home Guard, his name's Flod. He's organizing a search party, plus there'll be eight officers from Strömstad, and the three of us from VGM. All we need now is a couple of dogs . . . Can you fix that? Terrific!"

He ended the call and turned to his colleagues with a satisfied smile. It would take a while to gather everyone, so he and Flod had arranged to meet up at 7:30 in the morning at the T-junction in Holekärr. It would still be dark, but it would start to get light around an hour later—at least as light as it was going to be in the middle of winter . . .

"Holekärr is just a tiny dot on the map, and I don't know much about it, but it's less than a mile from Vasseröd, so we can all head over to Andersson's cottage together."

Embla got out glasses. She didn't bother with plates; they usually ate pizza straight out of the box. She looked out the window. It was pitch dark, with sleet sliding down the glass. Her heart sank at the thought of tomorrow's task.

"He can't possibly be alive," she said.

"No," Hampus agreed.

A small child couldn't survive without food or water for over a week. Not to mention the cold.

"What if he's not there?" she went on.

"This is the first real lead we've had, and it explains why we haven't found him in the local area. It's worth a shot."

Göran sounds determined, but even he must have his doubts, Embla thought. She filled a jug with water and added a handful of ice cubes from the freezer. As she put it down on the table she asked the question that had been troubling her ever since the conversation with Pernilla.

"Why would Ted kill Viggo?"

Neither of her colleagues had an answer.

EMBLA AND HAMPUS couldn't stop yawning; Göran had woken them at six. The weather was still appalling: strong wind and horizontal sleet. They met very few cars along the road.

They could see the blue lights from some distance away as they approached the T-junction in Holekärr. It turned out to be the dog team, and behind their vehicle was the Home Guard's minibus. Two patrol cars from Strömstad arrived seconds after the Volvo, which meant a total of twenty-two people. Pretty good, given the short notice.

Göran spoke to the guy in charge of the Home Guard and to the police officers involved. They agreed that VGM would lead the way because they had some idea of the route. Embla switched on the car's GPS just to be on the safe side. Pernilla had thought the area in which the cottage lay was called Skogkas, and to Embla's surprise a flashing dot appeared when she keyed in the name.

The convoy set off. They knew that the lake was on the right-hand side of the road, but it was impossible to catch even a glimpse of the water in the compact darkness. There were no lights in any houses; the few individuals who lived there in the sticks were obviously still sleeping. Then again, according to Pernilla the area consisted mainly of summer cottages, and of course most of those would be down by the lake. The forest itself was desolate and deserted—ideal for anyone who wanted to move around unseen in the winter gloom.

Hampus was the map reader, and had Pernilla's directions on his knee.

"Take a left opposite the white building up ahead; that's the one that used to be a grocery store."

"GPS says yes," Embla confirmed.

They turned onto a steep, narrow dirt track. Brush and overhanging branches scraped against the sides of the car as they bumped along over deep potholes filled with water.

Embla was acutely aware that they might well find Viggo today—and that he was probably dead. There was also an illogical feeling that if they didn't find him, there was still a faint hope that he was alive. She knew it was stupid, but she couldn't shake it.

They jolted uphill for around a third of a mile before the terrain finally began to level out. They were still surrounded by dense forest, and the rain was hammering on the roof of the car. Visibility beyond the beam of the headlights was zero.

"We should be just about there now," Embla informed her colleagues. She stopped after a few yards more, opened the side window, and peered out. "Can either of you see anything that resembles a house?"

"No," they answered in unison.

The other vehicles parked behind the Volvo. Even with the help of their headlights, Embla couldn't see a thing. With a sigh she realized they were going to have to get out.

The search party gathered next to the minibus. The leader of the Home Guard divided them into groups and told them which way to go, exhorting them not to leave big gaps between them. Before they set off he issued a final instruction:

"Maintain radio contact."

The four groups moved away, leaving Göran and Flod, whose first name was apparently Bengt, by the vehicle.

Each team consisted of five people. Embla and Hampus were with Patrik Lind and Alice Åslund from Strömstad, plus a young guy from the Home Guard who introduced himself as Linus. He was in his early twenties, below average height and pretty skinny. His green uniform was several sizes too big. He didn't say a word as they plodded along by the beam of their flashlights, tapping the ground with sticks as they went.

Suddenly the radio crackled to life.

"Group West have found an old house with a small shed next to it."

Then came Flod's voice: "Okay—how far from our location?"

After a mumbled consultation, the first voice said: "No more than a hundred yards. There's a narrow path."

Embla was in Group North. They stopped and discussed how best to proceed. While they were talking she swept her flashlight over the surrounding undergrowth. She saw a glimmer, and the hairs on the back of her neck stood on end when she saw someone shining a flashlight at her. Then she realized it was her own reflection in a windowpane.

"There's a house here, too," she said.

They reported back to Bengt Flod and Göran before

pushing their way through the vegetation to take a closer look.

It was a completely derelict structure. The porch roof had fallen down and lay in a heap on the top step. One of the two windows was broken, and scraps of gray fabric that must have been a lace curtain were fluttering in the wind.

"No one's been here for a very long time," Patrik Lind said with certainty.

"This could be the dilapidated cabin Pernilla mentioned," Embla suggested.

They scanned the area, and the beam of Hampus's flashlight picked out an old outhouse. The roof had fallen in and the door was hanging drunkenly on one hinge. A few feet away there was a small shed. The door was barred, but there was no padlock. When Embla went over and opened it, she was met by the acrid smell of rotten wood and mold. However, there was another odor that she immediately recognized. Her stomach turned over—not because of the stench, but because she knew they'd found the boy. Although of course it could be a dead animal. Hopefully.

Cautiously she stepped inside. An old cart took up most of the space; the wheels were missing, so it was propped up on large stones. There were a few rotten poles in one corner; otherwise the place seemed to be empty.

But that smell . . .

Slowly she shined her flashlight over the earth floor and the walls. Below the roof on one side she saw a wide shelf. Near the edge was a paper bag with something inside it. When she stood on tiptoe she could just see a blue-and-white patterned blanket right at the back, by the wall.

PERNILLA ANDERSSON REACTED with surprising composure to the news that they'd found Viggo. Embla had expected a total collapse, floods of tears and hysterical outbursts, but instead she became silent and still. Her face stiffened into a mask, and her eyes looked like two pools with not a ripple to stir the water.

A patrol car came to take her to the mortuary for the formal identification of her son. Before leaving she put on a long black cardigan instead of the bathrobe she'd been wearing for over a week, but she didn't bother changing the black tights and faded yellow T-shirt.

First she identified the blue blanket with white dots as Viggo's comfort blanket. Her voice sounded strangely toneless. She then followed Embla and Hampus into the room where the little body lay beneath a sheet. Hampus folded back the top section and moved aside to let Pernilla step forward. She stood there motionless for a long time, staring at her son's ashen, sunken face. Then she turned on her heel, grabbed her sobbing mother by the arm, and pushed her toward the door.

"Okay, that's it," she said without a trace of emotion. She paused in the doorway and looked back at Embla and Hampus. "I want to talk to you. Right away!"

Her voice was thick with something that could be interpreted as grief and suppressed tears, but the fire in her eyes revealed a burning rage.

PERNILLA DIDN'T SAY a word during the drive home; the only sound was her mother's weeping. Embla parked the Volvo by the gate. Viggo's toys were still strewn around the yard, as if a little boy might run out and start playing with them at any moment.

Without further explanation Pernilla invited them in. She marched upstairs, straight into the master bedroom. The double bed was unmade, and judging by the stale smell, the room hadn't been aired out for a long time. Pernilla went over to a low door and opened it. As Embla had guessed, it led to a built-in closet, very common under the sloping roofs of older houses.

Pernilla turned and jerked her head toward the closet. "In here."

She reached inside and switched on a bare bulb. Another jerk of the head told Embla and Hampus that she wanted them to follow her in. Hampus almost had to double over to avoid banging his head on the door frame. Pernilla was already over by the far wall, pressing on the tongue-and-groove paneling. After a moment there was a click, and she pushed one piece of wood to the side, revealing a space big enough to hold the sports bag they could now see.

"Ted's grandfather built this house. I presume this secret compartment was made to hide his homemade schnapps. And Ted . . ." Her voice broke and she fell silent.

Göran, who was still in the doorway, passed each of his colleagues a pair of plastic gloves. "Put these on before you bring out the bag, and take plenty of photographs before you touch anything at all."

Hampus went to the car to fetch a sterile plastic sack, then they carefully edged the Adidas bag inside. It seemed pretty new. They decided not to open it until they got back to the Shore House.

Embla gently led Pernilla down to the kitchen. Her mother was sitting at the table, seemingly incapable of doing anything. *Please don't let her have a heart attack or a stroke*, Embla thought.

Pernilla went over to the stove and said in that curious monotone, "I'll make some coffee."

Embla didn't have the heart to ask for tea. As the coffee began to drip through the filter and into the glass pot, Pernilla came and sat down. She clasped her hands and placed them on the table.

Impulsively Embla covered Pernilla's hands with her own. "Thank you for showing us the hiding place," she said.

There was no reaction from those dead eyes, but a slight tremble passed through Pernilla's body.

Encouraged by this, Embla continued. "Does Ted realize you know about it?"

Pernilla glanced at her, a defiant glint in her eye. Then she slowly shook her head. "No. He thinks he's so fucking smart, but he forgot to close the compartment one day back in the fall. I got home from work and went into the closet to look for something, and I saw it. I didn't say a word, so no, he doesn't realize I know."

It was good that she'd started talking again. There was a little more color in her pale cheeks, and her expression had changed. Embla was still afraid she would break down completely when the shock subsided, but at the moment she seemed reasonably calm.

"The compartment was empty, but a week or so later I went back to see if I could open it. Ted was in Norway, and Viggo was asleep. It was really difficult, but I managed it—and that time the bag was there."

"Did you look inside?"

"Yes. There was a set of scales and a whole lot of little plastic bags, plus an empty jar Ted had asked me to bring home when I was working in the candy section. There were some packets of powder in the jar. I knew . . ." She stopped abruptly, and her face stiffened once more.

Embla quickly stepped in to keep the conversation going. "You knew it was drugs."

Pernilla lowered her head and looked at Embla's hand, still covering hers. Slowly she withdrew her hands and hid them on her knee beneath the table.

"I've thought for a long time that . . . that he was on something. He's been . . . strange. But you don't want to believe . . ." She straightened up and stared at Embla, eyes wide with fear. "You won't tell him it was me who showed you . . ."

"No. We'll say we found the bag when we searched the house," Embla reassured her.

However, it was as if fear dug its claws into Pernilla when she thought about the possible consequences of what she'd done. She stood up and began to pace back and forth, then suddenly she turned to Embla and snapped, "Can't you just finish up and get out of here!" She shot out of the kitchen and they heard her stomping up the stairs.

Her mother, speaking for the first time, said quietly, "Losing a child . . . it's the worst thing that can possibly happen."

BACK AT THE Shore House they opened the sports bag. They lifted two sets of fresh prints, one from Pernilla and one from Ted. The others were blurred and presumably belonged to whoever had sold the bag to Ted. The bag contained a set of electronic apothecary's scales, a pack of latex gloves, several sturdy mouth guards, a scoop, lots of small plastic bags, two round tins with DREAM DUST on the side, and a plastic jar. The smell of marshmallow bananas still lingered in the jar. Göran counted the bags: three hundred and seven. In a side pocket they found twenty-four more.

Göran tested the contents of one of these with his portable kit and was able to confirm that it was cocaine. He was also able to establish that it was purer than the coke normally sold on the street. He tested one of the bags from the jar; as he suspected, this coke had been cut with something else. It seemed likely that was where the Dream Dust came in.

THE TEAM AGREED to keep the news that they'd found Viggo from Ted Andersson until the medical examiner provided a preliminary report on what had happened to the boy. Ted already knew his son was dead; they would have to try to find out in subsequent interviews how he had died. Meanwhile they decided to go for David Hagen and Ted on the murder of Robert Halvorsen.

During Wednesday night and all through Thursday the two men were questioned at length in the custody suite at Trollhättan. Both realized they were in trouble, and blamed each other for the stabbing. However, the investigators were more inclined to believe Hagen. The very fact that he was prepared to talk provided a clear indication of how worried he was at the prospect of going down for homicide.

According to him, the New Year's Eve party had gotten off to a good start, with plenty of food and drink. After midnight some people started asking where they could get more cocaine because they'd used up all they'd brought with them. Hagen had called his friend Ted, knowing he'd have a supply at home.

Both men worked on baggage transporters at Gardermoen Airport in Oslo, and had known each other since they were kids, when Hagen was living with his mother in Strömstad. They'd lost contact when he went to join his father in Oslo in his early teens, but they'd met again at Gardermoen and embarked on a fruitful joint enterprise. They had been smuggling drugs, mainly cocaine, via passengers' luggage for many years. Usually the narcotics were inserted in a particular suitcase immediately before it was loaded onto the aircraft. Someone at the plane's destination would be told which case to look out for. It would be quickly removed as the baggage was unloaded, then reported missing. It would usually turn up again before too long, with the explanation that it had somehow ended up on the wrong carousel. The owner would be relieved, and that was the end of the matter.

Hagen's gang also imported narcotics from Denmark by sea, and Ted was responsible for taking some across the border into Sweden. When he traveled home on his days off he carried a delivery from Oslo to Strömstad for further distribution down the coast and in Gothenburg. An extra income, easily earned, even if it did involve a certain element of risk.

Hagen called Ted around an hour after the clock struck midnight and asked him to bring over some coke. Ted assured him it was no problem; his wife and son were asleep, so he could set off right away. Halvorsen came over just as Hagen ended the call. He was furious and accused Hagen of stealing coke from him. There were inconsistencies involving those Hagen was supplying, plus he'd had complaints that the coke had been cut too much and was too weak. Hagen in turn immediately suspected Ted, but couldn't put the blame on him in order to protect himself because Halvorsen was unaware of Hagen's "little arrangement" with Ted.

When Ted arrived at the party, Hagen told him about Halvorsen's accusations. They both knew how dangerous it was to incur the Norwegian's anger. Ted had given Hagen the coke and said he'd fix things.

Around half an hour later, Hagen heard a woman screaming in the hallway. Everyone rushed in and found Halvorsen unconscious and bleeding from several deep stab wounds to the stomach.

There was no sign of Ted, and Hagen thought it was best to disappear before the cops showed up.

His willingness to talk about Halvorsen's murder was surprising, even though it was likely that not everything he said was true.

He claimed that Ted had given him the expensive hunting knife when they met in Strömstad the day after the fire, and that Ted had said something to the effect of, "I want you to scare the shit out of Kristoffer Sjöberg—in fact why don't you fix him for good? Don't forget I fixed Halvorsen for you."

Pedophiles and those who murder small children aren't too popular in criminal circles, which was why Hagen agreed, after a brief hesitation. Kristoffer might still be a teenager himself, but according to Ted he was definitely a child killer, and Hagen believed him. However, during the interviews he insisted over and over again that he'd never intended to kill Kristoffer, but only to frighten him into keeping quiet by threatening him with the knife.

Embla didn't believe him, not for one second.

You were worried about yourself, too, she thought. *If*

Kristoffer survived he'd be able to identify you as one of the men who were at Breidablick the night his father was burned to death.

When questioned about the arson attack at Breidablick, Hagen refused to say a word.

However, they should be able to charge him with inciting the murder of Robert Halvorsen, drug smuggling, and probably arson and the attempted murder of Kristoffer Sjöberg. All of which added up to a lengthy sentence, but at least he wouldn't go down for killing Halvorsen. That would make his life behind bars a little easier; being convicted of taking out a gang leader is never good if you want to survive a spell in jail.

GÖRAN SIGHED AS he ended the call. He stared gloomily into space for a few seconds, then pulled himself together and turned to Embla and Hampus. "That was the medical examiner. Preliminary tests show that Viggo's body is full of cocaine."

Cocaine? A six-year-old child? Why would Ted give his son cocaine? All three pondered this extraordinary news, but couldn't come up with an explanation. They were sitting in a depressingly bare room at the police station in Trollhättan. The walls were painted in a horrible shade of gray-green, with mottled gray vinyl flooring. After Göran's revelation the place felt even more claustrophobic.

"We've got the tow bar from Ted's car with Viktor Jansson's blood on it. He's definitely linked to that murder. We have a knife that's a perfect match with Halvorsen's injuries. We know the knife was stolen on the night Halvorsen was stabbed. That was confirmed by

Hans Joffsén, who owns the house where the party was held. We also know that Ted was there, thanks to the photograph taken at the party. David Hagen has told us that Ted "fixed" the problem of Halvorsen. Ted will be charged with at least those two homicides, and he's going down—I don't care how good his lawyer is."

As if by chance he glanced at Embla, and to her chagrin she felt herself blush.

Göran frowned, then suddenly he slammed down his hand on the table so hard that the others jumped. "Enough! Time for Ted Andersson to start talking! I want to know exactly what happened on the day Viggo died."

THE TIME HE'D spent in custody had taken its toll on Ted. He was still trying to be cocky, but it was obvious that he didn't feel well. He didn't have much of an appetite as a result of stomach pains, and had lost a few pounds. His face was gaunt, his complexion had taken on a sallow tone, and his eyelids were swollen. During the interview he sweated profusely and kept complaining that he couldn't sleep.

When he was told that Viggo had been found, he fainted. Before anyone had time to react, he slid off his chair and onto the floor. When he came to, he started yelling, "Why haven't you arrested that fucking pedo? It's Kristoffer fucking Sjöberg who should be sitting here, not me!"

Göran calmly cut him off. "He has a cast-iron alibi for the time of Viggo's disappearance. You don't."

There was no point in Ted's continuing to blame Kristoffer. He knew that the autopsy on his son would reveal the cause of death.

A six-year-old whose body was full of cocaine, wrapped in his comfort blanket, and hidden in an isolated location to which Ted was connected. There was no way out.

However, despite the compelling evidence against

him, it took several lengthy and difficult sessions before Ted finally accepted that continuing to lie would get him nowhere. He was suspected of having deliberately poisoned his son with cocaine. Faced with that accusation, he gave in and began to tell his story. The thought of being convicted of the murder of his own child was unbearable, even for him.

According to Ted Andersson, everything had gone well as usual. Before they drove over the Svinesund Bridge, they exchanged a few words with the customs officers on duty. After all those years Ted and Johannes spent commuting between Sweden and Norway, their faces were very familiar.

Needless to say, Johannes knew nothing about the cocaine in the spare tire compartment in the trunk. Only Ted and David Hagen were aware of their valuable cargo. The fewer people who knew, the better. David didn't want to cross the border too often in case the customs officers got suspicious. He already had several convictions for drug-related offenses in Norway. He'd never told Halvorsen that Ted took care of the transportation to Sweden and the ensuing rollout along the west coast.

It worked perfectly, and if Ted cut the cocaine a little more, then he had enough for his own use, too. A well-earned bonus.

Ted dropped Johannes outside his house in Önnaröd, then drove straight home. Ted had been expecting a quiet Friday evening: put Viggo to bed, then share a couple of bottles of wine with Pernilla. He might even feel like a fuck, although the fat cow wasn't especially attractive these days. Hanne in the cafeteria at Gardermoen was a lot sexier; the very thought of her made him hard. They'd been together for two months now, and he really wanted to move in with her in Oslo. However, he needed the family as a cover for "The Business." It gave him cash to spend in Oslo and access to good coke. Pernilla didn't have a clue. As long as he gave her some money and a quick kiss and cuddle now and again, she was happy. Stupid bitch! But Viggo was a great kid. A bit of a mommy's boy, of course, but he'd soon grow out of that.

The evening had gone exactly as planned. Apart from the fuck. She'd crawled off to bed after a couple of glasses of wine. Which was fine because everything depended on the fact that she'd be working the following day.

On Saturday Pernilla was tired and slow, but she'd caught the bus to the Co-op in time for her shift at midday. She wouldn't be home until eight-thirty at the earliest, which was perfect.

As usual she'd made a huge pile of pancakes for Viggo. They were his favorite, and a special treat to make up for her not being around much on the weekends. Ted was going to finish off yesterday's family-sized pizza and wash it down with a few beers. First, however, he needed to focus on The Business.

He asked Viggo what movie he'd like to watch later while he was eating his pancakes.

"The one with the snowman! And the lady who's cold!"

The kid meant Disney's *Frost* or whatever it was called. He'd seen it hundreds of times. Definitely a girl's film—Pernilla was ruining the boy. Why couldn't he choose *The Terminator* or *Jurassic Park* instead of this crap? But the important thing was to keep him quiet for a while, so there was no point arguing.

Viggo was in his room, absorbed in some game on his iPad. It would be stupid to disturb him now.

Ted decided to make his preparations for The Business. He didn't want Viggo to hear him and find out what Daddy was doing, so he crept into the closet under the roof and opened up the secret compartment. He took out the Adidas bag and carried it into his bedroom. He carefully removed the items he needed and placed them on the desk in the corner.

With the empty bag in one hand he went downstairs, through the kitchen, and outside. It was pouring; he got soaked in the short distance between the house and the garage. He should have grabbed his jacket—too late now. He closed the garage door behind him before switching on the light. He opened the trunk of the Lexus and lifted the mat, exposing the compartment where the spare tire should be. In fact it contained several packages, each around the size of a house brick, wrapped in plastic and sealed with duct tape to make sure they didn't split. That would be a disaster—the whole space filled with cocaine. He smiled at the thought. Oh no, not the smallest pinch of the precious powder would be spilled. He transferred the packages to the sports bag and replaced the mat.

He hurried back indoors and upstairs. He checked on Viggo, who was lost in his game and didn't even notice him. Good, he could carry on with his preparations. He closed the door to his bedroom as quietly as possible, then locked it and pulled down the blinds. Made sure there were no gaps . . . the neighbors couldn't see in, but you never knew . . . the cops could be watching him. The idea that the cops might be onto him had come into his mind more and more recently. Not that anything had happened—it was just a *feeling*. Better to be on the safe side with the blinds drawn.

He put the bag on the floor next to the desk. Of course he ought to have his own room from which to run The Business, but there were only two bedrooms. The cellar wasn't an option; it was filthy and poorly lit. And someone could peer in through a cellar window, so he just had to make the best of things.

Everything was neatly laid out: a set of digital apothecary's scales, a Stanley knife, a measuring scoop, and a box of small plastic bags, perfect for one or two grams of cocaine. Plus two tins containing a mixture of bicarbonate soda and something he'd bought online. It was called Dream Dust; he didn't really know what kind of crap it was, but it looked like cocaine, so it suited his purpose.

He felt a pang in his stomach—not of hunger, but *desire*. He picked up the knife and made a hole in one of the larger packets; he couldn't suppress a gasp of relief. Hands shaking, he measured out a line on the edge of the desk. Careful, careful, not too much. This was strong stuff. Greedily, he inhaled the white powder. An explosion in his chest, a rush throughout his entire body and up into his brain. He was suffused with intense happiness; he felt really good. That was the best thing about coke—it worked fast. If only Hanne were here now! He was so horny! Somewhere deep inside a little voice made itself heard. He had to sort out The Business. It mustn't take too long. He walked around the room on a total high, trying to pull himself together.

Through the wall he could hear the plink-plink of Viggo's computer game. Good. After a while he was able to focus, and sat down at the desk. He scooped some of the powder from the large package and tipped it into one of the small bags. He had no intention of cutting it; he was keeping it for his own use. He sealed the bag by pressing the edges together and moved onto the next. Thirty bags. Thirty grams—that would see him through to the next shipment. He would have liked to take more, but he didn't dare. Even if Halvorsen was out of the picture, there were others in the organization who might know about the accusations against David Hagen—and indirectly against him. These were dangerous guys to do business with, but who was taking all the risks? *Ted, that's who.* Which was why he was entitled to a little bonus from The Business. He'd come up with a brilliant way of taking his own coke back into Norway: he stuffed the bags into the battery compartment of an old flashlight, which he casually left in the side pocket of his car. If anyone started fiddling with it, which had happened on a couple of occasions, he simply said there were no batteries in it, and that was the end of the matter. The ploy had worked perfectly ever since he'd been involved in The Business.

He placed his own bags on the flat base of the desk lamp; it was important not to mix them up with the rest. Then he began to cut the cocaine in the packages with the mixture in the tins. One measure of coke, one measure of Dream Dust. Fifty-fifty. The customers paid for two grams of cocaine but received only one. He dropped these bags straight into a large plastic jar; he'd asked

Pernilla to bring it home from the Co-op when she was working in the candy section. It was full in no time, and the contents would bring in a good profit. He was pleased, very pleased.

He heard a scrabbling at the door.

"Daddy I'm hungry!"

Fuck, the kid needed feeding.

"Coming!"

Just as he unlocked the bedroom door he heard a knock on the front door. Who the fuck was that? On a Saturday? The cops? Before Ted could stop him, Viggo raced down the stairs. Ted stiffened, but told himself to relax. No need to be paranoid. He gave himself a little shake and headed for the hallway.

"Who are you?" he heard Viggo ask.

"My name is Staffan Eriksson," a deep voice replied.

Ted felt a surge of relief as he realized it was the carpenter who was going to help with the new deck. He stepped forward with a big smile on his face. Eriksson was wearing robust work clothes and didn't seem bothered by the wind and icy rain.

"Had you forgotten we were going to talk through the details of your new patio?" he asked.

That was exactly what Ted had done, but he attempted to play it off. "No, no, but my son, Viggo, is hungry. I'll just give him something to eat, then I'll be with you. Come on in."

Eriksson stepped inside and dripped quietly onto the rubber mat, a puddle quickly forming around his feet.

By the time Ted walked into the kitchen, Viggo had piled almost all the pancakes onto his plate and topped them with a small mountain of jelly.

"Sugar, too," he said firmly.

The important thing was to get him back up to his room, then deal with the carpenter as quickly as possible. All this was interfering with The Business. Ted searched the kitchen cupboards, his frustration growing by the second. No sign of any sugar.

"You'll have to manage without sugar," he said crossly.

"Nooo! I want sugar!"

Viggo rarely caused any trouble, but he chose that particular moment to throw a tantrum. Maybe he felt safe because Eriksson was there. *Don't lose your temper, not now, stay calm. Breathe!*

"There is no fucking sugar! Get to your room and eat your fucking pancakes!"

For once Viggo's expression was defiant, but fuck that. He wouldn't sulk for long. Fucking baby.

Viggo stomped upstairs with his plate. Ted thought it might be best to try to look a little more paternal in front of Eriksson.

"I'll bring you a can of Fanta!" he shouted up to Viggo.

He took the stairs in a few strides. Viggo was sitting in his kid-sized armchair from IKEA with the pancakes in front of him on the table. He didn't say a word when Ted put down the can and opened it with a hiss. He kept his eyes fixed on the screen and started the film.

Ted ran back downstairs and pulled on his boots and waterproof jacket. They went outside. The rain had eased off, but it was still windy. Eriksson asked if he'd made a sketch of the patio, but of course neither Ted nor Pernilla had remembered. He attempted to describe what they wanted. The window on the gable end was to be replaced with patio doors, giving direct access from the house. He'd already bought plinths and timber for the deck; that was what was under the tarps. Needless to say, he didn't mention that an old friend had gotten him a good deal. The greenhouse had been ordered but wouldn't be delivered until the end of March. They discussed the choice of roofing material for a long time. Even though the rain had settled into a steady drizzle, they were both drenched. Before he left, Eriksson said that because it hadn't been a particularly hard winter, the ground was unlikely to be frozen deep down, so he would aim to start work around the end of March or the beginning of April. They shook hands and Ted hurried back indoors.

He hung up his wet jacket and kicked off his muddy boots on the mat by the door. He could hear the music from that fucking girlie film. With a sigh, he went into the kitchen to reheat yesterday's pizza in the microwave.

With the hot plate in one hand and a bottle of beer in the other, he went up to the bedroom. He mustn't waste any more time; he had to finish off The Business. He was due to drive to Gothenburg on Monday, delivering this shipment along the way, and on Wednesday he was going back to Oslo. Back to Hanne.

He paused outside Viggo's room. The door was closed, and he decided not to open it. The kid was watching his film, eating his pancakes, and enjoying himself. No point in disturbing him and risking another tantrum.

When he walked into the bedroom it occurred to him that he'd forgotten to lock the door when the carpenter arrived. His heart rate shot up and he felt his chest tighten with fear. There was no room for any slipups. He looked over at the desk in a panic, but everything was just the same as he'd left it. Nothing to worry about. Ted sank down on the bed, ate his pizza, and drank his beer. Okay, he was ready to get back to work.

The same routine was repeated over and over again: one measure of coke, one measure of Dream Dust, seal the bag, shake it, drop it in the jar. After a while he'd lost all sense of time.

It was the silence that crept into his consciousness. The film must have finished a while ago, but there wasn't a sound from Viggo's room. He must have fallen asleep. So much the better—that meant Ted could get on with his work in peace. Feeling pleased with himself, he glanced down at the jar, which was almost full. One more package to cut, then he'd be done.

For some reason he suddenly felt the urge to count his own supply. The thirty bags that constituted his little bonus. With a smug smile he began to count.

Twenty-seven.

An ice-cold hand gripped him by the throat. Feverishly he counted again.

Twenty-seven.

There were three missing. Someone had stolen . . . He tried to think clearly. The only person in the house apart from himself was Viggo. Had he been in here during the twenty minutes Ted had spent in the yard with Eriksson? Ted shot out of his chair so fast that it crashed to the floor. *Fucking kid! Just you wait . . .*

He flung open the door of his son's room, then stopped. It was unnaturally dark and silent. By the light of the streetlamp outside he was able to make out the shape of the child on the floor. Ted's legs were as heavy as lead. He didn't want to do it, but he moved slowly toward Viggo's motionless body. He couldn't speak. He dropped to his knees beside his son. He leaned forward and put his hand in a pool of vomit. Disgusting! The kid had eaten so much he'd thrown up, made a mess all over the floor! Why hadn't he come to tell his dad he didn't feel well? That great big pile of pancakes . . . no wonder he got sick! It might be better to lift him onto the bed. Gently he turned him onto his back.

He let out an involuntary scream at the sight of Viggo's face. It was covered in vomit, the eyes half-open. When Ted touched his hands, they were limp and cold. Way too cold. And those empty eyes . . .

Only then did he realize that Viggo was dead.

Fear overwhelmed him and for a long time he couldn't think straight. How was this possible? How? Who could have . . . ? His gaze fell on the low table and the remains of the pancakes. Beside the plate were three small empty plastic bags, neatly arranged in a row. Viggo's scissors lay on the other side. The scissors he'd used to cut open the bags.

Viggo must have gone into the bedroom while Ted was out in the yard. He'd thought the powder was sugar! He'd taken three bags and sprinkled the contents over his pancakes. The strawberry jelly had masked the taste of the cocaine. Not the cut mixture, but the good stuff that Ted had put aside for himself. Three grams! That was the equivalent of six grams when it was cut . . .

Even if he'd thrown up a lot, it was still enough to kill a little boy. Panicking, Ted ran back to the bedroom to grab his cell phone and call an ambulance. Just as he was about to key in the number with shaking hands, he came to his senses. He couldn't call the emergency services.

The police would come and start poking around.

There was bound to be an autopsy, and they'd find out that Viggo had consumed a large amount of cocaine. That couldn't happen. The Business would come to light. Several years behind bars . . . An end to the good life in Oslo with his pals. And Hanne.

He flopped down on the bed. *Think, Ted! Think, for fuck's sake!* He sat there whimpering and rocking back and forth. He spent some time bashing his forehead with his clenched fists before the solution became clear: Viggo must disappear. Like Amelie.

The first job was to pack everything on the desk into the Adidas bag. Nothing relating to The Business must remain in the room. He carried the bag into the closet and tucked it away in the secret compartment. He made sure the piece of tongue and groove was securely in place, then went down to the kitchen. He rummaged around in the cupboard until he found what he was looking for: a bottle of window cleaning fluid and a roll of paper towels. Best to start with the room he'd been working in. He sprayed the desk and gave it a good wipe. He did the same with the floor all around the desk. He switched on the main light and surveyed the results with a critical eye: excellent. Not a trace of powder remained.

Now for the worst part. *Don't think, just do it! This is about your future! Just do it!*

He went back to the kitchen and stuffed the used paper towels in a plastic bag. Behind the bathroom door he found a mop and bucket. He filled the bucket with hot water and soap, then trudged up the stairs to Viggo's room.

He wrapped the boy in his comfort blanket, which he'd left on the floor. There was vomit on the blanket, so it had to disappear, too. He avoided looking at the little bundle while he was cleaning the floor. Instead he concentrated on doing the best job he possibly could. It was hard to see if he'd gotten everything because he didn't dare switch on the light. He'd have to check later. Afterward. When he came home.

He rinsed the bucket and the mop over and over again. There mustn't be the slightest hint of vomit left. It would contain cocaine, so if it was ever analyzed, he'd be done for.

A thought struck him: What was he going to tell people? They'd wonder how Viggo disappeared.

Outside. He must have been outside. But why would a little boy go out to play by himself in such terrible weather? *Think* . . . Yes! He'd been out playing with his little LED flashlight, of course. That was one of his favorite things to do when it was dark. Brilliant idea! Ted congratulated himself. He could do this!

Quickly he gathered up his son's boots and outdoor clothes and stuffed them in a paper bag.

It was completely dark outside; the clock on the microwave showed 15:12. Time to go. He switched on the light in his and Pernilla's bedroom to make people think he was home. He didn't dare turn on the light in Viggo's room. Not yet. Not until the boy was . . . gone. He went downstairs and made sure the kitchen light was off; he couldn't risk anyone seeing him carry the child out the back door. The door—he needed to put it on the latch. He had to move fast, nothing must go wrong. He put the bag of clothes next to the Lexus so he wouldn't forget it. *Quick, get a move on!*

The body didn't weigh much; he was so little. Ted

made every effort to avoid looking down at the blanket cocoon in his arms. He made his way down the stairs, through the hallway and kitchen. As he opened the kitchen door the rain and cold air struck them. Good, nobody in their right mind would be out and about in this weather. He pushed up the garage door with one hand—*inside, quickly now!* He let out a huge sigh of relief as the door slid shut behind him. Clutching his lightweight burden, he moved toward the trunk, then stopped. Putting the kid in there felt wrong. He opened the back door instead and gently laid the blanket and its contents on the seat. He stuffed the bag behind the front seat.

He slipped out of the garage, ran indoors, and turned on all the lights upstairs and downstairs. He also switched on the TV. It was essential to give the impression that the family was home.

HE HAD TO keep himself in check, make sure he didn't exceed the speed limit. He couldn't risk being pulled over by the cops. It was raining hard again, so there was also a danger of hydroplaning. The glow of Strömstad disappeared behind him. There were lights in the windows of isolated houses along the way, but he didn't meet many cars. The only sound was the monotonous swish of the windshield wipers.

After a while he saw the streetlights of Skee. His confidence began to grow as he drove through the community. He'd acted with icy composure—he was a smart guy! He'd done everything right. It was all going to be fine!

His mind felt calm and clear, which was why he was totally unprepared when his whole body started shaking.

Great hulking sobs forced their way up through his throat, and he could hardly breathe. Shit, he needed a fix! But he'd forgotten to bring his own coke. In his haste, he'd put it in the Adidas bag along with the rest. What a fucking idiot! The only consolation was that he hadn't put his bonus packets in the candy jar, but had slipped them into a side pocket. At least he'd had the presence of mind not to mix them up.

He noticed a parking lot by the side of the road and slowed down. He turned in and slammed on the brakes. The shaking had increased, and he couldn't stop sobbing. *Get a grip, Ted, for fuck's sake! Get a grip!* Air. He needed air. He fumbled with the handle, managed to open the door, and tumbled out into the pouring rain. He walked around to the back of the car taking deep breaths, then blew his nose using his fingers. His dad had taught him that—the only useful legacy the old bastard had left behind. Apart from the house in Strömstad and the cottage, of course. The cottage that would finally serve a purpose. It was lovely out there—at least in the summer. Viggo would be happy there . . . The thought of his son brought on a fresh burst of sobbing. It couldn't be true! Viggo wasn't dead! No! He wasn't dead! It must be . . .

A heavy hand landed on his shoulder and his heart missed a beat.

"Hi, Ted—sorry if I scared you, but I can see you're not feeling too good," said a familiar voice.

Ted stood there gasping for air, his brain working overtime. Viktor Jansson. Viktor fucking Jansson, his basketball teammate in high school. Viktor fucking Jansson who was now a cop. Shit! Shit!

"No . . . not too good," was the best he could manage.

Viktor glanced through the side window and saw the bundle on the back seat.

"And you've got the boy with you," he said with a nod and a smile. "Fast asleep, I see. So where are you two off to?"

Considerately he pushed up his headlamp to avoid dazzling Ted.

Fuck! It's all going wrong! What do I do? Think, think of something to say! Ted had never had any difficulty in lying, but this might just have been the most brilliant lie he'd ever come up with. As if from a distance he heard himself say, "My mom died. I'm on my way to tell Grandma. I didn't want to break the news over the phone."

What the fuck? Viktor would remember that they'd met in the parking lot at a time when Ted and Viggo definitely weren't supposed to be there. And his mother wasn't dead. Unlike his grandmother. It wouldn't take Viktor long to find that out.

"Sorry for your loss—I can understand why you're upset. Drive carefully."

With another pat on the shoulder Viktor turned away, adjusted his headlamp, and got ready to resume his run. Ted's paralysis suddenly disappeared. He opened the trunk and took out the tow bar. He was behind Viktor in a second; the idiot never knew what had happened. A few blows to the back of the head, and the cop was out of the picture. Viktor fell facedown into the water-filled ditch. Ted grabbed his legs and pushed him all the way in. No problem.

He drove off with a screech of tires, but he was feeling much better now. The attack on Viktor had provided an outlet for his pent-up anxiety and filled him with fresh energy. *I fixed it! Fucking cop, poking his fucking nose in!* Elation carried him through the darkness. One last task—and he could do that, too.

He'd intended to hide Viggo in the earth cellar, but couldn't find it in the gloom. It might have collapsed. The cottage itself wasn't an option. If anyone came along and found the body, suspicion would immediately fall on Ted. It would have to be the neighboring cabin; he knew there was a shed. He drove another hundred yards along the track.

The darkness was almost tangible, and he hadn't brought a flashlight with him. The only solution was to direct the car's headlights at the old building and try to orient himself. The problem was that it was a bit of a walk from the track, and the beam didn't quite reach. He was also running out of time; he had to get home. It wouldn't be credible if he claimed the kid had been out on his own after six. The simplest thing would be to put the bundle and the bag of clothes on the shelf in the shed. He could come over in a few weeks and burn the place down. But not tonight; he didn't have the right stuff with him, not even a box of matches. He was secretly relieved that he wouldn't have to incinerate his son's body. The thought was almost unbearable, and he pushed it aside.

On the way back to Strömstad he called Viggo's best friend from preschool. His father answered almost right away, and Ted anxiously asked if Viggo was at their house. When he was told they hadn't seen Viggo, Ted explained that he'd just gotten in the car to go out and look for the boy. Viggo had been playing in the yard with his flashlight, and now there was no sign of him. No more than fifteen minutes without supervision, and now . . . Yes, he'd probably gone to visit one of his friends in the neighborhood. Thanks, I'll keep searching.

The dashboard clock showed 17:11. Perfect. Methodically, he began calling friends and neighbors to ask if Viggo was there, or if they'd seen him.

HE PUT THE car in the garage and took the big flashlight inside so that he could fill the battery compartment with his own supply of coke, but first he needed to check that everything seemed normal in the house. He left the flashlight by the door and took off his jacket. Fear gripped him once more. What if he'd missed something? A quick tour of the ground floor revealed nothing out of the ordinary. The plastic bag containing the paper towels he'd used to wipe up the vomit was in the trash can, the mop and bucket were drying in the cleaning cupboard.

He took the stairs in five strides and went into Viggo's room. There was still a faint smell of vomit. He opened the window and decided to have another go at the floor with the window cleaner. Ammonia masks every odor. Five minutes later he'd applied a liberal dose of the cleaner and scrubbed it energetically with more paper towels. Then he went back downstairs and emptied the trash can.

One last check. On the bottom shelf of Viggo's bookcase he spotted the boy's small LED flashlight. Thank God he'd seen it! If it was found in the house, his entire story would collapse. He went over and grabbed it; he'd be sure to get rid of it as soon as possible.

Think, Ted . . . There was no trace of the coke

anywhere . . . hang on! The bonus coke was still in the Adidas bag. Into the closet, open up the secret compartment. How many should he take out? He decided on three; the remainder could stay in there until it was time to travel back to Oslo. He carefully replaced the piece of wood, then tucked two of the little bags inside his snuff tin.

With shaking hands, he opened the third and drew up a line on the edge of the desk. He inhaled and immediately experienced the rush in his brain. As his body was suffused with *the feeling*, he slipped the bag into the pocket of his jeans. He would save the rest for later.

For appearances' sake he took a short walk around the local area and asked the neighbors he hadn't called if any of them had seen Viggo.

At 17:50 he contacted the police.

Here we go, he thought.

TED ANDERSSON WAS keen to tell his story in detail. It was important for him to stress the fact that he hadn't deliberately caused his son's death.

"He took the stuff himself!" he exclaimed more than once.

The traces of blood on the tow bar forced him to confess to the murder of Viktor Jansson. He realized it was pointless to deny his involvement when the police knew he'd been there, en route to hide his son's body by the lake.

When Chief Superintendent Willén asked why he and David Hagen had taken Johannes Holm with them to Breidablick to set fire to the workshop and beat up Kristoffer Sjöberg, Ted suddenly looked very tired.

"It seemed like a good idea," he said with a weary sigh, "at the time." Then he clamped his lips shut and refused to answer any more questions.

His lawyer, Nadir Khadem, certainly had his work cut out for him.

IT WAS THE Friday evening before the February school vacation, and Embla was packing for a trip to Dalsland with Elliot. She'd promised to pick him up at nine o'clock the following morning, and he'd already called twice to make sure that a) she'd set her alarm, and b) she was going to keep her promise to take him hunting. This was Uncle Nisse's idea. Elliot had been begging to go hunting for years, but he'd always been told he was too little. However, now that he was nine, Nisse thought it was high time to take the boy out into the forest. Embla hadn't been quite so enthusiastic, but with her two favorite guys united against her, she'd given in.

After some consideration they'd decided to go for foxes. Their numbers had increased significantly during the previous summer, and a cull was essential. The aim was to track down their quarry. Elliot had a lot of energy, and would soon get bored if they stayed in one spot.

When her cell phone rang Embla smiled to herself. Third call—she wondered what Elliot had come up with now. Without looking at the screen she answered, "Embla."

"Hi, it's me."

Her heart skipped a beat when she heard Nadir's voice.

"Hi—where are you?"

She asked the question mainly to give her a moment to pull herself together. They had spoken briefly three days ago, but she'd heard nothing since. Of course he had his hands full with Ted Andersson's defense, she'd thought.

"Still in Trollhättan. Ted's being questioned again tomorrow, but it'll be over by lunchtime because it's Saturday. I wondered if we could get together in the afternoon, or on Sunday evening?"

Without hesitation she replied, "No, Elliot and I are going up to Dalsland to see my uncle tomorrow. It's the school break."

There was a lengthy silence, then he said, "Do you have to go? Can't you go on Sunday instead?"

Go on Sunday instead? Both she and Elliot had been planning this trip since before Christmas. No chance! *Why should I reorganize my life to fit in with Nadir's schedule?*

"Absolutely not."

"But why? I mean, he's not your son."

That was when she got really mad. She tried to keep her voice neutral, but was finding it difficult to control herself.

"Listen, I have no intention of reorganizing my life to suit you. I spend a lot of my free time training. Meeting friends. Hanging out with Elliot. And hunting, of course."

She could almost hear him thinking.

"So you're saying there's no room for a man in your life."

"Not a man like you! Everything has to be on your terms—when you're free to meet up, when you can sneak away from your work and your wife. I'm not interested!"

"It didn't seem to be a problem in Strömstad," he said sourly.

"No, because you were meant to be a one-night stand. Then we met up a few more times. But now we're done."

"So you're finishing with me?"

"There's nothing to finish."

The silence was even longer this time.

"Is there nothing we . . . I can do?"

He sounded almost desperate. At that moment the devil whispered in Embla's ear. Of course there was something he could do!

With deceptive calm she said, "The only way we can have a relationship in the future is for you to get a divorce. But given what you've told me about your family and Soraya's, I realize that's never going to happen. So the answer to your question is no, there's nothing you can do."

She listened to his breathing on the other end of the line, then there was a click as he ended the call.

Her heart was racing, and she felt a little shaky. She took a few deep breaths to steady herself. She was surprised at what she'd just done, but knew that her true nature had taken control. She felt a certain sorrow—or maybe it was more like emptiness—at having broken up with him, but she knew it was the right thing for her in the long run. They would never be able to build a solid relationship; their lives were too different. He was bound by the ties of family and tradition, while Embla was anything but, and she enjoyed the freedom of her life. Had it been real love? Doubtful. They had both felt an irresistible sexual attraction for each other, which in itself was a huge positive. She had needed that release in order to get back to normal after the difficult months following her attack last fall. Had she used him? Maybe, but if so it had been mutual.

She quickly finished packing, then decided to make a cup of tea. She opted for a wonderful, soporific herbal tea containing lavender and lemon balm, which felt appropriate after her conversation with Nadir.

With the steaming cup in her hand she went and sat on the sofa. She downloaded a few tracks by Adele, and as the opening notes of "Hello" flooded the room, she leaned back and closed her eyes, sipping her hot drink.

She jumped when the sound of her cell phone sliced through the music. Who would call her at this late hour? It had to be Nadir again—why couldn't he take no for an answer? She glanced crossly at the screen, but the display showed UNKNOWN NUMBER. Not Nadir, then. Warily she answered.

"Embla Nyström."

No one spoke, but she could hear shallow breathing, with a faint rushing in the background as if the person on the other end was far away, or standing by the sea.

"Hello? Who is this?"

There was a sharp intake of breath. "Å . . . Åsa? Is that Åsa?"

Nobody had called her Åsa for years.

It was only a whisper, but she recognized the voice. It was a good thing she was sitting down, otherwise she would have fainted. Everyone called her Embla these days. That was her given name, but she'd hated it when she was little because it was so unusual. She had managed to persuade all her friends and teachers to use her middle name, Åsa, but as an adult she had switched back; the name Embla was quite popular now. But someone who hadn't seen her since she was a teenager would still call her Åsa, of course. And she knew that the person on the other end of the phone hadn't seen her for fourteen and a half years.

"Lo . . . Lollo!" she managed eventually.

There was a gasp, and the connection was broken.

"No! No no no!" Embla yelled. The shock was too much; she couldn't control herself. The tears poured down her face and her entire body was shaking. She realized her teeth were chattering, but there was nothing she could do about it.

When her sobs began to subside, she knew she had to talk to someone.

For the first time since Lollo's disappearance she felt ready to tell her story to someone who would understand and be able to help. And she knew exactly who to call. With shaking hands she searched the contacts list on her phone. She found the name; he would see from the display that it was her.

"Hi, Embla," Göran said in his calm voice.

She swallowed, then took a deep breath.

"Hi. Sorry to call you so late, but . . . I've just spoken to . . . a dead person."

Acknowledgments

I WANT TO thank my agent, Anneli Høier, for the fantastic work she's done for me and my books over the years. Anneli, you're pure gold!

Heartfelt thanks to everyone at Massolit Förlag, for all your support on this book. Special thanks to Helena Gustavsson at StorySide and to Sofia Hannar, my phenomenal editor.

I have moved the action to Strömstad with a certain trepidation. The town is well-documented as a classic crime novel setting through Gösta Unefält's award-winning books about *Polisen i Strömstad* [The Police in Strömstad], which have also been made into films. I have tried to tread carefully . . .

I love the landscape of Bohuslän and lived there for a number of years. I also enjoyed sailing along the coast, which I did many times. Strömstad is a wonderfully lively town in the summer but pretty quiet in the winter.

All the characters and events in my books are fictional. Many place names are invented. As usual I have maintained a very loose relationship to the geographical reality and adapted it to fit the narrative rather than vice versa.

Helene Tursten